For a moment, she simply accepted Brant's mouth over hers.

She gave in to its demands and let her lips fall apart. She felt paralyzed by the strength of her body's reaction.

When she responded, it was like a leaf getting swept away in a current of water. No choice, no other way. Time stopped, and the rest of the world disappeared. This was so unspeakably precious. Worth more than anything she'd ever had or known or felt in her life. There was no logic to a feeling like this. The feeling just *was*. This kiss felt like nothing else in her life. She would cross oceans for this. She would fight battles. The earth's magnetic field might shift for the sake of this kiss.

Dear Reader,

I had a wonderful time researching and writing this book,
as I did for the whole WANTED: OUTBACK WIVES
trilogy, of which *Princess in Disguise* is Book Two. I
spent two days on a sheep farm very similar to Brant's
and enjoyed several afternoons of horse racing, as well as
spending a morning with an old school friend of mine who
is now a successful racehorse trainer. All of it is as accurate
as I could make it, although of course any mistakes are my
own. Brant seemed exactly the kind of hero to belong in
the different worlds of sheep farming and horse racing,
and I love him almost as much as Misha eventually
comes to do!

Still, you may be thinking, a princess like Misha? Could
such a woman really exist? Well, true, she is a product
of my imagination, but she does have an inspiration in
real life—our own Australian Princess Mary, raised as a
down-to-earth Aussie girl with no inkling about her destiny,
but now married to Denmark's Crown Prince Frederik.
Misha is exactly the kind of daughter I think Prince
Frederik and Princess Mary might one day have—born
and bred to her royal role, but with strong streaks
of independence and common sense, and a taste for
excitement.

Happy reading!

Lilian Darcy

PRINCESS IN DISGUISE

LILIAN DARCY

SPECIAL EDITION®

Published by Silhouette Books

America's Publisher of Contemporary Romance

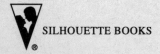 SILHOUETTE BOOKS

ISBN-13: 978-0-373-24766-0
ISBN-10:   0-373-24766-4

PRINCESS IN DISGUISE

LILIAN DARCY

has written over fifty books for Silhouette Romance and Harlequin Mills & Boon Medical Romance (Prescription Romance). Her first book for Silhouette appeared on the Waldenbooks Series Romance best-sellers list, and she's hoping readers go on responding strongly to her work. Happily married with four active children and a very patient cat, she enjoys keeping busy and could probably fill several more lifetimes with the things she likes to do—including cooking, gardening, quilting, drawing and traveling. She currently lives in Australia but travels to the United States as often as possible to visit family. Lilian loves to hear from readers. You can write to her at P.O. Box 381, Hackensack, NJ 07602 or e-mail her at lildarcy@austarmetro.com.au.

Chapter One

Sox was a terrific dog.

She was born to work with sheep, the kind of dog you thanked your lucky stars for over and over again. Brant could send her up the hill and she would muster the mob down to him all on her own. She would tear back and forth, ever alert for breakaways, pushing them toward the yard with scarcely a bark, and working on a level of instinct that training could never fully replicate.

She jumped fences like a kangaroo, and sometimes her eyes begged him with an almost Shakespearean eloquence for more work to do. Ple-e-ease, are we mustering sheep today?

She loved it.

Brant relied on her, and right now hers was the only ear he could confide in.

"Tell me those three lame ewes don't mean anything, Soxie," he said to her.

They were both riding the four-wheeler down the hill at

a considerable clip. It was a beautiful afternoon, unseasonably warm for mid-May. Fluffy white clouds floated in a blue sky, birds sang and in the distance on the road from Holbrook Brant glimpsed the red flash of a fast-moving car heading in this direction. The bright color toned with a pair of crimson rosellas who flew past, weaving an intricate flight pattern in the air and twittering as they went, then the car disappeared behind a stand of breeze-tossed, sunlit trees.

It wasn't the kind of day for bad news about his sheep.

Brant straddled the four-wheeler's wide seat, his hands and feet working the controls, and Sox sat crosswise on the back, craning around the side of his body, panting at him, waiting to find out what sheep-related adventure the two of them were going to have next.

Unfortunately, she couldn't reassure him about the lame ewes.

"It's not foot rot," he told her. He'd taken a good look at the hooves in question, had cleaned them out and pared them back, taking care not to draw blood or expose soft tissue. There had definitely been some inflammation and underrunning. "Don't tell me it's foot rot, okay, because I don't want to hear it. I am not contacting the Pastures Protection Board yet."

It could be foot rot.

After a long, crippling drought, there'd been a warm autumn with good rains, the right conditions to activate and spread the bacteria, and if any of those four thousand pregnant ewes he'd just paid top dollar for had been infected when they'd arrived here recently, then his entire acreage could soon harbour the disease.

The implications were too expensive to bear thinking about, and the worst-case scenarios could play out for almost a year.

Sox nudged her compact black-and-tan body closer to Brant, as if she could tell he was worried. He felt her warmth and her panting motion against his back. They swooped down the green, rolling terrain, over a well-worn metal grid and along the fence line toward the house.

Brant kept thinking about sheep feet, thinking about the ghastly prospect of disease, of a third of his stock's value and his year's income getting slashed down at a single stroke—six figures' worth of loss—thinking of all those months of extra work and expense and concern…

…None of which he wanted to share with his sister, because Nuala and Chris were getting married in a few months, Chris had his own stock and acreage to think about and Brant didn't want to rain on their parade.

And then he saw the bright red car again, just inside his main gate and definitely heading this way. It was a zippy little machine, gleaming and well maintained.

Not a farmer's car.

His spirits sank even further. He knew what kind of a visitor this would be.

Female.

A stranger.

A city girl.

Over the past few months he'd met enough women like this to last him a lifetime, and even the nicest of them hadn't struck any meaningful sparks. Recently, one of them—not the nicest—had spread his address around to some of her friends and now he had new ones dropping in unannounced at the most impossible times.

Such as when he'd just discovered that at least three of his new ewes had gone lame.

The red car dipped down into the creek and temporarily disappeared once more. Brant and Sox had almost reached the house. He parked the four-wheeler in the carport, chained the dog and went inside, kicking off his boots in the mudroom on the way. He found a note from his sister on the kitchen countertop.

"Don't forget Misha…"

Misha. Nuala's friend from Europe.

The red car.

He'd completely forgotten.

"She'll be here around three-thirty or four," Nuala's note continued. "I should be back, but if I'm not, be nice to her."

Be nice to the strange woman in the zippy red car.

Great.

Just what he felt like.

Since a self-invited international guest should start off in the right spirit of proving herself useful, Misha had stopped her little red rental car at Inverlochie's roadside mailbox on her way to her friend Nuala's Australian sheep farm and collected the mail.

There was quite a large sheaf of it, bundled together with a brown rubber band. Branton Smith, Inverlochie, Hill Road via Holbrook, NSW 2644, read the address on the topmost letter, in loopy purple handwriting. Misha had stashed the bundle neatly on her front passenger seat, along with the flowers she'd bought in Albury for Nuala. Both items sat on top of the case of wine she'd bought at a drive-through liquor store for Nuala's brother Brant, whom she'd never met.

But when she arrived at Nuala's and found Brant there to greet her, he didn't seem very pleased at what she'd done.

"You have to be Misha," he said to her through the open driver's-side window when she'd stopped the car in front of the low, sprawling house. His broad shoulders hunched with tension, his gray eyes looked smoky and hard, and his expression could only be labelled a scowl.

"I do have to be," she agreed, spreading her hands in mock resignation, "even when I don't want to."

Expecting a smile from him, she didn't get so much as a flicker.

"And I've brought your mail," she said, in case that helped.

It didn't.

He glanced down at the bundle of letters and groaned. Unless he was groaning at the wine and the flowers. "Nuala's not here," he told her. "You're a bit earlier than we thought."

"I probably drove too fast."

"You shouldn't, around here. We don't have those massive autobahn things you're used to in Europe."

"We don't have those massive autobahn things much, either, in Langemark. I'm pretty experienced on rural roads."

He didn't seem impressed.

Although he was impress*ive*, she had to admit—a taller, darker, stronger and way more masculine version of Nuala, who'd never had any trouble attracting the opposite sex. Brant wouldn't, either. He had wind-rumpled dark hair, strong cheekbones and chin, sinful lashes, muscles like braids of thick rope below the rolled sleeves of a gray-green, mud-stained sweatshirt, and that aura of basic maleness that aftershave could never disguise…or imitate.

There was something built in to the genes in this family that couldn't be explained purely by their hard-working farm background, their intelligence or their good looks. For a long time, Misha had thought that Nuala—loyal whirlwind, sexy tomboy—would end up with some European billionaire or aristocrat, but although she'd introduced her friend to plenty such men during Nuala's month-long stay in Langemark three years ago, Nuala had never been seriously interested.

"They're too civilized," she'd said. "They're tame."

Now she was home in Australia again, and happily engaged to Chris, the Farmer Next Door. Misha looked forward to meeting the man who was uncivilized enough for her friend.

…But back to Brant, who had just opened the car door for her.

Used to such attention, Misha dipped her head in acknowledgment, smiled at him from beneath her lashes and

began to climb out—knees together, pivot, leg slide, step—
only to catch him rolling his eyes and sighing between his
nice white teeth. Just in case she hadn't picked up on the
subtle body language, he looked at his watch and frowned
at the time.

He might be good-looking, but he displayed as much
charm as a paparazzo snapping a drunken heiress outside a
nightclub bathroom door, which wasn't much charm at all,
Misha knew, because she'd witnessed such incidents herself.

"Thank you so much for having me to stay, Brant," she
said, keeping her own well-practiced guard of charm firmly
in place. "It's so good of you, and it's wonderful to meet you
at last."

Reaching a standing position, she held out her hand but
he didn't take it. "You wouldn't want to," he said, showing
her a dirt-stained palm.

"Hey, I can wash afterward, can't I?"

Misha kept her hand where it was, and finally he responded by stretching out his own. She wished she hadn't
pushed the issue. His grip was brief and bone crushing, as if
to demonstrate that he was both busier and very much
stronger than she was. She knew those things already.

"The wine is for you," she said. "Just a small token of my
appreciation that you're able to have me here."

"No problem," he drawled. His mouth barely moved,
which allowed her to see its exact shape, and to realize that
it was perfect, not too fleshy, not too thin. With a mouth like
that, he should have a far better idea about smiling.

"And of course the flowers are for Nu. Will she be long?"
she asked, feeling fatigue begin to overtake her like the cold
winter mists that rolled over Langemark on dark December
days.

Determined to keep the press at bay, she'd flown anony-
mously in coach class from Europe to Melbourne. She'd had
a wait of several hours for her connecting flight to Albury,

followed by forty-five minutes of driving on the wrong side of the car, on the wrong side of the road, to reach Inverlochie.

Her cinnamon-and-cream Mette Janssen skirt and top were limp, and her feet had swollen inside her matching Furlanetto pumps. She should have thought the travelling-coach-class-incognito thing through a little better and worn flats.

It was three in the afternoon here, which meant it was six in the morning in Langemark, and goodness knew what time in whichever time zone Gian-Marco was in today. Spain, still? The Spanish Grand Prix had only just finished.

Nuala's brother looked at his watch again. "Not long. Maybe half an hour," he said.

"Right." At this point, half an hour was twenty-nine minutes too long, and any thought that involved Gian-Marco Ponti was a mistake.

To hide the sudden tears in her eyes, Misha leaned back into the car and snapped the release on the trunk, then walked around to the rear of the vehicle. Brant got there first, lifted the trunk lid and surveyed her Van Limbeck suitcases, her matching carry-on bag and her purse. He held out his dirt-stained hands again.

"Point taken," Misha told him, feigning a cheerful attitude. "I'll bring them in myself."

She'd already heaved the first one onto the ground before he answered. "Sorry, I meant I'd wash these hands, and then I'd do it."

"Well, if you can show me my room, wash your hands, and still beat me back out here, I'll very kindly let you bring the second suitcase, the wine, the flowers and the carry-on bag," she said, counting the seconds until she could be alone.

I'm a surly yob today, I should apologize, Brant thought, giving his hands a rough scrub with even rougher soap. He dried them on a towel he hoped was cleaner than the hands had been, and headed quickly back out to Nuala's friend's car.

Good.

He'd arrived first.

No dazzling sheaf of silky blond hair, no Scandinavian blue eyes, no hundred-watt smile, no smooth pancake-hued tan or willowy, well-engineered, designer-fashion-clad limbs in sight.

Now he could at least do the decent thing and bring in the gifts she'd brought, along with the rest of her luggage. He took the wine and the flowers first, then went back for a second trip. The heavy, expensive suitcase bulged and so did the carry-on bag, and he wondered what this Misha person had seen fit to bring with her. Twenty pairs of shoes?

What did she expect? Why was she here?

Nuala had been cagey about it. "Personal problems. She just needs to get away for a while. She needs some space and some anonymity."

Nuala was not her usual self, these days. The wedding was scheduled for the first weekend in September and it had gone to her head, the way forthcoming weddings apparently could even for the most down-to-earth of women. She spent hours on the phone to Mum in Sydney every week, and she was planning a visit up there soon, because Mum warned that she'd already slipped direly behind schedule in her quest for the perfect dress.

Brant was skeptical.

Behind schedule?

September was still more than three months away.

But he appreciated the wedding as a way to bring Mum and Nuala closer.

For a long time, the two of them hadn't seemed to have much in common. At heart, Nuala was such a country girl, while Mum had never been totally happy here. Less than a year after Dad's death six years ago, she'd remarried a friend

of theirs from racing circles—a wealthy Sydney business-
man. She'd signed over the ownership of Inverlochie to her
two children and settled to a life of socializing, race-going,
charity work and renovating Frank McLaren's Double Bay
mansion.

Brant and Nuala had both realized she would be happier
in the city, but it hadn't given them many points of contact.
Then Nuala had spent two and a half years seeing the world
in a way that Mum considered far too menial—camp coun-
sellor in the USA, chalet-girl cook in France, volunteer aid
worker in India. Now, with the wedding coming up, Mum
and Nuala had points of contact in spades. Although it irritated the heck out of him to hear this endless angsting over
guest lists and venues and color schemes, he didn't make any
attempt to get Nuala to tone down.

"I can't break her confidence, Brant," Nuala had said
about Misha. "But you should know before she gets here that
things are *very* difficult for her at the moment, and she needs
our absolute discretion and support."

Yeah.

Very difficult.

With top-quality European luggage and clothes that even
he could see must have serious designer labels.

He felt deeply, deeply sorry for her.

Forget the apology.

He was back to surly.

And for the first time in his adult life, he had overdosed
on women, especially well-groomed women who were making a big effort. He'd been out with at least a dozen different women this year and he'd had his fill of flirtatious games,
transparent agendas, the sound of ticking biological clocks,
misguided expectations, too much makeup, pushy seduction
attempts, attitudes of entitlement, airhead questions about his
farm, the whole gamut.

He had so much on his plate. Prices for his nineteen-micron wool were less than a third of what they had been a few years ago, and cross-breeding his flock with Border Leicesters to move into the fat-lamb market remained an unproven strategy at this stage.

With a pending contract sale on four thousand of his merino ewes that could be voided by the presence of disease, he did not need some pampered, impossibly gorgeous European trophy blonde from Nuala's frivolous chalet-girl past lounging around the property for the next several weeks, with no idea about what his way of life involved, expecting to be entertained.

He'd been to Europe, he knew the type. Like Nuala, he'd spent a chunk of his twenties travelling. He'd taken part in an agricultural-exchange program, spending six months in the USA, six months in the Netherlands, and a couple more months at either end of the exchange just playing tourist.

He'd had a Dutch girlfriend—Beatrix—for a short while, and he might have stayed in Europe longer, but that was when Dad had first become ill, and he'd chosen to come straight home when he heard the news, to take over the running of the farm. Beatrix hadn't wanted to uproot her career in journalism to come with him. He couldn't blame her for that. In terms of future lifestyles, the gulf between them had been pretty wide.

Before he reached the house, weighed down by the luggage, he saw Nuala's battered old four-wheel-drive utility truck approaching. He put the two bags down and waited for her, expecting her first words to be something about Misha. She would have noticed the car, or the bags at his feet. She'd be happy that her friend had arrived safely.

Instead, she jumped out of the front seat of the ute and announced, "Sage!"

"What?"

"We are going with sage and butter and cream. It's decided. I am *so* relieved!"

"Sounds a bit limited. I was hoping for steak."

"What?"

"Sage and butter and cream. Bit limited. Even for vegetarians."

"You twit, you know quite well I'm talking about the color scheme, not the menu."

"Well, more good news, in that case. Misha's here, so you can talk about the menu with her."

"Oh, she is?"

"You haven't noticed the shiny red rental car, or the luxury designer suitcases in my possession?"

Nuala didn't seem troubled that she'd missed these details. "She's early!" She grabbed his arm and lowered her voice to a confidential murmur. "Tell me! How is she? She is under so much pressure at the moment. How does she seem?"

And to his surprise, Brant discovered that he could tell her. "Bit brittle. Doesn't look as if she's been sleeping very well. And is she always that thin? She put on a good front, though, even if she doesn't look the gutsy type."

"Misha is incredibly gutsy. You will love her, Brant, I promise."

He didn't believe her. "Save your promises for Chris in September."

"So where is she? I hope she hasn't lost weight. She couldn't have had much to lose. She always keeps very fit."

"I sent her inside. You'd better grab her a towel and all that stuff."

"I made up her room this morning."

Behind their words came the sound of an engine, and they both paused to listen. "Is that on our road?" Nuala asked.

She looked up toward the trees, beyond which the farm track looped around the side of a hill. They both glimpsed another vehicle—white, this time, and not anyone they were expecting. The car nosed cautiously over a grid and around a puddle, as if the driver expected to lurch into a ten-foot-deep ditch at any moment and never get out alive.

"This is going to be one of your women," Nuala predicted.

Unfairly.

"*My* women?" Brant was really not in the mood for this.

"Well, they haven't been coming to see me!"

"Nu, they wouldn't be here if it wasn't for you! They wouldn't ever have heard of me. And they definitely would not have seen my photo on the front page of a national magazine. Do *not* call them my women, okay?"

"Sorry…" She shrugged and made a face and had the grace to admit, "It has been getting a bit out of hand lately, hasn't it?"

The white car made a final cautious curve around a final puddle and came to a halt, at which point Brant recognized the driver, with her sleek, plum-colored hair and not-so-sleek pear-shaped build. What was her name? Hell, his mind had gone blank! Lauren, he remembered, just in time.

They'd had a lunch date in Albury some weeks ago, after she'd written to him in care of the magazine. They'd spoken a couple of times by phone since. She'd seemed okay, but he'd made the mistake of giving her his address, since she'd seemed so interested in the farm. She'd passed it around, so that even though *Today's Woman* magazine's Wanted: Outback Wives campaign had officially closed now, he was still getting letters and drop-ins.

This time, she'd brought three of her friends.

They all grinned as they climbed out of the car. One of them tossed her hair, and another whispered something to Lauren that made her nod and twist her features into a raunchy look.

"Hi, Brant," Lauren said. "We have a proposition for you that's going to be great fun for all of us. Did you get my letter about it yet, or are we a bit ahead of ourselves?"

"Uh, I don't think I got your letter."

"Well, good, because it'll be much better to tell you about it in person."

A short distance away, the sliding door on the front veranda opened and Misha stepped out of the house, wearing sunglasses and a borrowed gray-brown felt farmer's hat pulled low over her forehead. "Nuala!" she said, her voice cracking, and the two women rushed up to each other and hugged hard then started talking in low, intense tones.

"This isn't a good time, Lauren," Brant told his latest visitor bluntly.

"Well, you know, we don't have to get going on it this minute," Lauren said, sparing a fleeting glance at Misha.

"Get going on what?"

Lauren dimpled. "We had this great idea, you see, kind of a reality-TV-show thing. Well, you know, not real TV, obviously, but the same way they do it on a lot of those shows. A process of elimination."

"A what?"

"You know, you're looking, the four of us are looking… Why don't we be, you know, upfront about that? We could all go out, for dinner tonight or whatever, and at the end of the evening, you eliminate one of us, and after we've been on, you know, four or five dates, there's only one of us left and that's obviously the one you like best." She paused expectantly.

Brant couldn't come out with a word, not even a strangled exclamation.

Lauren took note of his reaction and launched into selling the idea a little harder. "We just thought it would be fun. You know, you're stuck out here in the middle of nowhere, with nothing to do, we thought you'd appreciate a creative way to find the right woman. I mean, you must already have a creative outlook about it, and, you know, an open attitude, or you wouldn't have entered the Outback Wives campaign in the first place."

Her friends were making her awkward and nervous, Brant could see. All those awkward *you knows*. She hadn't been this silly—or else he hadn't been in such a disgusting mood—when they'd met for lunch. Hell, how could he deal with this? He didn't want to hurt her, but it was ludicrous to find himself in this situation.

As for his part in the Outback Wives campaign…

Nuala's idea.

Of course.

Brant and his other best mate Dusty had been seriously concerned about their friend Callan for quite some time. Callan had lost his wife to cancer four years ago, and he was still hurting about it, didn't have the slightest idea how to find someone new to share his life and help him with his two boys.

He had a huge piece of acreage in the Flinders Ranges in South Australia, and ran cattle there. It was beautiful country on a grand scale—the real outback in every sense—but it was arid and unpopulated and at their past few get-togethers Callan had seemed so lonely and lost, not meeting anyone new and not even thinking that someone new might be good for him.

Nuala had read about the magazine's quest to bring interested women together with single men in far-flung parts of the country. She'd suggested that Dusty and Brant take part and rope Callan in with them. As the classic line went, it had seemed like a good idea at the time.

Maybe it still was a good idea. Callan had been e-mailing a couple of the women who'd contacted him through the magazine, and Brant had an inkling that it had done him some good. They'd spoken by phone yesterday and Callan had sounded better—stronger and more upbeat. That flat, wooden tone had gone from his voice, and, Brant hoped, the thousand-yard stare from his eyes, also.

But Brant hadn't wanted his own face advertising the

whole Wanted: Outback Wives thing on the front cover of the magazine, he wasn't wild about the follow-up story he'd semi-committed himself to, and he definitely didn't want silly women showing up here with their reality-TV-style elimination games. Nor did he intend to tell Lauren or her friends that he'd only taken part in the whole thing for the sake of a friend.

He just wanted to get rid of her.

"I'm sorry," he said bluntly, in the end. "I don't think it would be fun."

He saw Nuala edging Misha closer, so that they could both hear what was going on…and, he hoped, help him get rid of the visitors. Nuala had begun to make covert can-you-please-wind-this-up signals with her finger. Misha had pulled her hat even lower. If she was that bothered by the relatively mild autumn sunshine, it was lucky she hadn't come in summer.

He added, "And I'd like to offer you a cup of tea, or something, Lauren, but I really can't today."

"Rain check?" Lauren brought out the dimples again.

"Uh, no."

"Oh, come on, Brant!" she wailed. "Where's your sense of humor?"

Not joking, he told her, "I left it in a sheep paddock about half an hour ago."

Then he shot a glance at Nuala, saw her eyes widen in alarm and cursed himself for letting the bitter line slip out. If he wasn't careful, she'd quickly guess that something was wrong. She knew as well as he did how quickly disaster could overtake a farmer's life. He was going to have to get his act down better than this.

"No, seriously," he said. "I'll have to call you, because nothing's going to work for this weekend."

"The weekend's not for another two days, Brant."

"For the next two days *and* the weekend," he corrected himself.

It took another ten minutes to fob Lauren off with the promise of coffee in Albury next week, get rid of the four women, apologize to Misha, agree with Nuala that they'd need to put a lock on the gate, and convince her—lying about it for all he was worth—that the comment about leaving his sense of humor behind in the paddock had been nothing more than a joke.

Chapter Two

Heading back into the house, watching Brant carry her heavy suitcase with no visible muscular effort about four paces in front, Misha said quietly to Nuala, "Would I be able to call, um, Thingy?" She couldn't even say his name, today, without getting the familiar tight, tearful feeling, along with a sense of confusion and disappointment and being totally alone.

"Of course." Nuala lowered her voice, but her brother could probably still hear both of them. "Use Brant's office, it's nice and private."

"Thanks. I so appreciate all of this, Nu." She hugged her friend again, knowing that Nuala would feel through their body contact that she'd lost weight.

"Oh, stop! Do you want to call him right now?"

"Get it over with, I think."

"So things are pretty bad?"

"We had a big fight, and I still have no idea if he was right about what he said or if I'm being an idiot even to consider believing him." She spoke faster, needing to get the basic story out and over with. "I mean, we're supposedly engaged. Although, are we? I don't feel I even know. Officially, we are. Officially, the wedding's at the end of September. Officially, I've been told that even if the whole relationship goes down the tube—and I don't know if it has—I'm not allowed to break it off publicly until some time in June."

"Why? Told by your parents?"

"By the whole country, practically. Well, you know, various advisers and government types. Christian and Graziella are having another baby."

"Oh, lovely!"

"It hasn't been announced yet. They're waiting another few weeks, until the end of the first trimester, and when they do announce it, they don't want the news clouded by anything negative from me. As well, there are these new laws in the pipeline, and a broken engagement could send the wrong message, influence the vote." She flapped her hands, dismissing the details until she and Nuala had more of a chance to talk.

Nu seemed to understand without the detail. "That's terrible! Even your parents are telling you that?"

"Mom and Dad understand that it's hard, but you know, duty comes first. Except duty just makes it harder to work out what's going on purely between the two of us. If we love each other, I should be able to believe him, and that's what he says."

"So he says those other women—"

"—are just Formula One groupies he has to fight off with a barge pole and if I really loved him, then I'd trust him when he says he hasn't slept with any of them."

"So he's turning it into your problem."

Misha's throat tightened again, and she felt a senseless need to defend her fiancé. "But maybe he's right and it is my problem…"

"Call him. See how you feel after that. Where is he?"

"I don't know. Spain? Monaco? I'll try him on his cell."

"I'm going to feed animals." Nuala squeezed Misha's arm. "We'll talk soon, okay?"

But when Nuala had shown her into Brant's very neat, business-like office, the phone rang before she could key in Gian-Marco's number. Hearing the shower running in the adjacent bathroom and guessing that no one else was available to take the call, she picked up. Took a message. Someone called Shay-from-the-magazine, saying that the photo shoot and story interview were scheduled for next week, and could they confirm a day and time? Could Brant please call Shay back?

Without giving her own name, and trying to make her light European-American accent anonymous, Misha scribbled down the details dutifully, like an executive assistant. But her heart was sinking. What was this about?

Surely—*surely*—Nuala wouldn't have done anything so crass as to organize a magazine story about her presence in Australia! Nuala knew how Misha felt about that kind of thing. It had to be something else, but anything to do with the press made her miserable and stressed at the moment.

She took a couple of minutes to coach herself into a more rational attitude. Those magazine photos of her fiancé and the dark-haired French actress could easily have been faked. If she loved Gian-Marco, she should believe him.

His proposal seven months ago had been so romantic, and perfectly staged in every detail. He'd taken her on a hot-air balloon ride over the vineyards and lavender fields of Provence, and asked her to marry him three hundred feet off the ground. They'd toasted each other with champagne and he'd given her an enormous solitaire diamond ring. He'd said he loved her so many times. But that was before the fight…

Knowing her stomach wasn't going to settle until she'd done the deed, she called him.

"Checking up on me?" was almost the first thing he said.

It was a short, tense conversation, and it didn't dampen a single one of her doubts. Had she heard a woman's voice in the background? Did Gian-Marco *want* to make her feel like a jealous, irrational hag? He'd succeeded.

And he'd made her cry.

Determined not to have either Brant or Nuala—particularly Brant—see reddened eyes and a swollen nose, Misha remained in the office for several minutes after she'd put down the phone, imprisoned by her tears, imprisoned by family expectations and relentlessly unfolding wedding plans that made it so hard to know her own heart.

She finally had her hand on the door handle ready to open it and make an urgent dash for the bathroom to tidy up the final smears of emotional evidence when she heard Nuala and Brant talking out in the open-plan living room.

She froze.

"By the way, who's Thingy?" Brant said. "The one she wanted to call."

"Her fiancé," answered Nu.

"Whose name she's apparently forgotten."

Nuala sighed like a teacher with a slow, stubborn pupil. "Brant, when a woman doesn't want outsiders to know who she's talking about, or when she's uncertain or upset about the relationship in any way, she prefers not to use the man's name, okay?"

"If you say so."

"Sometimes, in fact, in really dire situations, she is *unable* to use the man's name without crying."

Yep, thought Misha.

"So the use of the term *Thingy*…?"

"Indicates caution and doubt and problems."

Yep, again.

"If the relationship actually breaks up," Nuala continued, "the woman may look for a more distancing term such as *The Creep*."

The Creep.

Good one.

Must remember that, in case I need it.

"Right. But Misha isn't at that point with Thingy yet, right? So maybe I should know his actual name." Brant's patient tone was heavy and exaggerated.

"Um, it's Gian-Marco Ponti," Nuala said.

Misha held her breath, waiting for a reaction that didn't take long to come. Her parents had reacted the same way last year when they'd first found out she was going out with him.

"Gian-Marco—*that* Gian-Marco Ponti? The racing driver? Formula One? The Mercer-Fernandez team? In contention with Ferrari and Renault and—?"

"That's the one," Nuala agreed on a drawl. "And I should also mention—and I really don't want you to make a big deal out of this, Brant, because she'd hate it—but the thing is, she's a princess."

"Yeah, well, I'd already worked that out for myself," Misha heard. The tone was sour.

"You had?" Nuala said.

Damn, thought Misha.

If she couldn't even pull off the incognito thing for half an afternoon…

She used to be so good at it.

But her relationship with Gian-Marco had put her picture in more magazines over the past year than she'd featured in during the entire previous twenty-six years of her life. Her mother had always insisted on as much privacy as possible for her royal offspring, and even though Mom's own laid-back Colorado upbringing had been impossible to replicate for her children, she'd done her very best.

And then I had to go fall in love with a Formula One driver…

Way more people recognized her now than had recognized her during her chalet-girl ski season with Nuala three years ago.

"Expensive luggage, designer clothes," Brant listed in the other room. "She thinks a barrage of charm and a gorgeous smile can get her anything she wants…"

"Misha's not like that, but I actually meant—"

"…and she magnifies the kind of personal problem that everybody has to deal with from time to time into a piece of major tragedy and hysteria that requires everyone around her to drop everything and rush to her immediate assistance."

"She's not like that, either. She really isn't, Brant. It's other people who magnify her personal problems. Because the thing is—"

"Of course I could tell she was a princess," Brant continued, ignoring his sister completely. "Do you think she's the only one I've ever met? You've been a bit of a princess yourself lately, Nu, with this wedding in the works."

"Uh, yeah, point taken, but you see that's not the kind of princess I meant."

Approximately forty-five seconds later, Misha heard the explosion of disbelieving profanity that she'd been expecting for some time.

Out in the living room, Nuala lowered her voice to a hiss of warning and locked an iron grip onto her brother's arm. "Don't overreact, Brant, she hates that. Had you heard of her?"

"Of course I'd heard of her," Brant said, ready to overreact ten times more strongly, if he perceived the slightest need. "You've talked about her a lot since you got back from your trip."

"No, I mean, of course, yes, you've heard of Misha. But had you heard of Princess Artemisia Helena de Marinceski-Sauverin?"

And he had.

He wasn't proud about it, but thanks to a lengthy spell in a doctor's waiting room a couple of months ago after he'd gotten an infected barbed-wire gash on his hand, he was up to date on his celebrity-magazine reading, and he had indeed heard of the European princess who was about to take up temporary residence beneath his roof.

He'd heard of her elder brother Prince Christian, heir to the centuries-old throne of Langemark, and of his charming Italian wife Princess Graziella and their two young sons. He'd seen pictures of the two royal residences, the Gunnarsborg Palace and Rostvald Castle, with their stunning artwork, furnishings and decor. And he'd read about Princess Artemisia Helena and her American-born mother's alleged heartbreak at her allegedly wild ways.

Would the adrenaline junkie junior royal ever settle down? the magazines wondered. Close friends claimed that the princess's engagement and upcoming wedding to Gian-Marco Ponti was no more than a stopgap measure to keep Queen Rose from laying down the law about her daughter's wilful behavior. What did hip, sexy Artemisia Helena really feel?

Et cetera.

Shoot, it was embarrassing that he remembered it all in this much detail.

It was probably even more embarrassing that he hadn't had an inkling until now—hadn't recognized her when he first saw her this afternoon, hadn't ever thought to ask Nu about "my friend Misha's" background. Nuala had been deliberately cagey about it, he realized.

"I've read a bit about her," he confessed.

"But the magazines always get it wrong, you see. She hates the labels and the scandal and these supposed 'close friends' who are always ready to dish the dirt on her innermost feelings. She's really down-to-earth, she's—"

"Hang on a sec. Can I debate that last point? Down-to-earth in four-inch heels?"

"She has a public image to maintain, of course. But when she's in a situation where she can just be herself—*please* let her be herself while she's here, Brant, and don't go all weird with her."

"All weird?"

"You have to treat her like she's one of us. Take her riding, and skiing if she's still here when the season starts, do all that stuff with her, but she'll want to help out on the farm, too. She won't mind getting dirty."

"That I don't believe. Do you know how much I don't need something like this right now, Nu? A bleeping princess?"

"You're overreacting. Please just—" Nuala stopped. They'd both heard the click of the office door, and half a minute later, Misha appeared, signalling the end of the current opportunity to talk about her in heated whispers behind her back.

She smiled at them brightly. "Thanks for that. I got onto him. He's in Paris. I won't be making international calls every day, I promise. And I called my parents to tell them I got here safely. Now, once I've unpacked and changed, what do you want me to do? Cook? Clean? Brand? Shear?"

"Could you handling some mulesing?" Brant suggested unkindly.

It didn't faze her.

"Well, I'll give it a shot," she said energetically at once, then added in a somewhat less confident tone, "if you tell me what it is."

This was why it didn't faze her. Ignorance was bliss.

Nuala frowned at him, and he knew he was being a surly yob again, and that any minute Nu would want to know why. He didn't want to tell her about the lame ewes.

Okay, sis, I'll stop.

He mirrored the princess's smile, instead, feeling as if the stretch of his face muscles must look more like a grimace of pain.

"How about I just show you around the place?" he said. On the third-to-last word, his voice cracked like a fourteen-year-old's. He clenched his teeth harder and his jaw began to ache.

Chapter Three

"So, have you ever ridden a four-wheeler before?" Brant asked. He expected, and received, a negative answer.

"But I'd love to try," the princess added.

She appeared to be sincere. She'd changed out of the designer skirt and top and killer heels into running shoes, a Wedgwood-blue cotton sweater and jeans. All of these items might be designer, too, but at least they didn't look brand-new. The outfit hugged her whip-thin figure, but showed its strength, too. She had real legs, not feeble sticks. She had a couple of very definitely curvy bits, and a way of moving that said she wasn't afraid of using her body.

He unchained the dogs then handed her the helmet.

"Why do you keep them chained up?" she asked as Sox and Mon began to circle around the place, frantic with excitement.

"They're working dogs. If they're left to run where they like, they get all sorts of bad habits and they're useless."

"It doesn't seem very kind, to work them then keep them tied in one place."

He just grinned at her. "You watch them for a week, then tell me if they're not the luckiest dogs in the world."

"They look pretty happy right now," she admitted. "What breed are they?"

"Kelpies. Australian sheepdogs."

"And what are their names?"

"Sox and Mon."

"Short and sweet."

"Sheepdogs usually have short names. Yelling 'Marmaduke' across a paddock doesn't seem like fun after the first few hundred times, most farmers find."

She laughed. "Okay, Sox and Mon. Hi, girl. Hi, you. I love your tan eyebrows." She gave each of them a sturdy pat across their shoulders.

He showed her the accelerator on the four-wheeler's right handlebar, the hand brakes, the foot brake and how to work the gears with her left foot. She nodded, mentioned that she had a motorcycle license and had had a couple of rides in the past on a Ducati and a "Kwaka" 750, both impressive bikes. She seemed keen to get started.

And, wow, she wasn't like any other female city visitor he'd ever had here. She took a couple of experimental circuits around the grass and along the track at a sedate speed to get familiar with how the gears and brake responded, and then she gunned the thing. With the iffy starter on the two-wheel trail bike holding him back for a couple of minutes, he had trouble catching up to her, and he only did so because she stopped when she got to the first choice of route so she could ask which way they were going.

The magazines in the doctor's waiting room had been right about one thing, at least.

The princess was an adrenaline junkie.

"Over the grid and into the paddock," he told her. He had Sox on the back of the trail bike and Mon panting on the ground beside him. "From the saddle between those two hills you can see most of Inverlochie."

They pretty much raced each other up toward the saddle, peeling away from the track that led down to the shearing shed and careening across the grass. He would have won, except that he kept slowing to look sideways and make sure she wasn't doing anything stupid. Four-wheeler farm bikes had the dubious distinction of being the number-one cause of vehicular fatalities in this country, and it probably wouldn't be a popular move from an international diplomacy perspective if he killed the princess on her very first day here.

But, no, she had good instincts, picked the clearest trajectory, didn't crash over every bit of fallen timber or tip the four-wheeler at too steep an angle on the side of the slope. The sheep at the foot of the hill milled around and headed for higher ground and the dogs were so keen to round them up that he had to feel sorry for them.

"We're not working right now," he told them. "This is just for fun."

He heard the princess whoop and laugh and yell a couple of times, and when they stopped at the saddle she was breathless. Her cheeks glowed inside the confines of the helmet, and her hair soon recovered its bounce when she took the helmet off and tossed her head. "That was fantastic!" She climbed off the bike and spun slowly around, looking at the sky, the green paddocks, the distant mountains.

"You can get an even better view from the top of the hill," he told her, gesturing to the right where the slope grew much steeper, "but it's pretty tricky taking a four-wheeler up there."

"This is good enough," she said, and followed his arm as he showed her the fences that marked the edge of the property, the shearing shed at the bottom of the hill and the old fibro-cement cottage beside it that no one lived in anymore. "How many acres is it, all told?"

"Around three thousand."

"Does that give you a full-time living?"

"In this part of the country it does. It wouldn't further west. Out in the desert, my mate Callan needs six hundred thousand acres to run a viable herd of cattle, and our friend Dusty's station is even bigger."

"Wow! But I bet their land isn't so pretty as this."

"Callan's is rugged, Dusty's is flat and flood-prone. I like my land, and these rolling hills. Here, most years we can run around six thousand ewes, plus twenty-five hundred wethers, and right now we have sixty-five rams. I've never had to work off-farm, and Nuala and I can manage with contractors in busy periods, instead of having to employ another person full-time."

She asked several more questions, about the work that was coming up at this time of year, about his long-term plans, about the issue of humane farming practices, and he reached a conclusion that hadn't been covered in the magazines.

The princess was very bright.

He knew that Nuala, and Misha herself, would hate that he kept thinking of her as "the princess" but it was just so weird. His face didn't feel as though it fit him anymore. He couldn't find the right expression for it. Smile insanely? Hold his cheek muscles in deferential stillness, with tight, pruny lips and a sort of butler-like refusal to show inappropriate emotion?

Nu just treats her like a person, so do that, he kept coaching himself. But today wasn't a good day in that area. Even without the princess stuff, he was hiding his real thoughts, and his real self. He'd taken a gamble, temporarily overstocking his land so that he could buy in the new ewes he wanted before actually getting rid of the old ones.

The sale of those was already contracted, but the buyer hadn't wanted to take delivery for another three weeks, and, yes, it was risky to have so much stock here at once, but he'd done it because he'd thought the payoff was worth it and the risk was low. He was a good farmer, and he knew it. He could supplement the stock's grazing with feed grain if he thought they needed it.

If the new ewes had foot rot, however…

Smile, Brant.

Just keep smiling at Nu, smiling at the pretty princess, the way you smiled at all those women who liked your picture in a magazine, because you're keeping this foot-rot problem to yourself, smiling all the while, until you've had a better chance to check it out and you're sure.

No wonder he couldn't get a handle on how to behave.

He looked at the sheep on the hill, couldn't spot any obvious signs of lameness in the ones who were moving. It was getting late in the day and the sun had begun to dip toward the horizon. There was a broken bank of cloud in the west, and sun and shadow came and went across the ground, making the light change from soft purple to green and gold, and back again. To the east, the layered hills became higher and steeper and more thickly clothed in dark blue forest as they rose toward the Snowy Mountains, which didn't have any snow on them yet because it was only autumn.

"It's so beautiful. It's stunning, Brant," Misha said. "Absolutely stunning."

He blinked and looked, just as the sun broke from beneath the pile of western clouds once more.

Shafts of golden light radiated outward and washed between the eucalpytus trees, making them glow with rich, warm bronze and rust and tan. The new lambs in one of the lower paddocks looked as white, next to their dust-stained mothers, as the sulphur-crested cockatoos that squabbled in a nearby treetop. The water in the dams that had been filled by the recent rains looked like sheets of molten metal, and the grass was green, green, green.

It *was* beautiful.

How long since he'd really looked at it?

Too long.

Oh, hell, and this was why it was all worth it, all the worry over wool prices and the health of his livestock, the early-morning starts and long days, the frustrations with contractors, the filthy fingernails, all of it.

Because sometimes he got to zoom up to the green saddle of ground halfway up the hill, look at his very own land bathed in unearthly late-afternoon light, and take in deep, enormous breaths of his very own clean, beautiful air.

Today, as it happened, he was breathing clean air with a princess.

Princess or no princess, he knew he wouldn't want any other way of life.

"We should head back," he said, after several minutes of silence during which he forgot all about the princess thing. "It'll be getting dark soon."

Back at the house, Misha disappeared for a shower, Nuala was on the phone to Mum in Sydney, and Brant could smell Irish stew in a big pot on the stove. He set the table in front of the living-room fire that Nuala had lit, found some wet laundry in the machine and chucked it in the dryer, then came back into the kitchen to discover Nuala still arguing with Mum.

"Well, it can't be this week," she was saying, "Because I have my friend Misha here. I know that means putting it off until—" She stopped and listened for a moment. "And that's too late? Why is it too late?" More listening. "But what if I don't want a specially made gown? Can't I buy one off the rack?"

Apparently she couldn't.

"And you're right about the venue," she agreed. "If it's going to be in Sydney, then, yes, a decision's getting pretty urgent. I guess you're right about the wedding dress, too. Look, I'll have to see what Brant and Misha say. Chris will be okay with this week, and he won't mind that he can't come. He says I'm to organize it how I want. But it really can't be—?" She listened. "No, you have to pack and all that stuff. I know. Okay."

"What's up?" Brant asked when she'd put down the phone and made a resigned face in his direction.

"Mum says I have to come to Sydney *this week* to finalize the dress and the venue, because next Wednesday, a week from today, she and Frank are heading off on their cruise, which means Monday and Tuesday she has to pack and finish off her to-do list."

"So go to Sydney," he told her. Nuala had a tendency to complicate the most simple decisions lately.

"Well, I was supposed to help Chris with lamb-marking. He won't mind that, but—"

"You were supposed to help me with lamb-marking, too." It was only the mildest reproach. Brant knew Nuala's loyalties were in transition, between the farm she'd grown up on and the one fifteen minutes drive away where she'd be spending her future.

"I was going to split between you," she said.

"Go to Sydney," he repeated stoically. "Chris and I'll take turns helping each other. It's a twenty-five-day cruise, isn't it?"

"That was Mum's point. If we leave it much longer, she says I'll end up getting married in a thirty-dollar nylon dress at ten o'clock on a Thursday morning in the local Scout hall. I thought she was exaggerating a bit, there, but I don't want to arrange it all without her, and—"

"Get up at five, leave at five-thirty, you can be there by late morning. Stay until Wednesday and see Mum and Frank off on the cruise."

"And leave Misha alone with you?"

Oh.

Right.

The princess.

Who turned out to be listening in the doorway, with the

wet ends of her blond hair still curling around her swan-like neck. "It's fine," she said. "I can help with lamb-marking."

Brant and Nuala stayed respectfully silent.

"I *can!*" She went from zero to indignant in three seconds. "Gosh, Nu, you of all people, I thought, would *not* assume that I'd be too prissy for something like that! Forget the fingernails. Forget the engagement ring. I didn't even wear it on the plane. What does it involve? Getting a bit of wool grease on my hands?"

She was impressive.

"Um, not quite," Nuala said. "Bit, uh, messier than that."

"Well! Still! When have you known me to back down from a challenge? How many times in France did we climb the Aiguille Bleue together and ski the *couloirs* when no one else had made tracks there? How many times did I manage to cover cooking at your chalet as well as mine on the same night, without the guests ever knowing, so we could buy each other extra time off?"

"Half the season, Mish. We took turns."

"Exactly! How many drunken package tourists did I fend off with my psychotic-aromatherapist routine? Look at me, Nu!" She bracketed her hands on each side of her jaw. "This is more than just a princessy face, you know!" She batted her eyelids at ninety beats a minute and gave a toothy but still helplessly gorgeous grin.

Nuala was laughing by this time, while Brant was thinking, psychotic aromatherapist? Something stirred inside him, a giddy feeling he hadn't experienced in quite a while.

"Fine," Nu said. "Go ahead. Help with lamb-marking. But don't say we didn't warn you, Mish."

The princess put her hands on her hips. "Have I *ever* said that you didn't warn me? Have I *ever* acted unwarned?"

"I want to see the psychotic-aromatherapist routine," Brant blurted out.

"No chance!" Her blue eyes were sparkling.

Brant could see that she must have been great as a fellow chalet girl. He presumed she'd worked under a fake name, because she couldn't have had people knowing who she was. It must have been one of the most liberating periods of her life. He began to understand why she and his sister were friends.

But, thanks to his own insistence, he would be stuck entertaining her on his own for the next few days while Nuala went to Sydney, and somehow, despite everything she'd said, he didn't think lamb-marking would quite cut it as a way of spending ten or twelve hours every day.

He'd have to take her places. Dinner in that swish restaurant that had opened in what used to be the Bilbandra pub. A tour along the banks of the Murray River. Riding horses, if she knew how, which being a princess she probably did. They didn't keep horses at Inverlochie but he had friends who ran trail rides on their property.

There'd have to be some whole pretence to everyone about who Misha was. He remembered how she'd worn sunglasses and pulled one of Nuala's old hats down so low over her forehead this afternoon, when Lauren and her friends were here. It made sense now. He'd have to watch everything he said, put on a performance the way he had for at least seventy percent of the would-be Outback Wives who'd contacted him through the magazine since February. He could do it, all of it, but it was an extra effort he didn't need right now.

Great.

Just great.

His brief interlude of appreciating her humor and her evident gutsiness cut out and left him tense and sour again.

"Oh," Misha suddenly said. "There was a phone message for you earlier, Brant, I wrote it down but forgot to tell you. Shay-from-the-magazine? About a story and shooting some photos."

Nuala had heard something in her tone. "Not photos of

you, Mish, you know I wouldn't do something like that," she said quickly, and explained about *Today's Woman* and the Wanted: Outback Wives campaign. "They're doing a follow-up story about Brant, because he was their—"

"Don't say it," Brant warned.

"—number one—"

"Nuala…!"

"—and he got the most—"

"Stop!"

"Okay, okay." She was silent for a whole five seconds, then burst out, "No, I have to say it! He got the most letters! Women think my big brother is hot. That is such a hoot, Mish, but cute, too, do you know what I mean?"

At this point Brant just gritted his teeth and went to return the call from Shay Russell at *Today's Woman* magazine.

"Something's up with him," Nuala told Misha.

They were now sitting at the kitchen table drinking the first hot sips from big mugs of coffee while Nuala's fabulous Irish stew simmered on the stove and a long loaf of garlic bread got toasted in the oven. Outside the landscape had darkened. Dogs and chickens had been fed, Nuala had opened a bottle of red wine to let it breathe, and at some point she'd lit the fire in the slow combustion stove in the living room. From where she sat, Misha could see the flames leaping behind the glass and could feel the spreading warmth.

"But I don't know what it is," Nuala went on. "I'm sorry. I know I'm bugging him with the wedding details, it's probably that. The thing is, Mish, you've been a princess your whole life, you're used to it and it's a chore for you, but September is going to be my one shot at it, princess for a day, and I want to embrace it with my whole soul, because after that it's going to be pretty much muddy boots and sheep-smelling hands for the rest of my life—which, as a long-term thing, is far more the real me."

She gave a vague gesture that took in the high-ceilinged old house with its eccentric additions, as well as the fenced paddocks and rolling hills outside. A satisfied smile hovered on her lips, and Misha understood the reason for her happiness. She was where she belonged, and it wasn't hard to imagine how good it would feel to belong in a place like this.

"But Mum is ecstatic that I'm finally acting like a girl. She almost cancelled the cruise. Brant is being—" She shook her head. "I'm sorry."

"Hey," Misha soothed her. "I'll deal with it. I won't act like a girl for a second."

"He actually likes girls."

"I can see he has a strong personality, pretty intense in his reactions."

"He's one of the best men in the world to have on your side when you need him. But, honestly, there have been some really idiotic girls around since the totally-my-idea magazine thing." She thought for a moment. "I guess it's that as much as the wedding. I guess there's nothing else going on."

She frowned.

Brant came back from the office, poured coffee for himself and sat down at the table with them. "Story's set up for Monday," he said. "Misha, you'd better hide in the shearing shed."

"Hide in the—?"

"While the magazine people are here. If you don't want to get discovered and get your cover blown, that is. I can see the headlines now. Princess Incognito In Australia."

"I can see them, too," Misha agreed. "Although your subediting needs work. You have to get *Sex Scandal* or *Out of Control* in there, somehow. *Diet Danger* is a good one, too, if you're really stuck."

For the first time in four hours, he laughed—a surprised and almost grateful jolt of sound, accompanied by an electric flash of appreciation in his gray eyes and a lift of his strong jaw. Misha had never seen a man's face change so fast, with such a radical effect. She wondered what he'd look like when he wasn't stressed and in a bad mood.

Magazine-cover material, of course.

As Nu had let slip, it was official.

And then the phone rang and he lunged toward the office again with a frustrated, impatient growl. What had she been wondering just a second ago? What he was like when he wasn't in a bad mood? It didn't look as if she'd ever get to find out.

"Let the machine pick up, Brant," Nuala told him. "I'll grab it if it's Chris or Mum. Anyone else can go jump."

He slowed and the tightly wound energy drained out of him. He took his coffee and flopped onto the couch that sat in the corner of the big farm kitchen. All three of them listened to his to-the-point recorded announcement. "You've reached the Smiths at Inverlochie. Please leave a message after the tone."

Then they heard Lauren. "Brant, I'm so-o-o sorry about today. It was a dumb idea. My friends talked me into it. They're heading back to Melbourne on Friday, but I'm in the area over the weekend. You know, just sightseeing, doing some food and wine, and looking around. If you want to get together, here are the numbers where you can reach me."

She gave them—hotel and cell phone—then repeated them slowly.

"I hope you've written those down! Plus I'll drop in, shall I? See what you're up to? It would be great to hang out with you. I could, like, shear, or something. Or we could hit the pub for a beer. Whatever you want. Talk to you soon. Pick up if you're there…"

"She doesn't give up, does she?" Brant muttered, hauling himself up from the couch again, as if something was hunting him and he couldn't find a safe place to rest. The muscles in his forearms looked like rope about to reach its breaking strain. "Can we eat, do you think?"

"It's ready whenever you want," Nuala said, and Brant pulled the garlic bread from the oven with his bare hands, opened the foil and tossed the bread into a dish. It smelled like heaven.

"Guess you're not there," the voice continued on the answering machine. "So... You'll get back to me, and—"

Mercifully, the message timer that cut off the caller after thirty seconds spared them from any more of Lauren's perky desperation. Hauling the heavy cooking pot to the other table—the one in front of the fire that he had set earlier, ready for their meal, Brant uttered a single, blunt word. "Why?"

"Because the magazine people put you on the cover," Nuala said. She picked up the open wine bottle and they all moved to the other table to eat.

Brant had left his coffee barely drunk. "That doesn't make sense."

"But some people are like that," Misha said. "They zero in on the person they think everyone else is going to want the most."

"Usually that's you, Mish," Nuala pointed out.

Unnecessarily.

"I know." She controlled a sigh. "I've been thinking about that a bit, lately."

She'd wondered if this had been the attraction for Gian-Marco—that in a room full of interesting, attractive, pedigreed women, she was very often the one that men wanted the most.

Gian-Marco was a professional driver on the most high-profile racing circuit in the world. He hungered to win. But she'd thought until recently that it was the hunger they had in common, the love of a good healthy adrenaline rush, not the fact that he was an instinctive winner and she was just another prize.

Which was it, really?

The answer was important.

Answers to recent questions raised about his faithfulness by some pretty flagrant—if conceivably faked—photos in the press were important, too. If he was the kind of man who went all out with a woman and then stopped wanting her as soon as she was safely his, then the man she thought she had fallen in love with before their engagement didn't really exist.

This was why she'd fled Europe—to work out the truth about Gian-Marco and her own feelings in peace, without the pressure of publicity or wedding arrangements, and without the word *duty* ever getting mentioned. It had been a desperate action, and she wished she hadn't needed to do it.

Basically, she was a mess. She would seize on any distractions, any kind of healing that she could find, while she was here.

"You're lucky, Nu," she told her friend. "You and Chris want each other…love each other…for all the right reasons—for what you can share, not what you can get from each other."

"You see, you *get* that, Mish!" Nuala said, spreading her arms like an opera singer. "You understand. So many people don't. You see why I'm friends with this woman, Brant?"

"I'm certainly seeing a few things in common," he drawled. Misha wasn't convinced it was a compliment.

They settled down to eat. Nuala told Misha more about the whole magazine thing, about Brant's friend Callan who'd needed help learning to live again. "But I'm sorry I ever came up with the idea now," she said.

"Don't be," Brant answered. "Callan's sounded pretty good the last couple of times I've talked to him. I'm not sure if he's serious about anyone, but I think it's helped him to get over Liz. Even with all the crud I've been getting lately from people like Lauren, it was worth it. And Dusty's practically engaged."

"To that Mandy woman?"

"Why is she that Mandy woman? You've never met her. She could be wonderful."

Nuala shook her head and made some concerned clucking sounds. "I don't like the vibe."

"What vibe?"

"You told me about the magazine cocktail party. I could pick up the vibe from that."

"What vibe, Nu?" Brant said patiently.

"Well, as we've discussed, there are women who'll go right for the man they think every other woman in the room will want, and then there are women who'll grab the first one that's put in front of them. Mandy fell squarely into the second group, from what you said. See Dusty, grab Dusty."

"Dusty's pretty down-to-earth. Maybe that's what he wants."

Nuala looked at Misha and opened her hands. Can you believe anyone could come up with such a bizarre theory, and is there a chance you could possibly agree with him, her body language said.

Misha shook her head, slow and exaggerated. Not in a million years.

No, I didn't think so, said Nu's face.

Brant laughed again. "You two!"

"People sometimes thought we were sisters, in France," Nuala confessed.

"You look nothing alike."

"Some sisters don't. But thanks to Misha's total lack of imagination when coming up with a fake name, we were both Smith, we cooked in chalets next door to each other and we finished each other's sentences."

"Or, as just now," Brant suggested, "you didn't bother with verbal communication at all."

"That, too," Misha agreed.

It was so nice.

For at least twenty minutes.

Misha had a glass and a half of wine, which was about

twice as much as she usually drank. She had four pieces of garlic bread, and a large second helping of stew, and they talked about all sorts of things. Mostly she and Nuala did the actual talking, admittedly, but Brant's listening wasn't as morose and hostile as she might have expected. They didn't get anywhere near the subject of Formula One racing drivers or the ethics of the press.

And then the phone rang again.

The machine picked up. "Hi-i!" said Lauren brightly after Brant's announcement. "Look, I've just had a thought. How about a weekend in Melbourne? It doesn't have to be this weekend if you're not free, but we could arrange something for next weekend, or the one after. I know I'm being a bit pushy here, but I really, you know…this sounds stupid, I hate saying it into a machine, if you're there, do you want to pick up?" Several seconds of silent waiting. "I guess you're not. I guess you'll get this later. Well, anyhow, I really intuitively felt something between us. There, I said it. Doesn't it sound stupid?"

"Yes, love," Nuala commented to the answering machine in the other room. "It does."

"But didn't you?" Lauren plowed on. "Feel it? I felt that you did. I'm going to stop now before I really embarrass myself. I'm not used to being this pushy, but what's that ancient Chinese curse? May you live in interesting times? And I think we do live in interesting times. Different times. No one knows the rules anymore, and I think it's tough for women to—" The machine cut out again.

Brant had one hand over his face, his head bent forward, and the other hand gripping his wineglass so hard Misha expected to see the stem snap. She thought about teasing him, but then she might be the thing that got snapped instead. Even Nuala wasn't smiling.

"I'm sorry, sorry, sorry," she mouthed to Misha.

"Apologize to your brother, not me," Misha mouthed back.

"Do you know what we have to do?" Nuala announced aloud.

Brant groaned.

"No, this is the answer. I'm serious. This'll get rid of her, get rid of the other women, and get Shay-from-the-magazine off your back."

"What, Nuala?" growled Brant, from within the depths of his despair. Misha couldn't see his face at all, just some dark hair flopping over his hand, and his chin dropped toward his empty plate.

"Look, the only people you'll be fooling will be people who don't count, people you don't even know. I can tell you're stressed, Brant. I don't know if it's the fallout from the whole *Today's Woman* thing or what, but—"

"Of course it's not *or what*, of course it's the magazine," he cut in quickly. Misha noticed the uncomfortable way he shifted in his seat. "Just get to the point. If you have one."

"I always have a point. And it's this." Nuala paused, then announced as if she'd just invented sliced bread, "The two of you should pretend to be engaged."

Chapter Four

"I apologize on my friend's behalf, Brant," Misha said. "Her mind has been poisoned by reading too many bridal magazines."

Brant glanced at his sister, feeling sour. "She's leaving for Sydney first thing tomorrow, thank goodness."

"Although I don't think that's going to act as a detox, given the purpose of the trip."

Nuala clapped her hands. "You're ganging up on me! I love it!"

"Five-thirty in the morning, aren't you, Nuala." he said. It was an order, not a question.

He'd had enough.

And he didn't want to tell her about the lame ewes.

"Yes. Or maybe even five. Mum really wants to get in a solid day. She's putting together a schedule."

"Fortunately, it's not fatal," Misha promised him, eyes twinkling and inviting Brant to laugh.

She'd made him do so a couple of times tonight. The action had felt rusty but welcome, like when you oiled an old hinge and it finally began to work smoothly. Even though this latest business of the lame ewes had only started today, he'd had a background level of higher-than-usual stress for… hell…years. Wool prices, drought…

He'd craved a bold strategy that would pay off in one huge, giddy burst, but now he was back balanced on the knife edge of doubt and worry. He hadn't realized, until Misha had made him laugh, how little he'd been laughing lately, how tight he'd been.

"There'll be a long convalescence after the honeymoon, and then she'll be okay again," Misha was saying.

"If the rest of us live that long," he pointed out.

"And there may be a relapse when she starts shopping for baby clothes."

"I'll warn Chris," he drawled.

Misha looked at him, and the promise of a smile on her face was sexier than the actual smile would have been. She was pretty nice, pretty funny, pretty down-to-earth. She was also…pretty. Beautiful, actually. Those blue eyes were huge, and for a blonde—even a slightly salon-highlighted blonde— she had incredible lashes, thick and long and dark. That mouth, too, so full and lushly curved…

He took a breath that wasn't quite steady, and then he remembered.

She was a bloody princess.

A princess, and he had to entertain her without Nuala's help for the next six or seven days.

He woke at five-thirty the next morning—an early start, because usually he slept in until around six. Nuala was already up and dressed and packing a snack to eat en route.

She kissed him on the cheek. "Thanks for this, Brant."

"You should thank Misha," he answered. "You're skipping out on her more than you're skipping out on me."

"She understands. She's great."

He avoided the trap of agreeing with her, and headed out to the four-wheeler, unchaining Mon so that she could ride on the back. Breakfast could wait. He wanted to take a better look at those ewes.

They were sluggish at this hour, a little indignant at being disturbed so early. It was only just beginning to get light. Mon roused them into action and they milled down toward the mustering yard, where he could set up portable sections of gate and fence as well as making use of the permanent rectangle of enclosed grass.

His fences weren't in great shape. Merinos had such a strong herd instinct and such a docile temperament that they stayed put, but the crossbreeds he was getting into now tended to push against sagging sections of mesh and barge their way through, especially the lambs. He was going to have to repair or replace quite a number of stretches soon.

Between the two of them, he and Mon got a couple of hundred ewes into the yard and closed the gate. The light had grown stronger, and the sky pale at the horizon. He could watch the animals as they milled around and see if any of them seemed lame, have a good look at some more feet, clean them out and settle his doubts.

These ewes had come with a written guarantee as to their condition, but a lot of farmers were doing it much tougher than he was right now, and sometimes a seller conveniently overlooked a problem. Guarantees weren't always accurate. Nor were they always enforceable. He'd had these ewes for over two weeks. The seller would have a good case, at this point, for claiming that they'd left his land disease free, and that the problem must lie in Inverlochie's soil.

As far as he could tell, only one out of this batch of ewes looked lame. After checking some healthy feet and some that had more dirt packed into them than they should have, he got hold of the lame ewe and took a look at hers, with their two surprisingly dainty sections, like the chunky heel of a fashionable shoe.

Her front right foot didn't look good. It showed separation of the hoof from the horn, reddening in between the two sections of hoof and a soreness that looked like abscesses. As he'd done yesterday, he cleaned it and pared it carefully, then imagined having to do the same to his entire stock.

One ewe in two hundred, and only one of her feet. Did it mean anything?

He told himself it didn't, that foot rot wasn't the only reason for red, sore feet, especially when only one of the four was affected, and decided he'd monitor the situation for a bit longer. He wouldn't rope the Pastures Protection Board in yet, because then the whole thing would be out of his control. He let the sheep out of the yard and back into the paddock. Typically, having not wanted to be yarded in the first place, they now didn't realize that they were supposed to leave and Mon had to race around convincing them.

She didn't have the same razor-sharp instincts for the work that Sox did, but she was a good dog if she was given the right instructions. He whistled and yelled, "Wa-ay back, back around, back around," and off the sheep started, and just as they really began to push along up toward the saddle he saw…thought he saw…a couple more of them limping.

Feeling as if he had a rock in his stomach, he went back to the house for breakfast.

Having a diploma from a very prestigious French gourmet cooking school under her belt, as well as four months' experience cooking three meals a day plus afternoon tea for a chaletful of hungry skiers, Misha could whip up a good breakfast. She could also interpret the state of a kitchen sink, dishwasher and draining basket to determine how many people had already eaten that morning, and Brant hadn't.

Still dozing at the time, she'd heard the two vehicles before dawn—Nuala heading for Sydney and Brant on the four-wheeler going off to do something important with sheep. By the time she heard the four-wheeler coming back again, she had apricot-oatmeal muffins fresh from the oven, coffee grounds sitting in the plunger waiting for their boiling water, and grilled tomatoes, mushrooms and bacon ready to serve on whole-wheat toast.

She could have done a pretty amazing cheese omelette with herbed scones, also, but had decided to save her really star-quality cooking ammunition for another day. Somehow, it had become important to her overnight, while she slept, that Branton Smith should not have any reason to conclude she was a lazy ditz with an overdeveloped sense of entitlement.

She wasn't any of those things, and she would have thought the fact was obvious, but he wouldn't be the first man to make all the wrong assumptions about her, despite the evidence.

Gian-Marco...did he have her all wrong, too? Should she give him back his ring? How much would that hurt? She wasn't wearing it at the moment—the stone was just so huge, it got in the way—but maybe she should put it back on.

She heard Brant out in the mudroom, kicking off his boots and washing his hands, and then he appeared with his bare, brown feet scuffing the floor below his jeans. The jeans hung low on his hips, showing off the lean length of his body.

Timing it perfectly, Misha put bread in the toaster and boiling water in the coffee plunger, then went to meet him wearing Nuala's old, oversize blue-and-white-striped chalet-girl apron. "Ready for breakfast?"

If she'd hoped for hungry, lit-up eyes or an appreciative

sniff of the fabulous aromas she'd created…well, bad luck.
"You didn't have to do this," he growled.

"No, I know that, but I wanted to."

"What is it?"

She told him.

"You really didn't have to. I'm okay with toast and coffee."

"There are those things, too. It's all ready."

He followed her into the kitchen, where she had everything set up at the old table, instead of at the more formal one in the living room where they'd eaten last night. Sitting down and reaching at once for the coffee, he said, "I was thinking you might like to go riding today. We don't keep horses, but I can tee it up with some friends. They have a beautiful property with river frontage and sections of rolling, wooded country that are great for trail riding."

"I thought we were marking lambs today."

"*We* are not marking lambs any day. Chris and I can mark lambs tomorrow."

"He called. He says he'll be here by nine."

"I'll call him back and cancel."

She sighed. "I know why you're doing this, Brant, and you don't have to. I won't let you. You have to get those lambs marked…" For some reason she kept picturing hot-pink felt-tip pens being involved in the process. "…and I'm a fast learner. I got the impression it's messy…" She'd probably get completely encrusted with pink ink. "…so just lend me some old clothes."

He looked at her in total silence for at least thirty seconds, and his body language shouted, *You're really asking for it, aren't you?* so clearly that she almost laughed. "Chris is coming at nine?" he finally said.

"Yep."

"Meeting us up at the yard?"

"So he says."

Another beat of silence, then, "I'll lend you a shirt."

* * *

Ten hours later, Misha no longer had any illusion that pink ink was involved in the lamb-marking process. She was encrusted, yes, but the substance was much darker in color and consisted of bodily fluids she didn't want to examine too closely. Standing under a flood of hot shower water, she understood the reason for having a nail brush right there in the soap dish, and she used it energetically on her fingers. She also treated her hair with conditioner and three lots of shampoo.

Any princess in her right mind would be back in Albury by this time, totally traumatized and waiting with hysterical impatience for the next flight—especially since they were lamb-marking again tomorrow, at Chris's—but Misha actually felt…good.

Tired.

Satisfied.

With a sense of freedom she hadn't felt in months.

And *clean,* thanks to this heavenly steaming water.

She now knew how to pick up a bleating, woolly bundle, lay it in the worn old cradle and hook its hind legs into the two spiral-shaped curls of metal that kept the bleating bundle in place. She knew where to stick the needle that vaccinated the little guys against about six different diseases at once.

She knew how to rotate the cradle around to Brant and Chris who tackled the next much messier stages in the process, and she knew how to unhook the hind legs of the docked, marked and—where applicable—castrated lambs and swing them back down to the freedom of the grassy yard where their mothers would join them as soon as each batch was done.

She had helped to muster each successive paddock full of sheep into the yard. She'd wrestled with "wet" and "dry" ewes who didn't want to be sorted into the right group and

tried to go through the wrong race into the wrong yard. She'd
yelled at the mothers and talked baby talk to the lambs and
combed her fingers through the incredibly long, fine, soft
crimp of their wool. Shearers had the softest hands, she'd
learned, because of the lanolin.

Brant and Chris, she thought, had been grudgingly impressed. Chris seemed like a great guy, the steady, physically
adept, rough-hewn and slightly uncivilized kind that Nu had
always wanted. He had very sexy eyes. And Brant had looked
a little more relaxed today. If he'd frowned a bit at some of
the sheep and wrestled a few of them into a position where
he could examine their sheepy feet, it couldn't mean anything
bad or serious, because he'd told Chris cheerfully, "Just
checking. They're fine."

For the icing on the cake, after the long day, she might just
manage to get her aching body dried and dressed and drag
herself into the kitchen to knock together one of her chalet-
girl dinners, if she could find some decent ingredients. She
had already assured Brant confidently, out in the sheep paddock half an ago, that she would do so. "It'll take twenty minutes."

"Yeah? I don't think so, Misha, after you've been standing
in this sheep yard or riding a four-wheeler for nine hours."

"You wait."

"Let me get on the phone when I'm back at the house and
get something else fixed up for us."

It had sounded like an empty threat and she'd ignored it.

Filo-pastry parcels filled with herbed chicken, maybe,
she decided as she turned off the shower water. With steamed
vegetables and a soup. She remembered how she and Nu
used to cut the timing too fine sometimes on a really good
skiing day, zooming back down the powder-covered slopes
on their last run, yelling to each other about garnishing tricks
or side dishes to jazz up a meal.

Twenty minutes would be a stretch, but she could do it in

forty. Brant would soon learn that it was never safe to set her any kind of a challenge.

There was a knock at the bathroom door.

"I'm almost done," she called out, wrapping herself in a purple towel as big and thick and fluffy as a sheep's fleece.

"No, it's fine, I'll use the laundry," Brant called back. "I just wanted to tell you to put on a dress for tonight."

She opened the door. "*What?*"

"Suggest that you put on a dress. Might want to. I mean, it's up to you." He seemed disturbed by something. Her reaction. Or maybe the towel. "I thought…but if you don't have dresses…if a dress is too princessy…"

"Look, I said I was happy to cook for you—and Chris, if he's still here."

"He's gone home."

"But, I'm sorry, that doesn't mean you can dictate what I wear while I'm doing it."

"No. No!" He shook his head, as if irritated at her misunderstanding. "I thought we'd eat out. Didn't I say that? I made us a reservation at Tarragon."

"At what?"

"The best restaurant in the area. It used to be just the Bilbandra pub, down the road, but some corporate types in Sydney bought it before the Olympics—that's not important. There are new owners now, who've opened a restaurant. Called it Tarragon. You worked hard today and I was never seriously going to let you cook. Sheesh, of course not! I thought you realized."

They looked at each other, a little taken aback by how quickly they'd both misunderstood.

A little disappointed, too, in Misha's case, about how it felt.

She'd been so relaxed with him today. She'd had that sense of marvelling disbelief that always came when she was doing something different, rising to a challenge. Hey, I'm working on a farm with sheep, and I'm doing a pretty good job. Nuala had had it the time she'd come to stay in Langemark. Hey, I'm in a palace with eighteen-foot-high ceilings, eating my banana with a gold-filigreed knife and fork.

It didn't matter what kind of circumstance gave you the feeling, it was the feeling that counted—that you were really alive, stretching yourself, receptive and sizzling and on fire, making memories that made you believe in yourself and that would never go away.

"Sorry," Brant said gruffly.

"My fault. I jumped to the wrong conclusion."

"No problem."

In her initial anger, Misha had opened the bathroom door too wide. Now, after yelling through it about wanting her to wear a dress, Brant was standing too close. He hadn't showered yet, but he'd washed as far as his elbows and stripped off his outer clothing. He wore only stained jeans and an ancient white T-shirt, so threadbare it was almost transparent. She could see the strong shape of his chest and stomach muscles, and the curved line where his tan ended at his collarbone.

She saw his gaze flick to her shoulder. Droplets of water still clung there, because she hadn't really had a chance to dry off yet, she'd only flung the towel around herself—thank goodness it was big—and tucked a corner in at the top.

She took in a breath of air that suddenly felt overheated and too rich, and backed away from the feeling, away from their shared realization that she was dressed in a towel and he was wearing a see-through shirt. They were alone in the house, and she had a strong inkling that he was thinking about this, too. Thinking about what could happen, if either of them wanted it to.

Her body crawled, and parts of it suddenly ached. It confused her, made her think about Gian-Marco and what he might be doing right now. Was he with the actress? Did he miss her and think about her at all? Did he still value his prize princess, now that he'd won her?

"Maybe not a dress," she said.

But I'll wear Gian-Marco's ring. See how that feels.

"Whatever you want. It's a nice place. They have open fires. And tablecloths."

"Wow! Tablecloths! I don't think I've ever seen one of those!"

Brant's teeth threatened to grit together. "As opposed to throwaway place mats, I meant."

Again. Missing his point. What was wrong with her?

And why was she so disappointed about it?

"I'm sorry," she said, closing her eyes. Which helped more than it should. "I'll be ready in five minutes."

"You're really into these impossible promises about timing, aren't you?"

Her eyes flew open again.

He was grinning.

She grinned back. "You just wait and see!"

Misha really was ready to leave by the time Brant had finished his shower and dressed.

Okay, so those activities took more than five minutes, but she hadn't been through the hour and a half of obsessive grooming he'd envisaged, nor did she look overdressed. Her makeup was so subtle he decided she might not even be wearing any, and she had her hair in a little knot at the back of her head, with some wispy bits hanging down. She wore plain black trousers, a soft, silky pale blouse-type thing and a neat, shimmery, darker jacket-type thing on top of that, sewn with some beady bits.

Or something.

Oh, and earrings. Gold. Little.

It was possibly fortunate that he had not gone into the field of fashion journalism.

Their thoughts had travelled in a similar direction. "These are made of wool," she said, running her hands down the side seams of her trousers. "Is there any chance it could have come from Inverlochie sheep? They were designed and made in Italy."

"It's possible," he said. "Inverlochie wool is fine enough for that high end of the market."

"They feel fabulous. Some wool is too prickly and thick, but these are so soft and light." She ran her hands over the fabric again, making a swishy sound against her thighs.

Brant wished she would stop doing it. He kept thinking about her wrapped in that purple towel, earlier—the way it draped her body but left her shoulders bare, the contrast between the dark, plummy color of the fabric and the shimmery blond of her hair, the suggestion of her nakedness beneath.

"That's one of the goals with superfine wool," he managed to say. "The softness, the way it can be spun and woven very fine. It was tough for us when the bottom fell out of the market. I was proud of our beautiful wool, but no one will pay us what it's worth anymore."

"Competition from synthetic fibers?"

"Basically, yes."

It was ten minutes to seven. They needed to get going. He grabbed a bottle of the wine Misha had brought yesterday, and they went out to the car. As usual, he didn't bother to lock the house.

"I suppose that seems strange to you," he said, because it always seemed strange to city visitors and they always commented.

"Um, no, well, we never lock up at home, either," she answered.

"Oh, you don't?"

"Because there are always palace guards."

"Oh. Right. Of course."

She laughed. "I know. It's bizarre. You don't have to say it."

You're a princess.

How could I forget?

I wish you hadn't reminded me, because I can feel this getting weird again.

"What do we do tonight if you're recognized?" he asked.

"It won't happen," she predicted confidently. "I mean, I know people are always spotting Elvis in their local supermarket—"

"Yeah, all the time, around here, and you should see what he buys!"

She laughed again. "But with celebrities in living form, it tends to be different. I am so-o-o *not* where anyone would expect me to be, in a place like this. No one will make the connection. I'm not that well-known. Sometimes I'll get accused of looking like someone famous, but it's usually an actress. And I always do my hair and makeup differently when I'm being just Misha, and I have a couple of other strategies. Seems to work."

She flicked a blond strand behind her ear.

She looked like a pixie on a hot date.

Except that this was as far from being a hot date as Misha was from her family palace, he reminded himself quickly. He'd been on at least a dozen dates like this over the past few months, thanks to the Wanted: Outback Wives campaign—evenings spent entertaining women with whom he had nothing in common.

It was a Thursday night and Tarragon was half-empty. The two fires in the open grates were lit because of the evening chill, and two or three couples sat at the tables, as well as a party of four on the far side of the room. Misha took off her jackety thing….

Brant, he coached himself, it's a jacket, okay? Not a *jackety thing*. Just because it seems too clingy and shimmery and beady and soft for a jacket, and it probably cost about five thousand dollars, that doesn't mean it's not a jacket. Get over it.

…and then she looked around. As always, she seemed interested in what she saw, ready to find it new and fascinating, ready to ask questions.

Oddly, this suddenly left him feeling flat.

She's eaten fancy meals like the ones they serve here a million times. Her main goal for the evening is not to be recognized.

Oh, yes, and to stay awake.

He saw her hiding a yawn behind her hand. Maybe she'd have liked it better if he'd run into town for pizza to eat in front of TV. He found himself hoping for something different, to keep her entertained…and to keep her eyes open. Irish folk musicians. A knockdown marital argument at the adjacent table. An oil fire in the kitchen.

"I liked Europe," he said, abrupt and desperate.

"Oh, good," she murmured politely in reply. "When were you there? Which places did you see?"

He told her about the agricultural exchange in Holland eight years ago, and the travel he'd done, how he'd liked the sense of history and the subtle shadings of culture. "Australia must seem so brash and young to you."

"I like that," she answered. "I love the space. It gives you a freedom to be yourself. I think Australians carry the freedom with them when they travel. And I loved the smell of the air when I was driving here yesterday, so tangy and fresh."

They continued this polite and overcareful complimenting of each other's heritage for a bit too long, then took refuge in the menus that had arrived. They ordered, and about a minute afterward, the "something different" that Brant had hoped for actually happened, and he remembered the old saying, "Be careful what you wish for."

Lauren Whatshername arrived with her three friends.

Brant saw them as soon as they came in, but was able to watch them being shown to a table and set up with menus and big, paper-parasol-decorated drinks before they saw him. He didn't mention it to Misha, who had her back to them, but that turned out to be a mistake because when two of the friends came over in a posse, leaving Lauren and the third friend hiding and whispering intensely behind their menus, Misha was unprepared.

"I don't know how you can do this to a wonderful girl like Lauren," the first friend hissed in Brant's face, leaning toward him over the table.

Misha jumped.

"She is the best, sweetest, nicest person," said the second friend, nipping past Brant's far elbow in a flanking pincer movement worthy of Napoleon in battle against the Russians. "She has the worst luck with men, time after time, and *this* is why. Because there are people like you, who just trample on her good intentions, hurt her, betray her, lie to her—"

She shot a narrow-eyed look in Misha's direction, and Brant discovered that Misha had picked up the wine list and positioned it so that it shadowed the guarded expression on her face.

"I can't believe you can sit here like this with someone else, ignoring her," the friend continued, "when all she wanted was to make a connection, develop a friendship. She trusted you enough to be open with you about how she felt, and you couldn't even return her call."

Which was true.

He'd gone to bed early last night, he'd woken at five-thirty, and he'd been marking lambs all day. He'd forgotten all about it.

"Couldn't even come over to our table and say hello," said the second friend.

"He's reserved, sometimes," Misha murmured suddenly, from behind the wine list. "It can take a while for people to see past that."

The older couple at the next table had heard the indignant

voices and were looking in Brant's direction. The woman muttered something to her husband and he raised his thick gray brows.

"You *put* yourself in that magazine, Branton Smith!" said Friend One. "You sent a message. Lauren, like a whole lot of other women, took that message in good faith—"

Misha put down the wine list. She was now wearing a pair of large reading glasses with pearlescent red rims. They didn't suit her at all. "The thing is, he met me," she said to Lauren's friends. "And as of last night, we're engaged. So I'm afraid for Lauren it's hands off." She smiled sweetly. "Can you tell her? Sorry to be blunt."

She took Brant's hand across the table and squeezed it with the grip of a woman strong enough to wrestle lambs in and out of lamb-marking cradles for hours at a time. Lauren's friends looked shocked. They turned open-mouthed, wide-eyed faces to Brant, who hadn't a clue what to say.

"I hope she'll be happy for us, and understand about Brant not calling her back," Misha went on. "This is very new, and we're very excited about it. See my ring, isn't it gorgeous?"

She held out her left hand, showing what had to be Gian-Marco Ponti's engagement gift. Brant hadn't even noticed she was wearing it tonight, even though the solitaire rock in the middle of it was huge. Had she spoken to her fiancé again? Or was she simply celebrating the fact that she had clean hands?

She frowned at the ring for a moment, and he saw her eyes cloud with a distant expression that she quickly schooled away. He guessed she had to be well trained in hiding her feelings in public. Maybe she could give him a few lessons.

"And…well…I guess we're just not thinking straight, either of us," she finished prettily. Not for the first time, he noticed how perfect her English was. "We apologize."

She beamed at Brant, beamed at Lauren's overemotional friends, beamed at the couple at the next table, beamed at her ring and wiggled her hand to make it twinkle in the firelight.

None of it worked.

"You *two-timed* her?" Friend One said to Brant.

"You wrote to him?" Friend Two asked Misha.

Misha nodded, still smiling widely in the ugly red glasses. Nobody would have recognized Elvis in those glasses, let alone a privacy-loving European princess. Brant guessed that this was the whole point.

"Isn't that romantic?" she said to Lauren's friends. "I wasn't hoping for anything as special as this. We've been so lucky."

"When did you write?" said Friend Two.

"The day I bought the magazine with his picture on the cover."

"So you must have written to him before Lauren even got to see the magazine?" She made it sound like a flagrant case of insider trading.

"Yes, but it's taken us a while. He was cautious about it."

"So Lauren never had a chance," said Friend One to Brant, "And you couldn't *tell* her that?"

"It's been hard…" Misha murmured.

Lauren's friends were not sympathetic to how hard it had been. They huffed indignantly back to their table. A word that might have been *witch* floated back to Brant's ears, and he could see them delivering a full report to Lauren and Friend Three seconds later. Four pairs of cold, resentful eyes lanced dagger-like looks across the restaurant.

"Well, I tried…" Misha muttered. "It's a good strategy, but when people have that kind of a martyr complex, and have friends with a full-blown case of Martyr by Proxy Syndrome, what can you do? Or should I ask, do you and this woman have a large slice of shared past that I don't know about?"

"Just coffee."

"How much coffee?"

"One cup each." Brant realized he needed to seize control of the conversation. "What," he asked her, without moving his lips, "was that stuff with the ring all about?"

"You have to trust me," Misha replied in an undertone.

She was still gripping his hand, and she looked into his eyes as if they were pools of liquid mist. It was an impressive performance.

"Here's the thing, though," he said. "I don't."

"Really, Brant, because this is my best area. I lost my virginity to the tabloid press a long time ago and this is the best strategy, the best we can do with the material available. Nuala was right last night. Fake romance. Used all the time."

"Yeah?"

"Generates publicity for bad movies. Douses scandal about unsavory sexual practices. Or in our case, gets rid of pushy women with martyr complexes and overinvolved female friends, and explains presence on sheep farm of strange and suspiciously royal-looking European visitor."

"Royal-looking? Not in those glasses."

"I know. Hideous. Don't you love them? I keep them specifically for when I suspect I'm in the presence of serious celebrity magazine junkies."

"You're as crazy as my sister, do you know that?" Brant told her.

And she also somehow managed to make the strategy of a pretend engagement sound like good, clean fun, which was a whole concept he'd sort of forgotten about just lately.

"Shared craziness has been the basis for a beautiful friendship," she said. "We can keep up the engagement idea for the magazine interview on Monday if you want, so that you don't get inundated with more visits and letters, or we can drop it in an hour when we leave here. Up to you."

"Can I get back to you on that?"

"Sure. As long as we make it convincing while we're doing it. Because I like a challenge."

He caught the twinkle in her eye and couldn't help laughing. "So do I, Mish. Always have."

"There you go. We can improvise."

She made the last word sound astonishingly sexual, although he didn't think she had any idea that she'd done so.

"Let's improvise," he agreed.

"Right now?"

"Um, sure." What did she mean by that?

He found out seconds later when she leaned forward and kissed him on the mouth across the table.

Chapter Five

Brant's lips tasted sweet and warm and shocking. They made Misha tingle. They were like a mouthful of champagne when you expected plain water. The soft, intimate contact sent a jet of sensation pulsing through her body.

She sat back at once, startled by what she'd done. It was over so fast. You could hardly count it as a kiss. She'd intended it as a bit of silly pretense, and it was. In which case, why did it feel so significant? Why had his eyes darkened? Why was all this heat flooding into her cheeks?

"Oops," she murmured, staring down at her gleaming white plate. "We can just rewind that moment, if you want."

He didn't answer, and she felt worse. She'd expected him to meet her halfway and agree that the moment hadn't even happened. Trivial impulse. Rational adults. Business as usual. That kind of thing.

Or, even better, laugh it off altogether.

"Say something, Brant," she blurted out.

"I'm trying to think of something funny about frogs, but nothing's leaping out at me."

She laughed. "Frogs? Leaping out?"

"You know. Kissing them. But I'm not a prince and you're already a—" He stopped. "And you have probably heard dumb jokes about frogs and fairy tales your whole life from every mortal you've ever met."

"Mortal? Um, Brant, I hate to break it to you but I'm actually not a fairy princess, just the regular kind."

"Sorry. I do know that. But what's the opposite of royal? I'm sorry." He dropped his voice to an anguished murmur. "Granted, we'll go with pretending to be engaged, tonight and then on Monday with the people from the magazine, but do you mind not kissing me again unless you really have to?"

"Sure," she said brightly. "No problem. You know, it was only for authenticity."

And it's still burning on my mouth. It lasted a quarter of a second. He's begging me not to repeat it. I'm obsessing about it. What's going on?

"But we can get authenticity…um, somewhere else," she finished.

"It's not that I didn't like it, as such."

"Oh, *as such*?"

"It's just that Nu told me you were engaged to Whatshisname…"

Misha let out a helpless sigh the moment she heard her fiancé's name, even though Brant hadn't actually said it. He noticed the sigh, and she was angry with herself for not managing to hold it back. She needed to get a grip, or the first thing that would happen when she flew back to Europe would be a front-page photo of *Princess Artemisia Helena In Tears After Mystery Trip*.

"…and I wanted to make sure you know that I'm well aware of the boundaries," Brant finished.

"The real question for me at the moment is, is Whatshisname aware of the boundaries?" she said, almost as if she were talking to Nu.

The fact that she trusted her friend so completely gave her an instant passport to trusting her friend's brother, also. This was probably a mistake.

"Yeah, my sister mentioned that issue, too," he said.

"Oh, she did?"

"No detail." He raised his hands, fending off any suggestion that Nuala might have been indiscreet. "Just enough to fill me in."

Their appetizers appeared, and they both began to eat. Misha had already forgotten what she'd ordered, and hardly noticed what she put in her mouth.

"Did you see any of the pictures?" she asked. "Of Whatshisname and the actress, I mean."

"No, I didn't."

"Lucky you. There were two of them, actually. A brunette and a blonde."

She had a sheaf of the pictures in an envelope in her suitcase. They had been taken from several different European tabloids and magazines, and helpfully cut out and mounted on sheets of pristine ivory card stock by the press office at the palace— although admittedly she'd had to lean on the staff pretty hard to get them actually to give her the pictures. They'd fobbed her off about it for days, probably under orders from the queen.

"You could argue that two women are better than one," Brant suggested. "Because it means he's not seriously involved with either of them."

"I thought of that."

She hadn't had a chance to show the pictures to Nuala yet, and suddenly, she wondered what it would be like to get a man's opinion, instead. A whole lot blunter and less supportive, probably. The trouble with having a friend you trusted and who really cared about you was that she tended to tell you only the things you wanted to hear.

"But you're not convinced," Brant said.

"Ask me in the morning, and again in the afternoon and you'll get two different answers. For a start, I have to work out my definition of *not seriously*."

And when you didn't know what things you wanted to hear, it could get messy. With the wedding only just over four months away, was she seriously considering breaking off her engagement, once the palace had decreed that she could? Would she only pretend to end it, as a piece of strategy, to try and get an emotional reaction from Gian-Marco? What did it say about her feelings, and about him, if she could even consider playing such games? Why was honesty such a rare commodity in her life?

And, forget all this complex analysis, how did she *feel*?

"How's your meal?" Brant asked, as if he knew she had too many questions running in her head and wanted to help her shut them down.

She looked down at it vaguely. "Oh, fine."

It was…oh, right, mushroom risotto.

Perfect princess food.

She ordered it at restaurants all the time, or requested it to appear on formal banquet menus. Not too much chewing, neat and easy to sneak into your mouth during breaks in the conversation, and no sloppy sauce to splash on your outfit. Sometimes, if the food was wrong at official functions, or if someone kept her talking too long, she didn't manage to eat at all.

One memorable time, when she'd had nine official lunches and dinners in four different countries in one week, she'd eaten mushroom risotto eight times. She thought this probably didn't happen to the British royal family. They probably had their menus coordinated at an international strategic level to avoid repetition. But Langemark was a pretty small country, and she wasn't the heir to the throne.

Thank goodness!

For that blessing, a lifetime supply of mushroom risotto was a small price to pay.

Brant did one of his silences, and she belatedly realized she'd said something wrong. It took her the rest of her appetizer to backtrack through the past few minutes and work out the problem, at which point she sounded too fake and forced when she told him, "Really, it's delicious. This is a lovely place. Thanks for thinking to bring me here."

"The next time we're not cooking, we'll have takeaway pizza by the fire," he told her.

"Can I tell you something?"

"Go ahead."

"Pizza by the fire would be a huge treat."

The tension drained out of him, and she knew she'd gotten the problem right. He had wanted to treat a princess in the manner to which she was accustomed. This princess would prefer anything but, and it had taken her too long to get the point across.

Misha had forgotten to take the red glasses off.

Brant had forgotten about them, too, while they sat talking over their meal. At first, he would look up from his plate and get startled by the unexpected sight of such large, ugly frames in such an impossible pearlescent red color, but once they'd become absorbed in what they were saying, he didn't notice the glasses anymore.

At some point, Lauren and her friends must have left, because when he and Misha finally stood up to go, their table was empty and already set with new silverware and crockery. At some point, also, time had speeded up, because it couldn't possibly be almost eleven o'clock as he stopped the car in front of the darkened house.

He intended to open the door for Misha, but she darted out of the vehicle before he could even get to the door handle on his own side. She waited for him, leaning a hand on the engined-warmed metal of the car, and she wore that little smile he was beginning to recognize and understand. She'd jumped out of the car so fast precisely because she didn't want the fuss of someone standing there doing all the work for her.

"Thanks for a great evening," he told her, meaning it. He hadn't thought about the farm, his finances or his ewes' feet in hours. "I know it would have been nothing special for you, getting dressed up and eating fancy food. In fact, I'm sorry I put you through it, but if it's any consolation, it was special for me. Time out. I don't get enough of that."

"You're welcome, Brant," she said. "And if I seemed too blasé about the food, I'm just a spoiled brat who doesn't know when she's well off."

"You're not a spoiled brat."

"You wait." She grinned at him. "I can be when I want."

"How often is that?"

She spread her hands and shrugged. "When the palace says I'm allowed to."

"The big, bad palace. Can I tell you something? Don't get upset about it."

"What?"

"Did you know you were still wearing those glasses?"

Her mouth dropped open and a hand flew up to her face. She burst out laughing. "And you couldn't tell me until now because they make me look so unbearably sexy, right? You thought the entire restaurant needed such a vision of loveliness to gaze at all through their meal."

She snatched them away from her face, and folded them. "Next time, I'm going to wear the wig."

"You don't have a wig."

"Trust me, I have a wig. Gorgeous synthetic chocolate-brown curls. It's for emergencies only, but a princess has to be prepared."

"Wear it on Monday," he told her. "I want a pretend engagement to a woman with pretend hair."

She laughed. Possibly she was even blushing a little. "But, as previously discussed, no pretend kisses?"

"Uh, no. If that's okay." They walked toward the house in silence, feet crunching softly on the mix of damp earth and gravel. "I mean, I wouldn't want you to think—"

"That you hadn't enjoyed it *as such*," she mimicked, and he groaned.

"Is that what I said?"

"Yep."

"Is there a way I can save us both from embarrassment on this subject, by explaining better what I actually meant? That I actually did enjoy—"

"Don't think so. Better stop before the hole gets even deeper."

"Right." He thought it already had.

They went into the house and he told her goodnight, hoping they'd both have forgotten about that sweet, unexpected and far too pleasant press of her lips on his by the morning.

The horses broke from the barrier on the far side of the course and belted around the rail, their initial tight grouping soon strung out so that individual horses and their jockeys' colors were easier to see. Brant nudged Misha, his gaze fixed on the distant movement. "Can you see him, pale blue and white, about a length and a half behind the front runner?"

"Yes, but he's closing in, I think."

She willed Trans Pacific to reach the front, willed those powerful, elegant legs to drum even faster, to lengthen their stride. She had her hands clenched into fists, and her neck craning to see better. She'd been to racing carnivals before. The most glamorous such events in the racing world—Royal Ascot in England, the Kentucky Derby—but this was so much better.

It was the first time she'd dressed like this, for a start.

Baseball cap, running shoes and a borrowed windproof jacket of Nuala's, instead of the usual heels, floaty fabric and pretty hat. The fashion photographers would have dropped her from their roster of targets after a single glance.

If they'd been here.

They weren't, of course.

At a country race meeting on an ordinary Saturday in late autumn, there was no one to photograph, and the only press coverage of the event would consist of dry listings of results in the sports pages of a few newspapers tomorrow.

For the first time, Misha could actually watch the races, read about the horses and their form, watch them warming up or giving their jockeys trouble on the way into the barrier, as they got ready for the start. It was so much more interesting than tottering around in the wrong shoes in the most exclusive enclave of the members' section, getting fawned over by dignitaries she didn't know, and very often with goose bumps all over her. Today, she was actually comfortable.

And there was plenty to look at. Several old-fashioned wooden bookies' stands had been set up in the no-frills pavilion between the public grandstand and the members' area, while the bookies kept their cash in cavernous bags made of cracked leather so old that she wondered how many generations had used them before.

Some of the bookies covered race meetings in the capital cities, while others took bets on this track's events. The bags and stands were complemented by nifty little computerized ticket printers, and there was a confusing selection of race-viewing on TV screens, also, to bring the atmosphere into the twenty-first century.

A rather red-faced groom-to-be was having a bucks' party before his upcoming wedding, and there were families treating the day as a picnic. The racing club had provided a free jumping castle for the children, but many of them were more interested in rolling down a short but steep section of grass, which had a great view of the winning post. They had red cheeks and grass marks on their arms and legs, and didn't seem the least bit interested in the thunder of hooves galloping in their direction, louder by the second.

Four young women had set up a gourmet meal for themselves on a picnic blanket, and were wearing adorable hats that they must have made themselves—pinned and folded confections of tulle, feathers, beading and silk flowers. Misha couldn't imagine what the bucks' party guests were thinking of. The girls looked pretty and sweet, but not one of the men paid them any attention.

The horses galloped into the straight on their way to the winning post. From this angle, their wildly working hooves seemed to tangle together and it was impossible to see who was in front. Not Trans Pacific. At least two other horses challenged him and each other for the lead.

But as the field came closer Misha could see that the jockey was really making Trans Pacific run, standing high and forward in the saddle and urging him on. He passed one horse, then another, and as the thoroughbreds swept past her she yelled out, "Go, Trans Pacific! Go!" and saw the horse overtake the leader fifty yards short of the winning post. He came home a comfortable two lengths ahead.

The other thing she'd never done at the races before was to bet.

"How much did we win?" she gasped out to Brant. She grabbed his arm and bounced up and down.

"Seventeen dollars and fifty cents."

"Is that *all?*" But she was still grinning.

He grinned back, under his farmer's felt hat. "We only put on five dollars, and he was running at three and a half to one."

"So we've made twelve whole dollars and fifty cents profit. When we've split it between us, I can just about buy a cheap bottle of wine. This is incredible!"

"Careful, or you'll get seriously rich this afternoon. It'll go to your head and you won't know what to do with yourself."

"Why didn't we put more on? A thousand, or something."

"Because Trans Pacific might have lost. You said you wanted to have fun. I wasn't going to let you lose a bundle on a horse I thought might not live up to its promise."

"Even though you own it."

"Part of it."

"Which part?"

"Well, the legs obviously. The money drains right down through them and into the ground with a hobby like this."

"Seriously?"

"Seriously? I own twenty-five percent and so does Callan. Dusty owns forty, and our trainers usually take out a ten percent ownership, also."

"No, but I meant seriously there's no money in racing? Because I can see how much fun it could be."

"There's a lot of money in racing, but you can never guarantee that you're going to get any of it. The costs are enormous and the results are uncertain. You can have a slew of poor runs, but your costs are just as high when you lose. You can have wins, but if they're not the right ones you don't make much. They reckon only about ten percent of race horses turn a profit during their career. When you do win, your jockey gets a percentage, so does your trainer. The prize for first in this race was $3,500. Which makes my share around $750."

"So why do you do it?"

"Because it's fun, and because it's a good way to make sure I don't lose touch with my mates."

"Callan and Dusty. Nuala has mentioned them."

"Between us we own seven horses now. Bought a couple of new ones a few months ago, but those aren't in serious work yet. Four of them are trained here—the stable's on the far side of the course—the other three in Queensland, not too far from Dusty."

"Do I get to meet your trainer?"

"She'll be in the mounting yard. Let's head over."

They clomped along through the lush grass to where jockeys had dismounted, flimsy racing saddles had been removed and weights were about to be checked. "Rae!" Brant called to a wiry woman in her forties. "Someone wants to meet you."

"Oh, don't say that." Misha pulled the dark blue baseball cap down her forehead and pushed her sunglasses further up her nose. "Michelle Smith, okay?" She squeezed his arm.

He ignored her. "Mish, this is our trainer, Rae Middleton. Rae, Misha wants to know how she can make a lot of money out of racing without doing any work."

Rae let out a warm laugh and her eyes crinkled up. Nice eyes, in a lively, no-nonsense face. She looked as if she spent a lot of time squinting at horses on the far side of a training track. She also looked as if she really enjoyed what she did.

"I think they had the technique down perfect in that *Back to the Future* movie," she said. "All you need is a thoroughbred racing website with a good archive of past results…and a time machine. But where's the adventure in that?"

"None," Misha said. "Which is why Brant actually got it the wrong way around. I'm interested in what it's like making a tiny bit of money out of racing by doing a lot of work."

"Aha!" Rae's eyes lit up. "Now you're talking!"

The three of them talked together for about ten minutes. Mostly this meant that Brant asked Rae questions about things like nominations and acceptances, starts and wins, gear changes and barrier trials, and Rae answered him. Misha struggled to understand most of it, but found it interesting all the same, and when she managed to slip in a question and they explained something, she understood a little more. Then Rae had to go and talk to a jockey before the next race.

"You never introduced me properly," Misha said to Brant when she'd gone.

"And did she mind?"

"She didn't seem to. She just talked to us. It was great."

"I'm learning, you see. Soon I'll be able to write the book. The care and feeding of a princess in disguise."

"You've improved markedly with the feeding since Thursday night, I have to say."

Today, they'd had steak sandwiches for lunch, eaten standing up on the grass beside the track, with slatherings of tomato ketchup, mustard and fried onions. Last night, dinner had been a reheated quiche that Nu had left in the freezer, along with bread and cheese and olives and salami, laid out on the coffee table and eaten while watching TV.

"Anything that liberates you from silverware and small talk, right?" Brant said.

"Pretty much. You have no idea what a great change it is to have my mouth really, really full!"

"Let's go and look at the next starters in the mounting yard. We have to make a considered decision on the best option for our five dollars."

"Five dollars again? We're going all out!"

They stayed until the last race, losing their five dollars on every one, and then he took her to the local pub for a drink on the way home. For dinner they zipped around the kitchen together with rock music playing, and made spaghetti Bolognese and salad.

Brant's recipe.

Misha had never learned to cook anything that simple.

"I know it involves eating with silverware," he said, "But I thought a single fork was a pretty good compromise."

Misha called home again that night and told her mother, "I'm glad I came."

"Have you made a decision, sweetheart?"

"Not yet. I'm still clearing my head. And you know, they're on the bottom of the world down here. Upside down. All the locals walk around with their feet on the ground and strangely enough it doesn't look as if they're going to fall off, but that's only because they're used to it. I think I'm going to need a little more practice before I can steer myself in the right direction without the blood rushing to my head."

"That's my crazy girl."

She lowered her voice to a more serious pitch. "But do you see what I'm saying, Mom?"

"I see what you're saying." Her mother the queen sighed at the far end of the line. "I do. Believe me, I would never choose to put this pressure on you, to make you wait for Christian and Graziella's pregnancy announcement, or make your private life into something so political, but the fact is, leaving aside any gossip and scandal, your actions influence the whole country, and—"

"I know. It's time the outdated divorce laws in Langemark were changed, but if I'm seen to behave in a shallow and fickle way by cancelling my engagement four months before a massive royal wedding, there could be a backlash against the morals of the younger generation and parliament will vote the other way. I got a letter about it from Dad's senior adviser, just in case I forgot our riveting conversation on the subject."

"And he sent a copy to me. And I'm aching for you, honey, but I agree with him. Right now, duty to Langemark comes first, your heart comes second."

"Have you seen it, by the way? My heart? I think I might have forgotten to bring it with me."

"I'll check your room," her mother drawled, and they ended the conversation soon after.

On Sunday, Brant took Misha horseback riding. Anticipating the possibility and hoping for it, Misha had brought her riding gear with her. Two-tone jodhpurs in cinnamon and sand that fit her like a second skin, almost-new custom-fitted riding boots in polished black leather with classic brown tops, a cheeky little stretch top that matched the jods, a jacket that matched the top, and a crash helmet covered in black velvet.

Brant looked appalled at the sight of her.

She glared at him. "It's what I have, okay? I meet with a consultant about my wardrobe. She calls me Your Highness, rules me with a rod of iron and doesn't offer me the combat pants option. I can put on jeans if you promise you have cream for chafed thigh skin."

"The jods are fine. But maybe the boots could get swapped for an old pair of Nu's? Those ones could get wet, or scratched or—"

"And here I thought we were spending the morning in a dressage arena."

He looked sideways at her. "You're telling me that's the kind of riding you want, today?"

"Please! No!"

She emerged from her room ten minutes later wearing Nuala's elastic-sided boots, Nuala's wind jacket and a hot-pink T-shirt of her own. "Better?"

"I really do like the jods."

They were out of the house and on the road by seven, driving for about twenty minutes toward the mountains, where he had friends with a farm that took vacation visitors in a set of cute little cabins on the property. Since schools were in session at this time of year, the place was quiet and they had their pick of the trail-riding horses, all of them looking glossy-coated and well fed.

They each chose one of the largest and most spirited animals, then took a grassy, forested route that led to a stretch of tumbling mountain river. In the shade, the air was crisp and cool, but the sun's heat still packed some power, even in late autumn, and the contrast between cool shadows and open glades felt delicious in Misha's lungs and on her skin.

They'd packed picnic supplies for a morning snack, but

nothing fancy, just a flask of hot coffee, some cheese and biscuits, apples and slices of chocolate cake. They tethered the horses by the river, spread their rain jackets out on the grass to sit on, and ate to the sound of water gurgling over smooth-worn river pebbles, and birds calling in the thicker, wilder forest on the far side. The air smelled of eucalyptus and warm stone.

After they'd eaten, Misha took off her socks and Nu's riding boots, scraped her stretchy jodhpurs up to her knees and paddled calf deep in the water until her feet no longer felt the cold. The sun pressed with satisfying warmth on her back and the horses looked just as content as she felt. So did Brant. He'd stayed on the grass, and when she saw him lying on his back with his felt farmer's hat over his eyes, she thought he was probably asleep.

It was so peaceful here. No flashes of sunlight bouncing off a camera lens hidden in the bushes. No curious crowds watching her reaction to Gian-Marco's Grand Prix race when they should be watching the race itself. No palace protocol or palace staff, or even the discreet security guards who hovered in the background when she and Gian-Marco went clubbing or skiing or visiting friends.

Dad had wanted her to bring a couple of people. She'd had to fight hard to be allowed to travel on her own, and Mom had needed to step in and convince the king that she could be safe this way.

She felt incredibly safe, and incredibly free.

Giddy about it.

Ready to let it go totally to her head.

She didn't even mind that Nuala was in Sydney. She and Nu talked too much, sometimes. Women often did. They analyzed their feelings to death. This was what she needed. Simply the peace, simply the space. No pressure to make any decisions until she wanted to. No insistence from anyone that she had to present a clear and consistent picture of how she felt. For a little longer, she could simply *be*.

She trailed a stick in the water and watched the braided surface patterns making intricate shadows on the pebbled riverbed below. She saw a school of tiny, semitranslucent fish darting in miraculous unison, zipping out of her way then darting off in another direction when something else startled them. The cold water ruffled like lace around her calves. Past and future vanished for a blessed interval, and all she thought about was this: the sun, the river, the space and the peace.

Suddenly, Brant appeared beside her. Over the rush and gurgle of the water, she hadn't heard him.

"You're awake?" she said.

"Didn't mean to fall asleep."

"This is so beautiful."

"We should have brought a camera."

"No. No cameras," she said quickly. "Photos are so flat. Even videos. I want my whole body to remember this. My mouth and my ears and the soles of my feet. It's perfect."

"But we have to get back." She could see how reluctantly he said it. "I have the last paddock of sheep to muster into the yard for lamb-marking today, and Chris still has more he needs help with. We won't get anything done tomorrow morning, because of the people coming from the magazine."

She nodded, hiding what she felt. "Let's go, then."

Peace and space and breathing air into your lungs until your head went dizzy…those things never lasted for her. It was all right for Brant. He would come here dozens more times in his life, while Misha wondered if she'd ever have a perfect morning like this one again. They paddled back to the river bank, getting their wet feet encrusted with coarse sand and bits of grass.

"Did we bring a towel?" she asked.

"Forgot. We can sun-dry them, then use my jacket to get off the sand. I won't need to wear it. It's not going to rain."

So they lay in the sun for a few precious minutes longer, letting their feet dry. Misha wiggled her sandy toes in the sun, saw that her pink polish had gotten chipped in a couple of places by the river pebbles, and didn't care. Brant came over and offered her the jacket, but she shook her head. Please could she have just one minute more?

He misunderstood.

Leaning back on her hands in the grass, she watched it happening like a car-crash test in slow motion. He thought she wanted him to use the jacket on her feet. He bent down and folded the jacket so that the plaid flannel lining faced outward and started to brush the sand and slivers of grass away. It was soft and warm and tickly, like the feeling inside her on Thursday night when she'd discovered she was still wearing her horrible red glasses an hour and a half after she'd put them on and Brant hadn't said a word.

She laughed and wriggled, and he stopped. "Is that okay now?"

"There's a bit more sand on the side of my other foot, but it's okay. My socks won't mind."

"Let me get it. You don't want to have blisters when you're riding."

"Shall I do yours?" she said a little later, when she'd put on her socks and boots.

He just handed her the jacket without a word. She'd begun to work on his second foot before either of them spoke.

Brant said, "Tomorrow." Then he stopped.

She sat back on her heels and looked at him.

"Nuala's pretend engagement idea. Do you still want to go with that? We haven't talked about it since Thursday night."

"Do you want to go with it?"

"I hope it'll stop the phone from ringing so much. And it's probably not fair of me to tell you all this female attention is driving me nuts. I know you have your own problems…."

"Mmm."

"But, ah hell, Misha, it's driving me nuts. If the Outback

Wives thing would just go away after this article, I'd breathe a sigh of relief, and I think if we did a convincing engagement story I'd get left alone. But that's to my advantage, not yours. I wouldn't want to push you into it."

He flicked a quick look in her direction and somehow she knew he was thinking about the way she'd kissed him on Thursday night—that small, silly, innocent touch of her mouth that he'd begged her not to repeat. The moment felt awkward, so she quickly told him, "I'm okay. It's just for a few hours. How hard could it be?"

"That's what you thought about lamb-marking."

"And I did great at lamb-marking."

"You're right," he agreed. "How hard could it be."

They smiled at each other, then they had a fabulous long, easy canter back to the stables. It turned into a racing gallop two hundred yards from the end, and Brant and his horse won by a nose.

Chapter Six

"Are you really going to wear the wig?" Brant asked.

He'd had a call from Shay-from-the-magazine a short while ago, saying that she and her photographer should be at Inverlochie's front gate within half an hour. He planned to meet them there, to show them the way down to the house. He'd given Shay directions, but she was apparently convinced she would get lost in such a vast, impenetrable wilderness without personal guidance. About to jump in the four-wheel drive, he'd discovered Misha on her way to the bathroom armed with her hairy disguise.

"You said you wanted me to," she reminded him.

"I was only half serious."

"But I'm a hundred-percent serious about not getting recognized, Brant, especially by journalists whose job it is to keep up on Adrenaline Junkie Princesses who are Out of Control, so I'm going for major wig insurance. You're heading down to the gate?"

"I should. I got the impression Shay has never been out of Sydney."

"I'm thinking, don't mention me, okay? Just let me appear on the scene in all my glory. You won't recognize me. So don't gasp!"

Dimples popped into her cheeks when she smiled this kind of teasing half smile, Brant noticed. They were adorable, and they terrified him.

"Gasp? Oh, because supposedly you always look that way?" he suggested after a moment, a little too slow in grasping her meaning. What was wrong with him?

"Exactly!" she said, and dimpled again.

"I'm scared, now." Too true!

"As you should be."

They laughed.

Getting to be a habit.

And it was a habit he liked too much.

"You almost look as if you're expecting to enjoy this," he said to Misha, and she shrugged like a little boy whose mischievous intentions are written all over his face.

"Think it might be a bit of an adventure," she said lightly, and then disappeared into the bathroom before he could react. When the reaction came, as he went outside, it was that same lifting of his spirits that he kept feeling when she was around. On the one hand, he liked it. It was a breath of fresh air. On the other...

Yeah.

As before.

He was terrified.

As he climbed into the vehicle, he thought about everything that had been on his mind when Misha had first arrived five days ago and his gut lurched. The lame sheep, the gamble of overstocking his land, the never-ending quest to compensate for the plunge in wool prices, the possibility of having to drop out of the racing syndicate with Callan and Dusty.

This was by far the most obvious way to cut his expenses and yet he didn't want to consider it, didn't want to take the sensible approach. Their beautiful horses bound them together across Australia's huge distances. If Brant sold his share, he knew he could end up losing his friends as well. He'd almost prefer to lose Inverlochie itself.

Entertaining the princess had made him forget his problems for hours at a time, but when they came back, they flooded in with a vengeance.

"I'm not going to lose this place," he muttered to himself, guiding the vehicle around a muddy patch on the track.

He knew his stepfather wouldn't let it happen, for a start. One word to Mum, and there could be an injection of clean, healthy capital in Inverlochie's bank account within a few days. In a way, this made his situation worse. He simply couldn't see himself going cap in hand to anyone, let alone the man who'd married his mother just a year after a lifetime of hard work on this place had worn out his father's heart.

He wanted to solve his own problems, not look for handouts, even from family. In fact, he thought he'd probably sell rather than ask for help from Frank, Chris, the bank or anyone else.

He didn't blame Mum for marrying the man. He liked Frank. He didn't even blame her for never quite adjusting to the reality of being a farmer's wife. In the beginning, she'd had these rose-tinted, optimistic ideas about pottering around in a vegetable garden and making hot breakfasts at dawn. It hadn't worked out that way very often. She'd been needed too much for the heavier work.

Sometimes, during shearing, she would have to go down to the shed and work as the roustabout, sweeping the wool and dags from the lanolin-stained wooden floor, or lifting the light, greasy fleeces to the sorting table and picking out the matted or discolored pieces. She'd get yelled at all day.

"Wool away!"

"Wool *away*, dammit, Helen!"

Paid by the number of sheep shorn, not by the hour, shearers wanted their shearing space swept the instant a freshly shorn sheep scrabbled down the chute to the yard, so that they could get to work on the next animal on a clean piece of floor. They wore special soft shoes made of carpet to give flexibility to their feet as they twisted and bent to maneuver the animals around, and they could get half-crippled by bruised soles if pebble-hard, dag-encrusted bits of wool were left beneath them too often. It was like hiking with a stone in your shoe.

"Wool *away!*" while sheep bawled and shearing blades buzzed and the odors of lanolin and sweat and fermented grass filled the air.

Mum hated the yelling, the impatience, the swearing, the mess and the smell. After a few hours of it, her face would start to grow tighter and tighter. She would flinch at every raised voice and she would eventually, inevitably, flee the shed in tears before the end of the day.

Dad would always go after her, abject about having to put her through this kind of work in seasons when an extra man hired for the job was a luxury they couldn't afford. Mum herself had wanted to save the money so that Brant could go to boarding school in Sydney.

Hanging around the shed as a kid, Brant had seen the tension and the unhappiness, despite the love. From the age of eight, he'd begged to be allowed to do the work himself, but Mum and Dad had united on that issue. Not until he was older and stronger. They had let him start when he was fourteen, when he was home on breaks from school, and he'd dealt with the tongue-lashing and teasing from the shearers instead of his mother.

As for helping with lamb-marking, Mum hated the sight of such mess, and she'd never even tried. She'd loved Dad sincerely, but she was so much happier with Frank.

Brant couldn't switch allegiance in the same way. He

wouldn't tarnish his father's memory by failing with the farm while there was breath in his body, but he was on his own, dealing with Inverlochie's problems. He knew it, and he had better not kid himself about anything different.

He reached the gate, but there was no sign of the magazine people yet. He climbed out of the vehicle and let his eyes roam over the sheep he could see from this spot. Lambs lolloped through the green grass after their mothers on their woolly white legs, their recent experience in the marking cradle completely forgotten.

A couple of the mothers lolloped, too, and he tried to assess their gait from this impossible distance. Stepping over a rock? Compensating for uneven ground? He didn't think so. It was more than that. At least a dozen of this particular mob looked lame today.

He thought about his father again. Dad had always been such a responsible farmer. He'd planted tracts of his land with native vegetation years before environmental issues had become a priority for most farmers. He'd always studied the latest edicts on disease prevention. He'd cooperated with the authorities whenever he could.

In Brant's situation, Dad would contact the Pastures Protection Board. He wouldn't knowingly hobble another farmer with tainted stock. And the contracted sale ewes would indeed be tainted, if the new ones were. All a healthy sheep had to do was cross a path walked by a foot-rot-infected animal, and the bacteria could get passed on.

If this was foot rot.

Brant still didn't believe it could be, and that was the only thing holding him back, now, but the time had come to make sure. His inspection of those muddy hooves had been too governed by emotion and self-interest. He desperately wanted to see something less serious like dermatitis or shelly hoof, so of course he interpreted the signs to fit. The time had come for tests.

Tomorrow, he decided. He'd phone the Pastures Protection Board tomorrow. They'd send someone out to take a sample, probably on Wednesday, the day that Nuala was due back. Maybe he could get rid of the P.P.B. guy before she arrived and she still wouldn't need to know. As for Misha, she wouldn't even realize who the guy was.

He saw a white station wagon slowing as it approached the gate. Male driver, female passenger. It had to be Shay Russell and her photographer. He went over, opened the gate, introduced himself and welcomed them to his land.

He shook hands with Shay and the photographer, Mark, and promised Shay that she wouldn't see any snakes, while secretly hoping that the snakes chose to cooperate with this statement and stayed hidden or asleep. If Shay screamed, fainted and hit her head on the ground, his insurance situation might be unclear.

When they reached the house, he somehow expected to find Misha waiting for them, artistically posed in her fake hair and some designer farm clothes. Fringed white silk shirt and cowboy hat, maybe, above those glove-tight stretchy designer jodhpurs from yesterday. As Misha had suggested, he hadn't mentioned her yet, and now she was nowhere in sight.

"Can we use your dogs?" the photographer asked, and this was when Brant heard the four-wheeler roaring down the hill.

He looked in that direction, and Shay and Mark followed his gaze. Misha had left the helmet behind. She wore a wide-brimmed hat jammed down over the fake brunette curls, and sunglasses with silver lenses. A dark-brown, thigh-length oilskin flapped open in the breeze, above scuffed riding boots and jeans. She even had Sox perched on the back of the bike for that final authentic touch.

Mostly, sheep farmers hated to have their dog answering orders from anyone else, but this time Brant just grinned. It would be hard to imagine a more convincing performance as a farmer's fiancée, and Misha hadn't yet even opened her mouth.

Catching sight of them, as she approached at what seemed like sixty miles an hour, she lifted a hand and waved. The four-wheeler bounced over the rough ground without the slightest slackening of speed. Then she yelled at him, at the top of her lungs. "The mob from the creek paddock's mustered up to the hill, Brant, but there's a poddy lamb we'll have to go after later on, and a couple of them are scouring."

She'd made up this information completely, of course, but she and Brant were the only ones who knew that. Zooming in a wide arc around the rough dirt driveway in front of the house, she screeched the four-wheeler to a halt on the grass, cut the engine and clacked the gearing into Neutral with her left foot.

"Hi," she said breathlessly to Shay and Mark, swinging her leg over the top of the four-wheeler as if dismounting a horse. She smiled widely and stuck out her hand, giving each visitor a hearty shake. "You must be from the magazine. I'm Mish. Has Brant…?" She trailed off artfully, with her head tilted to one side.

"Mentioned you?" he came in, recognizing his cue. "No, I haven't had a chance…uh…sweetheart. Shay and Mark, this is Mish."

"Short for Michelle," Misha supplied. "But please keep it to Mish."

"My fiancée," Brant explained. The word sounded strange in his mouth. Coy and formal, yet intimate, too.

"Wha-a-at?" Shay wailed at once. "Your fiancée, Brant? But you're supposed to be our—" She stopped.

Bachelor-farmer poster boy, Brant finished for her in his head.

He felt a sudden rush of gratitude to Misha for getting him off the hook with her sparkly ring and brown wig, and to his sister for coming up with such a crazy piece of pretense in the first place. It was going to work, and he was going to need it.

"I mean, that's great." Shay pressed her fingers to her temples and squeezed her eyes tightly shut, adjusting her thinking the way an orthodontist adjusted a kid's braces. Then she widened her eyes and clasped her hands against her heart. "But please, please tell me you met through the magazine, or I'm not sure we'll still have a sto-o-ory." The wail returned to her tone.

Misha and Brant exchanged a quick glance.

"Isn't there always a story behind two people falling in love?" Misha said.

She pulled off her hat—rather carefully, Brant noticed, so that there was no danger of the wig coming with it—and did her dimpliest smile as she cast a glowing look in his direction. She came up to him and slipped her arm through his.

"Actually, that's sweet," Shay said. "It's darling. It is." She let out a whimper and flapped her hands. "Completely darling. And it's true. There always is a story. But this was supposed to be about how many le-e-etters you've had, Brant."

With a visible effort, she managed to contain and repress the wail once more.

"It was supposed to be about how impressed you've been by the wonderful city women eager to abandon everything they've ever known for the adventure of an outback romance," she went on. "And to be honest, how hot all these women seem to think—" She stopped. "Well, that was the angle I'd planned, anyhow, and not that I wanted to treat you as a sex object or anything."

She still looked very stressed.

"No, I'm sure you didn't," Brant told her kindly.

He didn't want to ruin her day by scuttling her story. But then, he didn't want to ruin the next six months of his own life with an overdose of the wrong women, either.

Shay commanded brightly, "Tell me how it all happened."

She had a very attractive smile. "You're right. We can work with this. Our readers really love the heartwarming stuff. It's heartwarming, right? Let me adjust my thinking a little—" She pressed her fingers to her temples again. "We'll have a great story. Maybe if we could feature two or three developing romances, over the next few issues, or even wedding bells and a baby on the way…"

She whipped out an electronic organizer and began keying in notes about the change in plan before Mish and Brant managed to answer any of her questions.

"Well, I am a city woman, originally," Misha said. She held out her arm so that Brant would come and hug her, and he did. She felt good—pliant and strong and warm. "So you still have that angle."

"A wonderful city woman," Brant corrected her. Hell, had he ever given a woman a look this dewy-eyed before? If so, had it ever been this easy? It felt like looking over the edge of a cliff and discovering that the sheer vertical drop went a lot farther down than you'd thought.

Misha added, "From Denver, Colorado." Which was where Queen Rose had been born and raised, Brant knew.

He approved that the princess had stuck as close to the truth as possible. Not that he was particularly familiar with the strategies involved in out-and-out royal lying, but a base level of reality had to make the fantasy easier, surely.

"Wow!" said Shay. "And you're going to make a life out here, now, Michelle? In the outback."

Misha laughed. The brown curls swung around her face. She made a great blonde, but she'd be pretty impressive as a brunette as well. "My fiancé doesn't consider this to be the outback. He thinks it's incredibly civilized. I mean, there's green grass and take-out pizza less than a hundred miles away."

Mark-the-photographer suddenly spoke, after he'd been standing in the background watching the conversation with eyes narrowed against the bright light like watching some kind of three-way tennis match. "I'm hearing an accent," he said, his own voice bluntly Australian.

"Oh, and you don't mean from Colorado?" Misha answered brightly. "Yes, my father's company sent us to the Netherlands for several years when I was in my early teens. I picked up the language, and an accent along with it, and I've never quite gotten rid of it. A few years ago, my father's company sent him here, to Melbourne, which is how I ended up in Australia."

"So the accent's Dutch?" Mark said. *"Houdt u van Australië?"*

Brant still remembered the Dutch he'd learned during his farming exchange, understood the simple question about liking this country, and detected an Australian accent thick enough to spread on toast.

Misha replied without batting an eyelid, *"Ja, natuurlijk, zeer."* Her Dutch accent was perfect. In Langemark, he knew, they spoke a closely related language. And naturally, yes, she liked it here.

The photographer nodded. "Just wondered. I've spent a bit of time there." Then he turned to Shay. "So we'll have both of them in the shots? And the dog?"

Sox had jumped down from the four-wheeler and was racing around as usual, begging for some work to do. Round up the visitors? Put them in a sheep yard? Bark at them and stop them from jumping through a fence?

"You want to do the photos first and then the story, or the other way around?" Mark continued.

"Photos," Shay said. "We need a couple of action shots first, then somewhere that looks pretty."

She eyed the house, but seemed unimpressed. Misha and Brant exchanged a look that said, what, she thinks the house isn't pretty enough?

Brant felt himself flood with a sudden, ridiculous desire for

all of this to be true. For Mish to be his fiancée, originally from
Colorado, totally at home on the farm, not in any way, shape
or form a princess, and completely in agreement with his own
opinion that the higgledy-piggledly old house, with the wisteria
twisting up the veranda posts and the galvanized iron roof
needing a fresh coat of dark green paint, was very pretty indeed.

"How about by the citrus trees?" Misha suggested.

"I think we need sheep," Shay answered. "You know.
Snow-white flocks gambolling in the meadows, or whatever
it is that sheep do."

"Paddocks," Misha said, as if she'd been using the word
her whole life. "And I don't know if you've noticed, but
these sheep aren't all that snow-white. They won't be until
they've been shorn in the spring, and then they'll be naked
and a lot skinnier."

"Right," Shay nodded, while Brant thought, wow.

This princess was seriously good at faking her identity.
She sounded as if she knew all about sheep. He remembered
all the questions she'd asked while they were marking lambs
on Thursday and Friday. Clearly she'd filed every bit of it
away for future use. He'd started to like this about her a
lot—that she was genuinely interested in all sorts of things,
even if she might never need to think about them again.

While Mark got out his camera equipment and stalked
around looking for somewhere prettier and more sheep-farm-
like than the house, Shay asked questions, all of which made
Brant realize that neither he nor Misha had done their home-
work on this.

Had they met through the magazine?

In the blink of an eye, Misha decided yes, which con-
formed with what she'd told Lauren the other night. "I don't
even buy *Today's Woman* normally," she confided to Shay.

Probably true. Brant didn't think it sold in Langemark.
And definitely not the Australian edition.

"But that month," she went on, "when Brant's picture

was on the cover, some strange intuition made me walk past the magazine rack and reach out for it. I wrote to him that same evening."

Lies, lies, lies.

"I don't remember your letter," Shay said.

"But I'm sure you didn't read them all," Misha answered without a flicker of hesitation.

"No, I'm afraid not. But I do wish I'd read yours."

Misha cast Brant a lingering glance. "It wasn't anything special," she said. "I'm not sure that it really matters how two people meet. The point is, we did, and from that moment things moved very quickly. I felt so at home the day Brant first brought me here. Some aspects of this life are a challenge, but I know it's going to work out for us."

All of which had to be lies, too, but she said it so convincingly that again Brant had this odd, wishful ache low in his stomach. He wondered how his life might have been different if Mum had felt this way about Inverlochie, or if his long-ago Dutch girlfriend Beatrix had.

"Could you get back on that quad bike thing?" the photographer asked, his equipment unpacked and ready. "Could the two of you fit on it together? Could we have you rounding up some sheep, or something? I mean, you could look as if you are. No need to do it for real."

"Well, as long as we don't have to do it for real," Brant said, and Misha rewarded him with a quick glance, her princess-blue eyes glinting like a naughty child's.

Mark directed them as if this were a Hollywood movie costing a hundred million dollars. He wanted Brant on the front of the bike, working the controls, with Misha squashed in right behind him, her arms wrapped around his body and her head resting on this back. No hats, please, or their eyes would be shaded too much. Sunglasses? Pushed up against their hair if they wanted.

Misha obediently and carefully lifted hers.

Mark wanted them in the middle of a mob of sheep, which meant they all had to head over to the gate leading to the creek paddock, Mark and Shay lugging the camera equipment while Brant and Misha puttered along in first gear. Then Sox and Mon had to corral some animals with their barking and running so that the reluctant sheep would stay in the frame.

"There! Stop right there!" Mark said. The sheep didn't listen, and the dogs were confused. A big woolly mass of ewe almost knocked the camera tripod over.

The photographer swore and Misha began to giggle. Brant could feel her body shaking against his back, and her laugh sounded like a mix of music, bubbling water and kookaburras sitting in an old gum tree. "Maybe I should get down with the sheep and Mark should put a pregnant ewe on the bike with you," she muttered.

"Stay put," he growled back at her, trying not to laugh himself. Also trying not to think that what he could feel most clearly against his back was her breasts. "He's an artist. Give him his creative space. And let's get this over with, because I'm marking lambs with Chris over at his place again this afternoon."

"Want me?"

She doesn't mean it that way.

"We'll manage," he said out loud.

"If I promise to be useful?"

"If you're crazy enough to want to be useful around here, you're always welcome, Misha, you know that." Brant heard himself putting too much meaning and importance into the words and had a fresh inkling of the trouble he was in.

Serious.

Painful.

"Closer!" Mark said. "Can you, Michelle?"

"Just call me Mish," she answered, and obediently slid her thighs right against Brant's on the four-wheeler's broad seat.

Oh, yes, he was in trouble, all right! He hoped he

wouldn't have to get off this bike too quickly because then it would show.

The camera clicked away.

"And you, Brant?" Shay said. "You trust this city girl?"

"From the bottom of my heart." His voice came out husky, and he had to cough to clear his throat. The whole performance came way too easily.

"That should be enough," the photographer said eventually. "Can we head back to the house for some static shots?"

Thanks to Brant's determined focus on thoughts of cold showers, they could.

The dogs pushed the sheep out of the fenced corner of the paddock and everyone came back through the gate.

Some minutes later, Mark was ready with his camera again. He'd chosen the citrus trees for one set of shots, and as a backup, the cane chairs on the veranda, angled to face a different way. "That way, we get the backdrop of this vine-thing and the paddock, but we don't have to see the peeling roof."

"I told you it needed painting," Misha murmured to Brant, as if she really had.

Mark posed them like dolls. Brant's arm around Misha's warm body, slightly stiff and rustly in his oilskin. Sox sitting in front of them on a convenient stump, tongue hanging out as Brant used his free hand to give her the muscular patting she liked.

Sunglasses back up, please, Mark requested.

Misha raised her sunglasses again and her wig slipped. Just a tiny bit. Brant was sure he was the only person who'd noticed. "Careful," he muttered, squeezing her.

"I know," she muttered back. "I don't like this guy, much. Sometimes I don't know which is worse, formal photo shoots or candid ones."

"Yeah? I'd have thought it would be no contest," Brant said. He kept his voice low. "At least today we have some control over how we look."

"But sometimes, especially if it's a formal portrait with…" She looked uncomfortable. "…you know…with the jewels…"

Oh, right. Of course. The jewels.

"…it just takes so long!"

"You'd rather be lamb-marking."

"Seriously, I think I would."

He couldn't manage to believe her.

Too much of him wanted to.

Mark clicked off his camera about a thousand times— maybe a slight exaggeration, but not much. Turn this way. Smile more. Smile less. Move your hand to her upper arm. Look down at Mish. Look up at Brant.

"You're right," Brant said in the end. "This gets boring very fast."

His arms felt wooden and stiff, even against Misha's pliant warmth. He tried to soften the pose, to make this look more genuine, but as soon as he did so, it felt *too* genuine and he wanted to take it further, into territory that was uncharted and forbidden.

She was a princess.

She was engaged.

She could never belong here, never truly fit into his life. He'd seen it with his own parents.

If he hadn't been pinned in place by the camera lens, he never would have touched her, because all this brought him was a strange regret that he didn't fully understand.

"I'd rather there was a whole rugby scrum of paparazzi hiding in the bushes so we could just get on with our lives," he told her, "and good luck to them if they caught us doing anything more scandalous than feeding the dogs."

Next they moved to the veranda and he had to stand behind Misha with his hand on her shoulder, which if anything was worse. He could see the side of her neck, its fine column tickled by strands of that ridiculous hair. He wanted to sweep the hair back. Or, no, even better, pull it right off, pick apart whatever pins or nets were holding her real hair in place and bury his face in the blond strands.

Fifteen different women he'd been out with since his face had appeared on the cover of the magazine, and not one of them had affected him like this.

"Now, shall we have coffee while we talk?" Shay suggested brightly. "We're running out of time." She looked at her watch after she said it. Brant suspected she tended to run out of time before she even got up in the mornings. She was an attractive women, intelligent and with a sensitive mouth, but she had an edge, and he could tell she was fairly driven. "But I really want to get to the heart of your romance, so our readers get that feel-good sense that true love really happens."

"Wow! And that comes with coffee included?" Misha teased.

Brant hid a snort of laughter behind his hand.

Mark commandeered coffee for himself but didn't stay in the room while they talked on the veranda. "Bathroom?" he asked, then put his coffee down after a couple of sips, disappeared in that direction and stayed away for quite some time.

"Tell me what it is you love the most about each other," Shay said, after she'd covered some more obvious questions such as what Misha did for a living. She was a gourmet caterer, it turned out, with a diploma from a French cooking school. "Brant? You first?" She added in a token fashion, "I know it's hard."

But it wasn't.

It was surprisingly easy.

"She's gutsy, she's hardworking, she's funny, she has more life in her heart and her mind than anyone I've ever met," he said, all of it true.

"And you, Misha?"

"He's loyal and funny and honest and honorable. He

works hard and loves his land and his animals, but it's not the only thing he thinks about. He knows there's a whole world out there, and he's a part of it, even when he's so far from what we'd think of as its center."

"You mean somewhere like New York?"

"Yes, or Paris, or Rome."

"And when's the wedding?"

They looked at each other.

"No date set yet," Brant began.

"September," said Misha at exactly the same time.

"Uh-huh," agreed Shay. "No date, but roughly September." She made a note in her organizer. "That's great. Maybe we could come back then and do a—"

"No!" Brant and Misha told her in one voice, just as Mark came onto the veranda again. "No wedding story!"

"Fascinating place," he said. "There's been more than one addition over the years, I'm guessing."

"That's right," Brant answered. "The original place was little more than a hut, but they built things to last in those days."

"Are you living here, Misha, or are you still based in Melbourne?"

"Melbourne," she answered. "I have things to wind up before I move."

Mark nodded and didn't ask any further questions. He seemed to have lost interest. Misha excused herself and slipped into the house for a moment, not returning until Brant had convinced Shay that she and her photographer could find their way back out to the gate without his personal escort.

"I'll be in touch if I have any more questions," Shay said, scribbling down some final notes. "Our readers are going to love the story, especially if I can track down a couple of other serious relationships. If we do another 'Wanted: Outback Wives' article later in the year, we'll get a whole lot more participants because of your own romance." She darted forward and gave Misha a quick hug. "Seriously, I admire you, being prepared to sacrifice so much."

I admire you, but I don't understand you at all, said her face.

"It's not a sacrifice," Misha told her, smiling. "I feel incredibly lucky."

When the car had driven away, she said to Brant, "I think the photographer was snooping in my bedroom."

"Snooping? You think he recognized you?"

"If he did, he didn't let it show. And Nu put my suitcase and my passport in that big closet in the laundry, so I don't think there was anything too princessy for him to find."

"That's good. Nu's not stupid."

"Now, thank heavens, I can take off this wig, because it's so hot!"

"And anyhow, you're better as a blonde."

"I'll take that as a compliment."

She pulled the wig from her head and shook out her hair. They grinned at each other, with the wig still dangling in Misha's hand, just as, in the distance several hundred metres away, Shay and Mark's car curved around the hill on its way out to the gate. The side windows caught the sun and flashed a sudden sparkle of light back toward the house.

Chapter Seven

"We'll make it to Chris's by one," Brant said, looking at his watch as he warmed up the engine of the tray-backed four-wheel drive.

Sox was back there, along with some equipment and a pile of old hessian sacks for her to lie on. She trotted back and forth impatiently with her tongue hanging out, ignoring the sacks, excited about going for a drive and hoping it had something to do with sheep.

"Is that what you told him?" Misha asked.

"I said I didn't know, because it depended on Shay and Mark, and when they left. Tried to phone him just now but he must be still in the paddock."

"Should we have brought him some lunch?"

"You mean those exciting peanut butter sandwiches I made? He's probably done his own." Brant circled up to the track.

Misha felt almost as happy as Sox.

Nobody would have believed it, but it was true.

She had a healthy appreciation for city life, high fashion, extreme sport, motor racing, fine food, politics, charity work and the arts, but still there was something about bouncing along in an old truck, hearing its bodywork squeaking, knowing you were about to spend the afternoon out in the fresh air and sunshine, working hard and getting dirty.

No. Definitely, nobody would have believed she would enjoy this.

Mom, maybe.

Langemark's beloved Queen Rose had had ranchers for grandparents on her father's side. She'd spent her teenage vacations branding cattle and riding fence. When Mish was a child, Mom had sat on her bed sometimes, just before heading out to a state dinner or a palace banquet all dressed in her tiara, her sparkling sapphire-and-diamond necklace and some long, glamorous gown, and she'd told Misha stories about her own childhood.

Mom had turned her back on her heritage when she'd married a European king because she'd fallen in love with him. She barely even returned to the United States for visits, because she didn't want to draw the huge, uncontrollable and intrusive machinery of the American press into her royal life.

She'd been so discreet about it that America almost hadn't noticed it had raised its own queen, but she'd paid the price. Those early stories were just about all Misha knew of her mother's family.

But maybe some of it had stayed in her blood, all the same.

The sun twinkled between the trunks of the trees as they drove. Misha lowered the window several inches and breathed in the air. The eucalyptus gave it a tang she'd never smelled anywhere else. They took the side road that led toward Chris's farm, and she saw horses grazing and a litter of rusty old machinery parts on a neighboring property. They had somehow acquired an odd beauty as they decayed.

Up ahead, the owner of the old machinery was moving

some of his stock across the road. He had gates open on both sides and dogs working the ewes and lambs, who bleated and milled around and threatened to go the wrong way. One of the dogs jumped up and ran across the sheeps' woolly backs like running across a piece of carpet, and the animals didn't even seem to feel it.

"Is it dangerous, moving stock?" Misha asked, thinking of cars coming too fast down this road.

"Can be," Brant answered, slowing the truck. "And it can muck up the ground. Mostly it's fine and there are a lot of reasons for needing to move them, but you don't do it for fun. It can spread disease."

"Really? Is that rare?"

"This guy here had a foot-rot outbreak a couple of years ago." He made a jerky, grinding gear change, slowing the truck a little more. "It meant Chris couldn't shift some of his animals where he wanted, because his property kind of encircles this one and there's a right of way that was contaminated."

He braked.

And slewed.

"What the—? Damn, do we have a flat?" he muttered.

Twisting the wheel steadily back the other way, he brought the vehicle to a controlled halt on the grassy verge fifty metres from the mob, and the farmer on his noisy trail bike raised a hand as if to say, "Thanks, mate, we'll be across in a minute, and out of your way." If they did have a flat, the farmer hadn't seen it.

Brant jumped out of the car and Misha followed. "Do we?" she asked.

But she could see it for herself—the rubber of the right front wheel squashed against the road like a strange kind of black fruit with all the pulp sucked out.

"Don't worry," Brant said. "There's a spare."

"Does Sox get to run around while it's changed?"

Brant looked at her. "She's going to be busy this afternoon, so she should really stay on the truck, but that bothers you, doesn't it?"

"Sometimes," she admitted. "Dogs are people, too."

He laughed, shook his head and clicked his tongue at such odd ideas, then whistled to Sox and she jumped down and began to nose around in the grass on either side of the road. "Happy now?" he said.

"Sox is."

What the dog's sense of smell told her appeared to be as fascinating as a fast-paced novel, and she did some digging, as well. Brant got out the hydraulic jack, the tools and the spare, and Misha felt useless.

Her least favorite feeling.

"Can I help?"

"Have you ever changed a tire before?"

"Um, no, not as such." Changing Lego wheels for her nephews didn't count. "But I'd never marked lambs before, either, this time last week."

He loosened a couple of nuts by banging on the handle of the whatever-it-was-called, then sat back on his heels and gave her the same look as before—guarded, cynical, half-amused. "Would you like to learn, in case the chauffeur ever has an off day?"

She flinched a little, because he'd sounded impatient about it, and as if he still thought she was very spoiled. But she told him cheerfully, "He might. And then he'd be really grateful that I knew how to hitch up my ball gown, put my tiara on the backseat of the Rolls and get down and do it."

He raised an eyebrow at this, but said, "Here, it's pretty easy," as he handed her the metal tool.

And it was easy, but it took a while—longer than if Misha hadn't made a point about learning to do it, and had just let Brant change the tire on his own. The sheep had all been moved into their new paddock and the farmer and his dogs

were nowhere in sight by the time the truck got moving
again.

Sox settled into her position in the back, chewing on
something. She'd already had a fabulous afternoon. You just
wouldn't believe who had passed this way over the past couple of weeks, and what they'd smelled like. Now she could
take a rest until the next fun thing happened.

Arriving at Chris's, they found him just shutting the last
piece of portable yard behind a sizeable mob of ewes and autumn lambs, and got directly to work helping him. For several hours, everything went smoothly. Just the usual mess,
and sheep who didn't know what they were meant to do
next.

"*This* way you great galoot!" Misha yelled, bracing herself against a piece of fence and pushing on a thick, woolly
rump.

She'd discovered that she liked the feel of the deep fleece,
and that she even liked the stubborn way the animals moved.
Their inches-thick coats protected them and you could handle them quite hard without them feeling anything more than
a friendly shove.

"Yes! There you go! See? Was it so hard to get with your
friends?"

This lot of ewes and lambs seemed extra skittish, and the
dogs were having trouble, particularly Sox, even though
Misha had seen how good she usually was at this, and how
much she loved it.

"Push 'em up, Sox!" Brant yelled. "Push 'em up."

The ewes bawled, some of their cries pitched high and others
low, while the lambs gave their little bleats, and Sox seemed
unable to handle them at all. Her running back and forth grew
rapidly more frantic, and instead of barking she began to howl.

"Sheesh, what's wrong with you, Soxie?" Brant yelled
again, charging across the yard to prevent a ewe from breaking away and tangling herself in a floppy section of fence.

The dog began to flinch and shake, and could no longer control her bodily functions. It was horrible to watch. Chris had stopped working. Brant had frozen for a moment, but now he raced up to Sox and grabbed hold of her, not yelling anymore but dropping his voice to a whisper.

"Oh, hell, Soxie, oh, hell. What's wrong with you?" he repeated. His gray eyes burned as he watched the dog writhe and heave and howl and squat on the ground. "Chris…" He swore a couple of times, almost on a sob. "I think she must have taken a bait." He patted the little kelpie, but even his touch and the sound of his voice seemed to trigger her flinching.

Chris strode over, not wasting any time. Misha knew exactly why her friend wanted to spend her life with this man. He was straight as an arrow and worked incredibly hard. He really knew what he was doing. "Have you baited your place lately?" he asked Brant.

"Before lambing, but I picked up all the ones that hadn't been taken after two weeks, I'd swear I did. I marked them all." He wiped a strand of hair out of his eyes, leaving a smudge of dirt on his forehead.

"Same here. Doesn't matter where she picked it up, anyhow. The point is to get it out of her. Do you have salt in your truck?" He put his hand on Brant's shoulder.

"Yes. Yes, I do. Misha, in the glove box there's a bag of it. Can you get it? We have to make her vomit."

"Not the vet…?" Misha said. "An antidote?"

"This is Ten-Eighty, it's bait for feral animals who'll take the lambs. There's no antidote." His whole face was screwed up and his lips looked dry and white. "We have to get it out of her stomach before she absorbs any more and just pray it wasn't a lethal dose."

Misha went to the truck feeling ill. Sox was a mess. She looked as if she was trying to bring up her stomach on her own but it wasn't happening. In between her convulsive heaves, she kept on howling.

Brant's expression got even grimmer. His jaw jutted and he had grooves of stress around his pale mouth. Misha knew Sox was his favorite dog—the best he'd had in years, he'd told her. "You couldn't put a dollar value on her."

She found the bag of salt in the glove compartment, searching there with shaking hands. She brought it to him, but couldn't watch as he struggled and struggled to get a dose of it down the writhing dog's throat.

"Sox, come on, girl," he begged her, still with that wrenching note in his voice that made Misha want to go close to him and just hold him like a little boy. "Come on and just let me do this. Sorry, sorry, I know you don't like it, but I have to do it, girl."

He pinned her hard against his body, forcing her to be still, and Misha could see the amount of strength he had to use.

"Come on, Soxie, you know I wouldn't hurt you." His muscles were like knots.

"Where can she have picked it up?" Chris said. He tried to get near enough to help, but Brant waved him away.

"I've got her now. Come on, Soxie."

"Brant, I'd swear I've got no baits on this place now."

"It can take hours to show symptoms. It doesn't have to have come from your place. But where's she been?"

"Beside the road," Misha said. Oh, dear lord! Her throat constricted and she felt even sicker than before. This was *her* fault. "Brant, when I persuaded you to let her off the truck when we had the flat, she was nosing around beside the road and she was chewing on something."

"Barry Andrews," Brant said.

He'd gotten the salt into the dog, at last, and the reaction wasn't long in coming. Sox was miserable and all he could do was croon to her in between trying to work out how this had happened and whether the dog had a chance at life. "Okay, Soxie, there you go. Okay, girl."

None of them thought about the sheep, who milled around

or stood and stared, bleating. "It has to have been one of Barry's baits," Brant finished.

"Barry? Yes, he never picks them up, he forgets where he's put them," Chris said, pacing in the damp green grass. "He would have baited before lambing, too."

"When, I wonder. That's the critical thing. Was he slack with that, too, so it's only just been done... Soxie, girl, it's okay. This is good, you're getting it up. Come on, girl, hang in there." Brant's voice cracked. "If he's only just done it a week or two ago, then the poison's fresh and it could be lethal. If she's showing symptoms like this... We'll know pretty soon, won't we?"

"Doesn't take long," Chris agreed. His mouth barely moved, but Misha knew he felt as bad as Brant. He was pacing back and forth, eyes narrowed and jaw set, looking at his own dogs as if fearing the onset of the painful symptoms in them, as well.

"Come on, Soxie," Brant begged. "Don't let any of it stay in."

"The vet," Misha said again. "Couldn't the vet do more?"

In her world, you had people for this stuff. Experts to turn to. The royal palace veterinarian. A royal purveyor of emetics for dogs. This was her fault for getting Brant to let Sox off the truck, and there just had to be a better and more certain answer than a dose of plain old salt. She wanted to cry. She wanted someone else to step in and solve this.

"This is all he'd do," Brant told her. "He might use something different to bring up her stomach, might have gotten it down her gullet a little more gently and quickly than I managed to, but the effect would be the same. We just have to wait now." His voice cracked again. "See if she makes it through."

"Take her down to the house," Chris said. Once again he put a hand on Brant's shoulder, trusting action more than words. "The sheep are bothering her. The noise. They get hypersensitive to light and noise when the poison starts to act, it's one of the symptoms."

"I know. I know. She's miserable."

"So let her have some peace and quiet, mate. Take her down."

Brant looked both vague and stubborn. "We have about sixty lambs still to do."

Chris turned to Misha with a question in his eyes.

"Chris and I can finish the lambs," she said at once, and was rewarded by the relief that flooded Brant's face.

"Thanks," he told her. "And this wasn't your fault. This happens. This is farming."

"She's getting quieter, now, don't you think?" Chris said.

The little black-and-tan stomach had stopped heaving, and the dog's trembling had eased. Brant took off his dirt-stained sweatshirt, laid it on the hessian sacks in the back of the truck and settled Sox tenderly on top, then drove slowly and carefully through the paddock to Chris's house, avoiding every pothole and every bump.

Misha's heart went with the man and the dog all the way.

Chapter Eight

Sox survived.

They didn't leave Chris's until well after dark, and this time Misha had the little kelpie on some old towels on her lap in the front passenger seat. The dog seemed limp and exhausted, laying her head down and not moving at all, but Brant promised the princess that it would be okay, now.

The poisoning had stopped its progression. It hadn't moved on to convulsions and coma as it would have done by now if Soxie was going to die.

In fact, she would have died already, he knew, because he wouldn't have let her go on suffering.

Misha was gentle with her, stroking her furry forehead and rubbing her softly between the shoulder blades. "Good girl," she crooned. "Good dog. Good little Soxie." Sox rewarded her with a faint lift of her tail.

"You got the lambs finished, did you?" Brant asked. He felt as washed out as Sox looked.

"Yes. That's why we were so late getting back to the house. It took awhile."

"I guess it is late," he said vaguely. "I lost track."

"It's after seven."

"So you've been working in the dark?"

"It was all right. Chris angled his truck so the headlights shone at us and we could see what we were doing."

"You're a star, Mish, do you know that?"

"I know I nearly killed your best dog today, wanting you to let her off the truck. What's so starry about that?"

"You didn't nearly kill her. You have to stop thinking that way, okay? Barry Andrews is not a particularly efficient farmer, but even if he was, it's pretty easy to overlook a bait, and impossible to make sure a dog doesn't get one. It's just one of the risks that has to be faced for the sake of protecting the lambs. Why do you think I keep salt in my glove box? Because it's a recommendation from the Department of Agriculture, since it's so easy for farm dogs to get hold of bait that's not meant for them."

"Have you ever had to use the salt before?"

"Not with Sox or Mon. Once, years ago, when Dad was still working the farm."

"Did it work that time?"

"No," he remembered, and could still feel the frustration and the hurt. "It was a fresh bait, on our place. A lethal dose. Baz died." He cleared his throat. "How 'bout we get pizza tonight?"

"Please!" she said, and they didn't talk about poisoned bait anymore.

"May I show you these?" Misha asked Brant. "Would you mind?" She had slipped along to her room a moment ago, and returned with a big white envelope.

"No problem. What are they?" Brant reached for the second-to-last slice of the ham-and-pineapple pizza.

They'd been so hungry after the difficult day and spartan lunch, they'd ordered a napolitana as well. That one was all gone, after a satisfying interval of munching in front of the television without the need for polite conversation. The princess had a healthy appetite, and when she'd finished eating, there was a shiny spot of pizza grease in the middle of her top lip.

"I mentioned them the other day," she reminded him. "I've been meaning to get them out, but…well, I just hadn't found the right moment, before this. The photos of Whatshis-name and two women, remember? One's the French ac-tress."

"Right. Okay."

"I'd…um…be interested in a man's opinion." She lifted her chin a little. "Your opinion."

This had him sitting up straighter, and banished the feeling of sleepy relaxation created by pizza, beer and a hot fire, on top of all the stress over Sox. He had shut the little kelpie in the laundry tonight instead of leaving her out in her kennel, and he kept checking on her at regular intervals. She still seemed listless but not in any of that awful pain and distress that had overtaken her out in Chris's paddock. She'd lapped at some water, but hadn't eaten yet.

Waiting for his answer, Misha held the envelope full of photographs in front of her like a piece of medieval armor. She stood several feet from the fire, looking like a small is-land of princess surrounded by a large sea of Brant's day-to-day life.

Her blond hair stood out against a backdrop of farming books piled on a shelf. Gold earrings glinted, while in a cor-ner of the ceiling above her head there stretched a dusty cobweb no one had had a chance to vacuum away. A pretty European-American accent swamped the sounds of bleating sheep and howling dog that still echoed in his ears.

She'd scrubbed herself in the shower at Chris's after the

last of the lamb-marking, having gotten too filthy even for a fifteen-minute homeward drive in a dusty old truck with a sick dog on her lap.

After the shower, she'd borrowed some of the clothes that Nu kept at Chris's, but while Brant drove to town to pick up the pizzas they'd ordered by phone, she'd changed again, this time into Princess Casual: designer jeans, a cream silk top, a pink cashmere sweater and a pair of glittery pink, beaded, thongy, sandal-like things that were more air than shoe.

Until now, she'd looked very relaxed and impossibly pampered, sipping on her beer, wiggling her bare pink toes at the luxurious heat of the fire, licking a bit of melted cheese from her thumb, as delicate as a kitten having a bath. The way she held those photos, however, told Brant that he'd better be careful. He'd better be quite clear on what she was asking for. He wished Nu were here, because then Misha would be showing *her* the paparazzi pics instead.

"I don't want to get pizza grease on them," he said. "Maybe I should go and wash."

"Oh, please do get pizza grease on them! I have! That's all they're worth. They should have great big splodges of rancid pizza grease all over them." This didn't explain why she clung on to them so hard.

"Are you sure?"

"Plus, the palace has duplicates."

Of course.

"It's not my idea that all this stuff gets collected and filed," she protested hotly, even though he hadn't spoken. "Don't make me apologize for it."

"I won't."

She shook her head slowly, clicking her tongue. She almost smiled, but didn't quite get there. "Your face says everything, you know."

"Sometimes, that's a good thing. I'm honest. What do you want me to do with them, Mish?"

She looked at him with her big blue eyes, as if willing him to come up with his own answer, but he really didn't want to get this wrong, so he waited and made her say it straight out. Eventually, she did, telling him in a strained voice, "I want to know, from a man's perspective, if you think he's sleeping with them. And… and if he is, if it's important, and what I should do about it."

Her face begged him to take her seriously, to realize that this was important in her world, the way saving Sox's life had been important to him.

"You think I can tell you all that from a few photos and some shallow press stories?" he asked her slowly.

"I think you'll seriously try."

Misha slid the pictures out of the envelope, her movements neat and efficient. They were matted onto pieces of thin card. She moved the two pizza boxes out of the way, then fanned the pictures out over the table and stepped back, awaiting his opinion. There were about ten or twelve of them, complete with loud headlines, extravagant captions and paragraphs of text.

He leaned on the table, studied the left-most photo in the fan she'd laid out and read the first headline and part of the first caption, wondering what it would be like to see his own name written there.

Playboy Formula One Star Branton Smith.

Nah. Not for him.

He could have been a Playboy Sheep Farmer if he'd given Shay Russell what she wanted this morning with the magazine story, but this didn't appeal, either.

He stopped reading, remembering that he'd never yet seen a newspaper article on the wool industry written by a city journalist that had managed to get all its facts straight. And he was sure Shay wouldn't have all her facts straight today, either. He should ignore the text of all these tabloid articles and just look at the pictures instead.

"So?" Misha asked, way before he was ready to make a comment.

He slid a covert look in her direction. She'd taken a step closer to the table, and had her hands clasped near her mouth with her thumbs sticking up. She bit on them nervously, her eyelids lowered a little so that her lashes screened the blue. The shiny spot of grease had gone from her lip because she nibbled at it when she wasn't nibbling on the thumbs.

What did she want? She was a princess. She had staff who sifted through every newspaper in Europe for any reference to her family, her friends or herself. She had professional people to deliver lines like:

"Tell them, No comment," or "Cancel your commitments for the next month," or "Break off the engagement," or even "It doesn't matter if he's sleeping with them or not, it's what these photos do to the public image of the royal family, and to your reputation. The palace will issue a statement."

So why was she asking him? Being Nuala's brother hardly qualified him for anything in this kind of area. What could he give her?

"Be honest," she suddenly commanded him. It answered his unspoken question. Honesty was the thing he could give her, when there were probably a lot of people in her life who never gave her that. "You have to be honest," she repeated, "or I'll be sorry I asked."

Commands, and now blackmail.

The blackmail worked.

For some reason, he didn't want her to be sorry she'd asked.

"Well, for a start," he said, straightening to face her. "I wouldn't take the slightest notice of what the captions say, or the stories themselves."

She nodded and shut her eyes for a moment, dismissing the point as obvious. She'd no doubt spent a good ten or fifteen years taking no notice of what was written about her.

"So we're down to the photos," he said. "The body language."

Did he know anything about body language? He pivoted back to the table and looked more closely, feeling Misha's arm brush his as she came beside him to watch his expression, her body still tight with tension.

Concentrate, Brant.

Seven pictures of Gian-Marco Ponti with a blonde. Five pictures of Gian-Marco Ponti with a brunette. In most of the pictures, the figures were grainy and unclear, but two of them—the ones in the French magazine—had been taken in daylight instead of at night. Both of these featured the blonde and Whatshisname at a pavement café table. They had coffee cups sitting in front of them, the blonde was leaning close, and Whatshisname was smiling.

The blonde's face didn't show, but her eagerness did. She had her wrist turned upward, and Gian-Marco was stroking it lightly with one finger. She wore a dark top, off the shoulder. It had to be cut pretty low, and the way she was leaning forward said very frankly, "Take a look. It's all yours."

Anybody would have said that these two people were having an affair.

Brant looked at the clearest picture featuring the brunette, taken outside a nightclub. The brunette draped herself over the racing driver like a fur coat. She rested her open hand against his chest, and her head on his shoulder, twisting her neck a little so she could look up at him. She looked quite drunk, and some of her makeup had smudged.

Gian-Marco had his upper body half turned away from her, and he pointed at something, out of the picture. His mouth dropped open, not in a smile but as if he was speaking. At first Brant thought that the racing driver appeared totally uninterested in the brunette, but then he ignored the turned face, the open mouth and the gesturing arm and focused on other things instead.

Gian-Marco was holding up the sagging woman, supporting her with the whole length of his body. He had his spare arm wrapped tightly around her waist, and he was frowning. He seemed angry, but not at the woman in his arms. When you looked closely, it was an incredibly protective pose.

Brant looked back at the pictures of the racing driver and the blonde.

"He doesn't care two hoots about her," he said, pointing. "This one, he cares about." He tapped the brunette on her grainy shoulder. Too late, he thought to ask, "Which one's the actress?"

"The brunette."

"She's the one featured in most of the rumors?"

"Yes."

"Ah."

Her breath hissed into her lungs. "Okay. That's what I thought. That's what the pictures said to me, too."

Standing beside him she looked smaller, suddenly—not the same woman as the one who'd done most of a seasoned farmer's work this afternoon with Chris's lambs, nor the accomplished spin doctor who'd answered all of Shay Russell's questions so smoothly in her curly brown wig this morning.

She said in a small voice, "He's having an affair with her, and you're saying it's more than just a one-night stand."

"But we could both be wrong."

Forget honesty.

Misha looked as if he'd hit her, and Brant didn't want to strip any more layers from her courageous heart.

"Yeah?" she said. "Could we?"

"I mean, of course the press are going to pick the most compromising pictures, aren't they?" he argued, with a good deal of energy. "They're going to go for the ones that most make it look as if something's happening. Even if it's not."

"That's true, too."

Brant felt foolishly rewarded by her approval until she added, with a brittle smile, "You see? Isn't this fun, fun, fun? Trying to work out who's lying, who's manipulating who, trying to hide your own feelings from public scrutiny before you even know what your feelings are."

"Woo-hoo, yes, it's great fun. I want to go on the roller coaster, next."

There was a beat of silence, then she drew in another of those hissing, unhappy breaths. "You thought I was spoiled, on Wednesday, when I arrived."

"Well, I— Did you hear me talking to Nu?" He wanted to tell her he'd already changed his mind quite thoroughly on this point, but she didn't give him time.

"And I am spoiled," she went on heatedly. "When I have needs, people rush to meet them. When I have whims, they're fulfilled. Physically, I never have to clean up my own mess. At home, I would never have tried to give that emetic to Sox today, I would have reached straight for the phone and the best veterinarian in Langemark would have gotten a high-speed police escort to the palace."

"That's not your fault."

She ignored him. "But emotionally, no one can help. Emotionally, I'm on my own. And when you don't know what to think or feel…" She'd switched pronouns—*you* instead of *I*—but Brant wasn't tricked into thinking she'd distanced herself. "…it's not useful to have people telling you what's in the best interests of your public image, or the best interests of the king and queen, or even the best interests of the Langemark economy."

"No, I'm sure it isn't."

"And if you are going to break off your engagement, Your Highness—" She adopted a deferential court adviser's tone. "—please don't do it yet, because of your sister-in-law's pregnancy announcement that won't be made for a few more weeks, and because of the effect your decision may have on the proposed changes to Langemarkian divorce and family law that are due for debate and voting before the summer recess in June."

"You've had that?"

"Said to me. In those words. Last week. *After* I'd cried on my mother's shoulder, but *before* the photos were matted onto the card. Sometimes the press office gets a little behind."

She was trying to make him laugh, but she had tears in her eyes.

"Really, though, Mish?"

"Yep, I was officially asked to maintain the public perception that Gian-Marco Ponti and I are engaged and that the wedding is going ahead in late September, no matter what my private feelings might turn out to be, because my ridiculous little personal life could affect the future of hundreds of other Langemarkian marriages, as well as public reaction to a new royal baby on the way. In that kind of hothouse, how can I know what to think? How can I know what to feel?"

"Oh hell, Misha." He hugged her without even thinking about it, wrapping his arms all the way around her warm body and pulling her close. Resting his cheek against her blond hair, he could smell the floral fragrance of shampoo.

"Not hell," she said into the shoulder of his shirt. "I'm one of the luckiest people in the world. But it's not always perfect."

Right now this part of it felt perfect to him. She felt perfect, in his arms, needing him. It was hopeless. He couldn't afford to feel so protective toward her. And when the protectiveness was tinged with…something else…he could afford it even less. On Thursday night he'd asked her not to repeat that lush pink strawberry of a kiss, and now, just four days later, he'd grabbed hold of her and didn't want to let her go.

Nice contradiction, Brant, but you know the underlying reasons are the same. You want her, the way Gian-Marco Ponti wants the blonde who's offering herself. But you would protect her the way he's protecting the brunette.

She swept into your life like a royal tornado and you already care about her too much.

You've gone all Sheep Farmer in Shining Armor, and it's lucky Nu isn't here or she'd guess.

And laugh.

And tell you very kindly not to be an idiot, because Princess Artemisia Helena de Marinceski-Sauverin is way out of your league and if you think she's going to hock a tiara or two to help you through the rocky stretch on the farm, then you're crazy.

Except that Nuala knew full well he'd never take that kind of help from anybody, let alone this woman.

"Sorry," she whispered.

He felt her arms snaking against his body, her hands coming to rest lightly against his back. He also felt the tremulous hold she had on herself, and sensed the questions zinging in her head. He could feel every delicate fingertip, feel the tickle of every strand of her hair.

"What for?" he asked.

He hadn't let go.

He couldn't.

"You said not to kiss you." Her breath made a puff of warm air on his neck, then she rested her lips in the same spot.

She wasn't kissing him. Kissing required movement, and at this point she wasn't moving at all. Neither was he. He didn't dare. His whole universe might explode if he moved a muscle.

"You're not kissing me," he said.

"A hug is pretty much the same." She barely lifted her mouth from his skin.

He could feel her breasts, neat and squishy. He thought they'd be exactly the size to fill his cupped hands, and desperately wanted to see if he was right, wanted to slip her body out of some pale, lacy wisp of a bra and touch her with nothing getting in the way. He wanted to know what her nipples looked like, and how her breathing sounded when she was aroused.

He'd only met her five days ago. How could he want her this much, with everything he knew about all the distances and differences between them?

"No...Mish...a hug is not the same." He struggled to speak without betraying his own uneven breathing. "A hug is completely different."

For a while, neither of them spoke and still neither of them moved. Brant felt the heat of the fire flooding through the room. He was light-headed, with the giddy optimism that Sox's heroic survival and two beers had given him, on top of hours of work outdoors.

Of course there was nothing wrong with his sheep. Of course it was okay to kiss a princess, even when she lived on the other side of the world and her monthly clothing allowance probably matched the size of his bank loan.

No need to let her go.

No need to think.

Just be.

"But it doesn't have to be different," she said, then slid her hand around his waist to the front and lifted it, running it up his chest to cradle his jaw. "It can be quite important and good. It can go places."

Her touch was so light. His skin tingled at the roots of his hair, and his whole body began to throb. She kissed his cheek, her lips soft and tentative as if she didn't know how she might react to the texture of his skin.

"All sorts of places, it can go," she whispered.

She was testing herself.

And him?

Her mouth moved closer to his, advancing just a tiny bit closer with each kiss, one soft, questing press after another.

He wanted *so much* to turn his head and meet her. Just an inch of movement would do it. He wanted to close his lips over hers and fill her mouth, take her whole mouth, kissing her until she gasped for air, clawed at his back and moaned. He was on fire.

Another few seconds and she would arrive where he wanted her. Their lips would meet, hers would part and he'd crush her with the strength of his kiss, taste her and drink her in and give them both a memory that would stay inside them forever.

He wouldn't be able to stop.

Another few seconds and he seriously wouldn't be able to stop, so any rational thinking needed to be done right now.

"Misha, what are you doing?" Her lips moved another fraction of an inch closer. His voice sounded like a rusty gate. He really didn't want to say the words. "Come on. What the hell are you doing? What do you want, with something like this? What would we really be doing here?"

She stopped. Dropped her head so that it was her forehead that pressed into his cheek, not her lips. They both stood stock-still. He could still feel her breasts. Her breathing went in and out like an air pump, fast and shaky. He could feel her hips, and the hardness of his own arousal pressing against her. He had his hands on the tight curve of her backside, and didn't even remember moving them down, but, oh, it felt good to have them there, locking her against his body.

"Trying to find out what it feels like to be Gian-Marco," she said. "I think that's what I'm doing. I—I'm not sure."

He should have guessed. He should have overcome the effect of pizza and beer on his mood. He should have sensed the hidden motivation just in her breathing, in her fingers, in her silence.

It kicked at him, painful and unexpected.

He was her little emotional petri dish, where she could cook up a couple of experiments about the kind of relationship she wanted with her European fiancé. Would she take lovers, after they married? What kind of men would she choose?

He, Brant, was only a struggling sheep farmer, safely distant from paparazzi and royal protocol.

Safely unimportant, like Gian-Marco's blonde.

Safe to test herself with.

Safe to kiss.

Safe to leave.

"And?" he managed to ask.

"I—I don't know." She pulled away, and wrapped her arms around her own body instead of Brant's. Her eyes glittered and swam. "Don't make me answer that question. Not tonight."

"I don't think we should try to answer it any night," he decided out loud, bluntly. "It's not my business what kind of a relationship you choose to have, or what you decide you want about faithfulness and trust."

She nodded, her cheeks stained with color. "No. Okay. You're right, I guess it isn't."

He dragged in another breath and spoke even more harshly, this time. "It's not my business, Misha, and I won't be used."

Her eyes narrowed. "Is that what you think I was doing?"

"Well, isn't it? What else could it be?"

"I—I don't know. And I'm sorry." She stepped back to the table and gathered up the forgotten photos like a pack of oversize playing cards, stacked them neatly and slid them back into the envelope. "Thank you for helping me with this." Her tone had changed. "With working out what was really going on in the photos."

"If we're right about it."

"Oh, I think we're right."

She gave Brant a polite little smile that didn't reach her eyes, and he could almost see the protective emotional shutters coming down. He realized just how much of herself she'd given away tonight, and knew without a doubt just how much she'd regret it later on.

He wished his sister were here.

Chapter Nine

Brant was over at Chris's when Nuala got back from Sydney at two o'clock on Wednesday afternoon.

He'd had someone out here inspecting some aspect of the property this morning, but he hadn't told Misha why. He'd been pretty vague about it. Farm admin. Routine. She hadn't questioned him more closely on the subject because, basically, they weren't really speaking to each other.

This was less awkward than it sounded. You really didn't need to speak to someone that much when you managed to avoid being in the same room with them whenever possible. Brant showered, Misha made coffee. Misha read by the fire, Brant stared at the computer in the farm office.

Easy.

She was dying to see Nuala—someone to *vent* to. When she saw the familiar car coming down the track, her heart went fluttery and light, but a part of this was awkwardness, she knew, rather than anticipation. What on earth was she going to tell Nu? The strange atmosphere between herself and Brant stuck out like a sore thumb and surely her friend would ask.

What's up with you two, anyhow?

Um, I sort of tried to seduce your brother. But it didn't work. He's angry with me—he has to be—and I'm angry with myself. What was I trying to prove? Why did I risk my friendship with you in such a stupid way, Nu? And my friendship with him. This hurt and confusion about Gian-Marco and the engagement is no excuse.

Nuala arrived like a whirlwind. She hugged Misha and started talking about the wedding before she'd even shut the car door.

"We've booked the venue—Randwick—lucky to get the date, apparently. It's gorgeous. I can show you on the Internet. Chris is going to be speechless. And I have the dress. Which of course he is *not* going to see until the day. Mum and I are looking at the different menus. They have such an incredible choice, I get hungry just reading the descriptions and it's so hard to decide."

"Will people really mind what they eat, though?" Misha asked gently. "I won't. We're all going to be there for you and Chris, not for the free food."

Nuala looked a little shocked. "I want to create memories people will treasure. Your jaded palate is in a different league from most people's, Mish, don't forget."

"Too true! Hey, though, you look gorgeous! The hair, the eyebrows. Did you have a facial?"

"All of that. Manicure. Clothes." She posed and beamed. "But meanwhile I've still only narrowed the choice of florist down to three. One of them does all this really sleek Japanese-style design but I'm not sure if that fits the rest of the mood. And invitations are still up in the air. Which is not so good because we're running out of time. The plain silver on white looks really good, but I don't think it goes with the cream and sage, but when I looked at sage for the invitations it looked hard to read and just not the right shade."

"Nu, you're forgetting to breathe," Misha said.

"Am I?" She slapped the flat of her hand against her chest and frowned. "Hmm, maybe I am." She gasped in a lungful of air, then asked, "Is Brant around?"

"No, he's at Chris's."

"Lamb-marking, still?"

"No, that's finished. Something else today. Crutching?"

"He's so good, helping Chris out. Has he been good?" She grabbed Misha's arm suddenly, and studied her face. "Has he looked after you?"

"Yes, he's been great." She had trouble with Nuala's searching stare, and tried to deflect her attention onto something different. "We had a scare with Soxie," she said quickly. "She took a Ten-Eighty wild dog bait. We think it was one Barry Andrews had put beside the road and forgotten about."

"Oh, poor Sox!"

"But Brant got her to bring most of it up and she's fine, now."

"Oh, poor, poor dog, I'll give her a hug. Gosh, and you're sounding like a farmer's daughter. I'm sorry, I haven't even called since Sunday, but Mum and I were just exhausted, you have no idea."

"I do, a bit."

"Oh, of course you do!" Nuala squeezed the air out of Misha's lungs in a fierce hug. "Sorry! How are you?" She pulled back, narrowed her eyes and studied Misha's face. "You look great. A lot better. Tell me how you are."

I sort of tried to seduce your brother, but it didn't work and I don't know what I was thinking. I actually looked better than this three days ago. Can you tell me why I'm so confused?

The words stayed inside her.

"Can we go into the house and have coffee?" she asked instead, thinking maybe they could talk then—around the safer edges of the subject, anyway. The coffee suggestion came out way too needy.

Try not to sound as if you're begging, Mish.

"Umm, not yet?" Nuala gave an apologetic wince. "I'm going to dump my bag and head straight to Chris's. Mum says he has to come up to Sydney as soon as possible and see the venue, see what we're planning—they got away on their cruise with no problems, it looks like a gorgeous ship—and I have an idea he's going to dig in his heels and refuse, but it's important, I want his involvement, so…"

"Breathe, Nu."

"I am. I promise." Nuala rushed into the house, dumped her bag of Sydney clothes on her bed, grabbed a glass of water at the kitchen sink and rushed back out to the car. "Talk later?" she suggested, through the driver's-side window.

Misha saw a huge pale-blue-and-gold ring binder on the backseat, and glimpsed the words *My Wedding Planner* in an elegant script. Chris wouldn't know what had hit him.

Nuala roared up the track, leaving Misha staring after her, with frustration throbbing at her temples and uncertainty turning the bones in her legs to mush.

Nu was back seventy-five minutes later, in just as much of a rush but a whole lot less bubbly.

Well, unless sobs counted as bubbles.

With the polite avoidance thing that was going on between herself and Brant, Misha had pleaded a headache—genuine, but mild—and hadn't gone with him to Chris's today. Instead, she'd spent much of her time sitting in the swing-seat on the veranda, drinking fizzy lemon squash and pretending to read a classic murder mystery.

The sun shone and the temperature had to be at least seventy degrees, unseasonable for late autumn and just gorgeous. Birds sang, sheep mothers called to sheep babies, and very occasionally came the sound of an airplane high overhead, or a vehicle somewhere in the distance.

So much peace and space, just as there had been three days ago, on Sunday, when Misha and Brant had gone riding by the river. Except that she'd stupidly spoiled it all by trying to get inside Gian-Marco's skin, get inside the skin of her planned marriage with him to see if she could live that way, each of them with casual lovers on the side.

I couldn't.

Five minutes of misunderstanding and layered motivations and chemistry like nuclear fission with Brant on Monday night, and she knew it as categorically as she knew her own name. It would tear her apart, having a husband and a lover at the same time. It would wreck her life.

But how unfair had it been for her to conduct such an experiment with another human being? Especially with someone like Brant?

He was probably right to be angry.

Was he angry? She didn't actually know, because he'd withdrawn so much—and so had she—that his attitude remained a mystery. Mutual courtesy could be a very effective shield.

And here was Nu back from Chris's in tears.

She barged into Misha's arms the same way Christian's little boys at home barged at their mother when they were having a tantrum. Her face was swollen and red and wet, and she probably hadn't been very safe behind the wheel. For several minutes, all she could say was, "C-C-Chris s-s-says… C-C-Chris s-s-says…"

"What's up?" Misha crooned. "What does he say, honey?"

Nuala gave one last gasping hiccup of a sob and grew suddenly calm. "The wedding's off," she said.

Brant approached the house not knowing what to expect.

He hadn't heard a single word of the argument between Nuala and Chris, but then he hadn't needed to. Slammed car doors, intense whispering over by the temporary yard full of

bawling ewes, Nuala's storming stride across an open paddock with Chris storming just as hard as he pursued her, an
ominous silence after they both disappeared behind some
rocks and trees, Nu's final departure with jets of damp grass
and mud flying from her back wheels as she gunned the
four-wheel drive over to the gate.

It told its own story.

He'd kept to his post beside the crutching trailer belonging to the hired team who'd come in to tackle Chris's pregnant ewes. Chris didn't want his animals to have a lot of dirty,
dragging wool around their back ends when they lambed in
the spring, so like most farmers, he got rid of it in a quick,
localized shearing before the pregnancies became too far
advanced. Brant and Chris had been rounding up mobs of
sheep and getting them yarded ready for the crutchers all day.

One of the hired men had been "feeling crook." Hungover,
Brant suspected. The man wasn't pulling his weight and
there was tension between him and the others. Equipment
had broken, ewes hadn't cooperated, even Chris's best dog
wasn't his usual self today. They'd both thought about Sox
and the bait, but Shep wasn't ill, just distracted for mysteri-
ous doggy reasons of his own.

Then Nuala had entered the mix, still dressed in an outfit
Mum must have bought her in Sydney, including shoes that
were probably now ruined by the mud and grass in the paddock.
She'd had her hair cut and somehow…erm…lightened, he
vaguely thought. Her nails were manicured and various uniden-
tifiable things had possibly been done to her face.

She glowed, basically, but she wanted Chris to stop mustering sheep now, this minute, and go back to the house with her
so she could talk him through her wedding planner page by
page and get his opinion on tiny little decisions that he wasn't
remotely interested in, during a long day of crutching sheep.

Should the rosebuds be apricot or peach?

Chris hadn't realized there was a difference.

And what did he think of her new look?

Chris confessed that he hadn't specifically noticed it was new. Although she looked great, of course.

How many choices of main course? Two, or three? And did enough people like pork? Or would fish be better?

"Do we really have to bloody do this bloody now?" Chris had said in frustration after several minutes.

Cue the slammed car door, after Nu had dumped the wedding planner onto the backseat.

When she had stormed off home, Chris came back to the crutching trailer without a word and they got on with the job. By the time they'd finished, the light had almost disappeared. The trailer and the hired crutchers jolted back toward town, planning a stop at the pub. Chris asked Brant if he wanted to clean up a bit and have a beer before he went home. Brant picked up on the signals and said thanks but no.

"Shall I get her to call you?" he asked.

"Up to her," Chris growled. "She knows the number."

Right.

Now, Brant parked the car beneath the carport and cautiously entered the house. Apparently Nuala and Misha hadn't heard him. There was music playing and a cooking pot lid jumping up and down on top of boiling water on the stove, and the sounds muffled his arrival.

The evening had already chilled down after the day's spring-like warmth, and the fire flamed in the slow-combustion stove, with its fan making a low hum. He stopped in the darkened corridor long enough to catch his breath, and watched the backs of the two women's heads as they talked.

"But there are two kinds of fights, Nu, don't you think?" Misha said.

She had her feet up on the coffee table, and was painting her toenails as she talked. There were cotton balls wedged between each toe, and it made Brant ticklish just to look at them. He had a deeply scary moment of remembering that she had really sexy toes, and wondering what color polish she'd chosen this time. Same pink as before? It was like an out-of-body experience, and he was glad when it ebbed away. He'd never thought about nail polish before in his life.

"What kinds?" Nuala asked her.

"Well, there's the kind that…oh…strips the whole relationship back to bits of crumbled bone, and there's the kind that's…well…cushioned by this sense of trust, even when you're yelling at each other."

"Mmm?"

"Don't you think this one with Chris might be the cushion kind, not the bone kind?" Misha capped the nail polish and sat back on the couch.

"You're talking about trust? I *trusted* that he understood that this wedding was important to me!"

"He does understand. But maybe you didn't pick your moment."

"We both said some horrible things. How do we backtrack from that?"

"Hot horrible things, or cold horrible things?"

Nu laughed. Sounded pretty creaky and tired. "Stop giving me these weird choices, Misha. Cushions and bones, hot and cold. Just make it simple and tell me what you mean."

"Well, my fight with Gian-Marco—"

Okay, I can't stand here listening, Brant realized. He entered the room and flung them a greeting. They turned toward him in surprise. He said, "I'm filthy," and went straight to the bathroom to shower.

"Tell me about your fight with Gian-Marco," Nuala said to Misha, when Brant was safely out of earshot and she'd jumped up briefly to add pasta to the wildly boiling water in the kitchen.

Brant had startled both of them with his sudden appearance. They'd been talking too intently to hear his car outside.

"Cold horrible," Misha said. "Definitely." She was thinking all of this stuff through as she went, none of it was related to any conclusions she'd reached earlier. "Just...cold."

She thought about it some more.

"No care, you know? I can remember in my teens when I used to fight a lot with my mother, I'd really yell at her sometimes. I'd fling all this hot, passionate stuff at her, but she knew—we both knew—that I didn't really mean it because it was all fiery and...I don't know if this is making any sense."

"Maybe," Nu agreed carefully. "Hot horrible can be good, you're saying."

"Yes, extravagant, wild stuff that gets vented out of your system. The next day, you won't even remember why you felt it so strongly, because the love will be back again. And the love is strong enough."

"Chris was busy. My timing wasn't great," Nu conceded. "I was so excited. You know, you noticed my eyebrow shaping and hair right away, and my hands, and my outfit, but Chris didn't at all. And I've ruined the shoes. But I guess..."

"Who do women dress for?" Misha leaned forward and began to take the cotton balls out from between her toes. "Who, really? Other women! Men don't notice details but they notice the result."

Which was pretty, in the case of her toenails. It almost made up for the fact that turning into a farm princess instead of the palace kind had temporarily wrecked her hands.

"If Chris thinks you're beautiful," she continued, "in a slimy oilskin with rain-drenched rat-tailed hair and a red nose—and he does, right?—then he might think you're twice as beautiful in a new outfit with a fresh eyebrow wax, but he won't have a clue what the difference is."

"So this was a hot fight, not a cold fight, and cold fights are the nasty ones. The deal breakers. That's what you're saying?"

"The theory is still evolving, but yes. That's what I'm saying."

Nuala slumped her head against the back of the couch. "It's exhausting, being in love and planning a wedding at the same time. People should do those two things separately." She blew a blast of air from her lips as she thought about this. "Boy, that didn't make sense, did it?" she concluded.

"So is the wedding back on?"

"If Chris wants it to be. If my apologizing is enough."

"It will be. He wants to marry you, Nu."

"Do you think so?"

"Are you kidding? The way he looks at you? You don't know how much I envy you, because I realize now that Gian-Marco has never looked at me that way." She managed to joke, "Or not when I've been wearing a slimy oilskin in the rain, anyhow."

Nuala closed her eyes for a moment.

"Mish, I've been a bad friend since you got here, flying off to Sydney and obsessing so much about my own stuff," she said. "Tell me more about the cold horrible fight you had with Gian-Marco. Tell me where you're up to in how you feel."

So Misha did.

She talked about understanding that she'd get torn in half if she tried to have a lover on the side, but not how she'd managed to discover this about herself. She talked about shattered trust and public pretense and the pressure of expectations. She talked about not knowing the exact moment when her feelings for Gian-Marco had begun to die, but realizing now that they *had* died, and she couldn't bring them back. Her words went all over the place, and her voice fogged up several times, but when she'd said it all, she felt better and clearer.

"Do you know what you're going to do?" Nuala asked in the end.

She felt a sudden icy certainty. "Yes. I know."

Showing Nuala the ring finger on her left hand, she slowly drew off the sparkling solitaire diamond set in its pink-gold band. "This is what I'm going to do. It's what has happened in my heart, already. Keep it safe somewhere for me while I'm here? I don't want to look at it. Or think about it. Or think about what this is all going to mean."

"Mean?"

"Princess stuff, Nu. Don't you remember what it was like when you stayed with me? St. Margrethe's Cathedral has its calendar blacked out for a week and a half before the wedding and three days after it. No other weddings during that time, no church services. The Langemark National Orchestra changed its summer touring schedule so we could have some of their musicians playing at the reception. When I flew out here, in my silly little emotional crisis, all these letters had to get sent from the palace, regretting that Her Royal Highness would be unable to attend this or that function, even though some events had been in my official diary for months. I've already disappointed people. There are rumors at home that the princess has had a breakdown."

"Oh, Mish!"

"The nation is worried about me. Meanwhile, I have a designer almost finished with my dress, thinking it's going to make her career in international fashion. Mette Janssen. She's lovely. I love her clothes. You've seen them. I wear them to pieces, but she's not really known outside of Langemark, and my wedding would have brought her name to the whole of Europe, and probably North America, too."

"You can't go ahead with a wedding so as not to disappoint the dress designer."

"I know. I know! But I am not supposed to do something like this. I am not supposed to set a whole royal wedding juggernaut in motion and then bring it to a screeching halt, just because the tiny issue of my fiancé's infidelity has put a slight dampener on the proceedings."

"Misha…!"

"And you can't tell anyone about it, okay? Not anyone. Not your brother. Not Chris. I don't think I can even tell Gian-Marco himself, yet, from what my parents were telling me about duty and secrecy before I left."

"That's hard!"

"It'll be all right. I'm not going back to Europe until Graziella's pregnancy has been announced, which should be pretty soon. I don't want to exist in that kind of dishonest limbo. And I don't want to see all the stories about Gian-Marco and that actress in the press while the palace is still pretending things are fine. I just…" She blinked back tears. "…need a bit more time here, where it's easier. If you'll have me."

Nuala hugged her. "If we'll have you? Mish, I'm telling you! We may refuse to ever let you go!"

Brant emerged from the shower, wrapped in a towel from the waist down and wishing he'd thought to bring his clean clothes along to the bathroom with him. It was a real nuisance only having one shower when you had a princess in the house. He found himself thinking about putting in a second bathroom, which was crazy.

He should be looking forward to getting rid of the princess, instead.

She and Nuala were still sitting on the couch in front of the fire as he passed behind them on the way to his room. They'd opened a bottle of red wine and got out cheese, crackers and olives, and they seemed to be talking about fashion.

Nuala looked much happier, he discovered when he'd dressed and returned to the warmth. She hopped up to drain her pasta and announced over her shoulder that they could eat whenever he wanted.

Her disappearance into the kitchen left Brant alone with Misha for the first time since Monday night.

He hesitated.

They'd been doing really well with keeping their distance from each other.

Why rock the boat?

He'd had the Pastures Protection Board take their sample from one of his lame ewe's hooves this morning. He'd seen the inflammation for himself, and so had the P.P.B. guy, but it could be shelly hoof or ovine interdigital dermatitis. Over the next week, he should just get on with his work, wait for their verdict, keep on staying safely away from the princess and eventually life should…might…get back to normal.

On the other hand…

He stepped several paces closer and asked, "Did you get her sorted out?" Probably not the best way of putting it, but he felt so awkward. His tongue had knotted itself, and so had his brain.

Misha nodded and said quietly, "I think they're going to be all right. It was just one of those pre-wedding emotional blips. She's going to phone him after dinner, when she's given him a bit more space, and I expect she'll go over there. They love each other. They both want to fix this, not make it worse."

"I heard you talking. Some of it," he added hastily. "Thanks. She wouldn't have been as honest with me, and I wouldn't have known what to say. I'm glad you were here."

Ah, hell, look at her, she was blushing!

It started him off, too. He could feel the color creeping all the way up his neck and into his cheeks, burning him like a fever until a sweat broke out around his temples.

"Um, that's fine, Brant," she said. "She's my best friend. I'm glad I'm here, too."

They both kept watching each other, poised in odd positions like wary animals pricking their ears as they sensed danger. Misha sat up too straight, her hands curved over her knees. Brant hovered halfway between the couch and the fire, blocking her heat.

He should apologize about Monday night, he knew that. He'd been considering it ever since, but avoiding her had seemed easier than working out whether he'd overreacted with his accusation that he was only her experiment.

Tonight it seemed much clearer.

He'd been emotionally wrung out on Monday night, after thinking for almost two gut-wrenching hours that he could lose Sox. Misha had acted like a trouper the whole day, with Shay, with Chris, with Sox herself. One tiny misstep, not even a real kiss, and he'd jumped down her throat. His over-sensitivity was far more his own fault than hers.

"Sorry about Monday," he said. "About what I said. You know, there are worse things than being someone's…um… experiment."

But were there worse ways to apologize? Doubtful. Oh, *shoot!*

She tucked in the corner of her mouth. "Lots of worse things, Brant. Still, you deserved better."

"No, no, hang on, I'm not angling for you to apologize, too."

"But how about if I do?" she suggested brightly. "Then we can forget the whole thing and not have to keep sidling out of the room like nervous little crabs when we see the other one coming?"

He laughed, washed with a major flood of relief at her down-to-earth attitude. "You know what? That's a really good idea!"

Chapter Ten

"What do you mean you can't find the sample?" Brant said into the phone, to a disembodied male voice at the Pastures Protection Board. "Your guy took it a week ago. He labelled it and dated it and filled in all the right blanks on the form." He listened to the voice at the other end of the line. "But you can't find it." He managed to keep his voice below a yell. "And that's why you haven't contacted me with a result. I see."

He resisted the temptation to throw the phone at the wall, and arranged to have someone come back out as soon as possible and take a second sample for analysis. He was told it couldn't be today, probably tomorrow, and this left him in a state of further restlessness and frustration. He'd called the P.P.B. lab expecting a result, which, whether negative or positive, would have triggered more phone calls and a lot of work.

Now he'd be in a limbo of uncertainty for at least another week, and he had nothing else prepared to do today. It was just after eight-thirty in the morning. He'd already checked the sheep before breakfast and they were all fine.

Fine, but lame, in that same slowly growing number of cases, mostly on the front feet. They'd had more rain over the past few days, and the weather was still warm, which would keep the infection brewing whether it was foot rot or something less serious. He hadn't cleaned out or pared any individual hooves this morning. At that point, he'd believed he'd be hearing a definitive verdict today, which would make cleaning a few hooves an academic exercise.

But no, thanks to a bureaucratic stuff-up, he'd have to wait. He hated the powerlessness of the feeling.

The house was quiet. A clock ticked on the kitchen wall and the smell of breakfast coffee lingered in the air. Nuala had already gone to Chris's. She'd spent most of her days and several of her nights there since getting back from Sydney just over a week ago, and Brant knew that she and Chris were both working hard. Chris had promised that he'd go to Sydney with her for a couple of nights very soon, once he was on top of various jobs he had to do on his property.

Here at Inverlochie, Misha had convinced Brant that she could help muster his spring-lambing ewes for the hired crutching team just as effectively as she'd helped with lamb-marking—"You've seen me on that four-wheeler, Brant. It's such a buzz, I love it!"—so they'd been working hard, also. Misha zoomed around the grassy paddocks with almost as much energy and enthusiasm as Sox, whooping when she went over a bump, and he smiled whenever he thought about it.

Crutching had finished now, however.

Brant had a long list of repair jobs to do, and somehow that out-of-the-blue second bathroom idea hadn't gone away. He wanted to look at the potential cost, and where best to put in an extension, but all of it could wait today. He was too restless to put his mind to some new project—especially when he didn't know why it had suddenly struck him as such a good idea.

And the princess was overdue for a royal tour.

He found her picking a bucketful of lemons and grape-fruit in the stand of citrus trees. "Smell them, Brant!" she commanded him eagerly. "I never realized fresh-picked lemons smelled so much better than the ones you get in a wedge on the side of your plate. They're like lemon to the power of ten."

She held one out and he sniffed obediently and of course she was right. It was like inhaling the color yellow, and you could almost feel the sweet, tangy fragrance bursting in your nose.

"Are you busy today?" he asked her.

"You tell me! I had plans for a lemon chiffon pie, and lemon chicken, and grapefruit sorbet—you may detect a citrus theme, there—but you know that, like any normal red-blooded royal, I'd far rather be covered in lanolin and dog hair and unmentionable sheep by-products, so…"

"Do you ever just sit down?"

"Nope." She grinned. "Not often. It's more fun to do stuff."

"Okay, in that case, would you like to climb Australia's highest mountain?"

Not what Misha had been expecting. In fact, she almost dropped her bucket of citrus on the ground. She thought about the suggestion for a moment, envisaging ice picks and belaying pins, ropes and harnesses, swirling mist and sheer, giddy drops.

"Sure," she answered. "It sounds great."

Then she envisaged her body roped against Brant's, his arms reaching across to help her find the right handholds, his weight supporting her and his muscles moving just beyond her reach, and liked this second set of mental pictures far too much.

"Be ready to leave in half an hour?"

"Fifteen minutes, if you want." She looked down at her jeans, peacock-blue knit top and once-white running shoes. "Do I need to change?"

"You're fine."

"I'm going to sack the palace wardrobe consultant and hire you."

They loaded day packs, water, hats, snacks and warm jackets, but Misha noted the lack of serious climbing gear in the back of the truck. "Do we hire the equipment?" she asked. "You know, the ropes and stuff."

Brant laughed. "No. We go up in the chairlift."

Inside the house, the phone rang and he raced for it before Misha could assimilate the chairlift idea. She noted that he hadn't been moving toward the telephone with such an air of dread over the past few days. Lauren hadn't called again after the awkward encounter at Tarragon almost two weeks ago, and the June issue of *Today's Woman* had appeared in stores on Monday.

Publicly, Brant was no longer on the market.

The fact seemed to have taken a certain weight off his mind.

And the chairlift was probably a good thing. Much better than being roped together.

Blinking in the bright light, she realized she'd left her sunglasses on the kitchen bench and went in to retrieve them.

"You are kidding me!" she heard Brant say. "For heaven's sake, if you want any private life left, don't tell Shay Russell about it because she'll want to do a story. Not planning to? Good." He listened for a moment. "Hey, don't thank me. I seem to remember you were ready to kill Dusty and me for this at one stage." He listened again. "But that was before Jacinda? Mate, if I was there I'd punch you on the arm until you had bruises. It's great news. Now, if we could just get some of our horses over the line in a big win or two, I'd start to think there was some point in the three of us being friends."

Misha found her sunglasses and saw Brant's camera sitting at the end of the bench. She picked it up, wondering about it. So often, she avoided going anywhere near photographic equipment. Cameras caused her enough trouble and irritation in her public life, why let them impinge on her private existence as well?

He put down the phone, after a bit more talk about racehorses, and saw what she was doing. "Want to?" he asked. "We can easily fit it in one of the day packs."

"Let's take it," she said, surprising herself. "If we don't end up using it, that's okay, too."

But it might be nice to have a picture of Brant to take home with her to Langemark…

"My friend Callan is getting married," he told her. "That was him on the phone just now, with the news. He sounded…" Brant paused, grappling with a typical male's total lack of vocabulary for occasions like this. "…pretty good," he came up with. "And guess how they met?"

"Can I go out on a limb, in the light of recent events and a couple of discussions with Nu, and suggest…*Today's Woman* and 'Wanted: Outback Wives'?"

"Do you think I should go back through all my letters and see who I missed?"

"No, I think you should be happy for your friend, because it's great for him, and while you're feeling happy, take me up Australia's highest mountain. In a chairlift? Seriously?"

"Well, not all the way."

"So, after the chairlift there's some kind of hired rollerskate arrangement for the last six miles?"

"Hired kangaroo pouches, so you were close."

"Okay, now I've stopped believing in the chairlift, too."

"Hmm, and maybe there's a little talk we need to have about Santa Claus."

"You are in a nutty mood today, Brant."

And your eyes are different. They're not smoking and suffering today. What's been on your mind, Brant? And what's changed?

"Yeah, I'm actually pretty happy about Callan," he said. "Gets a few things in perspective."

What "things" he didn't specify…and Misha still didn't know what to believe about how they'd get to the top of the mountain.

To begin with, they drove.

"Got to have a royal tour, Your Highness, while you're here," Brant said.

The country they passed through became wilder and more beautiful as they left the farming country near the banks of the Murray River and went higher into the mountains. This was part of a huge national park, and the ruggedly folded terrain was clothed in thick eucalyptus forest, some of it still showing the ravages of major bushfires several years earlier.

The air had its usual fresh tang, and they crossed over little mountain creeks that hurtled their way down the narrow ravine-like valleys. Beside one of them, they stopped to drink hot tea from a flask and eat the oatmeal and coconut cookies that Nuala had made this week.

They took photos—idiotic ones of Brant hanging from a tree and Misha gesturing at the landscape like a TV quiz show hostess presenting the major prize—and she couldn't remember if she'd ever had such fun being on either end of a camera lens. They even set the camera on a tree stump and posed on a rock with cheesy, frozen grins.

"How long did you set the timer for, Brant?"

"Fifteen seconds."

"This has got to be longer than—"

Click. Just when she had her tongue stuck between her teeth as she talked.

"Want to take another one?" Brant suggested, holding the camera between them so they could both see the tiny picture on the digital display. Their arms brushed together.

"Keep this one," she said. "It's more the real me than tiaras and smiles."

"I wonder if that's really true…" he said softly, but she let the comment go.

After winding upward through stands of huge trees and litters of moss-covered boulders they reached a gap in the terrain, and soon after that, an alpine ski village appeared, its pretty chalets perched on one steep side of the valley, while on the other the ski lifts marched toward the treeless peaks, across slopes still bare of snow.

"So we really are going up in a chairlift?"

"You didn't believe me." Brant sighed loudly. "There's just no trust anymore…"

She laughed at him and pelted him with a strikingly patterned piece of bark she'd collected earlier. He deserved it!

The chairlift rose almost two thousand feet above the village, a slow, spectacular, and near-silent drift skyward, which landed them above the tree line in a terrain of round granite rocks and low, gnarled bushes. Next, a metal walkway guided them to the top of Australia, at just under seven and a half thousand feet. They ate a distinctly chilly, windy, late picnic lunch right on the top.

Mount Koshuzko, the mountain was called. Kozushko. Kosziosko. Something like that. As they ate, Brant attempted to spell it for her but failed, and even though Misha knew five different European languages, Polish wasn't one of them, so she did no better when she tried. Eventually, they found a sign and read the correct spelling on that.

Kosciuszko.

"Why does your number-one mountain get a Polish name?"

"Because a Polish explorer was the first person to officially reach the summit, and that's what he picked."

"If you ever had the chance to name a mountain, what would you call it?" The wind whipped Misha's hair out of its ponytail strand by strand as they stood looking at the sign.

"Not something that hard to spell," Brant said. Misha couldn't see his eyes behind the sunglasses, but she had found herself helplessly watching the back pockets of his jeans every time he walked ahead of her on the way up.

Well, not watching the pockets, exactly...

"But what?" she asked him. Which was scarier? Wanting to see a man's eyes, or watching his... ahem... back pockets?

"Would depend what kind of a mountain it was."

"So you'd go for the literal. Mount Snow, or Mount Granite."

"Something like that. Mount Eruption. Mount Bloody Steep."

"Mount Blisters on My Heels."

"Have you? Got blisters?" He looked concerned and glanced down the mountain to where the walkway wound its way for three or four miles back to the top of the chairlift.

"No, I'm fine. Just kidding."

"We should be heading back if we want to take a break in the village and still get home before dark."

They'd already had such a good day. Coming down in the chairlift, Misha felt as if she could have jumped off it and soared right down to Thredbo village in the valley. In the distance to the east she could see the layers of blue-tinted hills getting lower, turning into farmland and disappearing toward a hazy horizon. They stopped in the village and had tall drinks of soda and lime on an outdoor deck in the three o'clock sunshine. They talked about skiing, and tried to imagine these slopes covered in snow.

"I bet you're good at it," Brant said.

"I'm fast. But I'm untidy. And sometimes I whoop and yell all the way down."

"Not very royal of you. I've heard your whoop."

"Not very courtly of you to point that out. Thanks for my royal tour, Brant. Can I tell you the best thing about it?"

"The ride in the kangaroo pouch?"

"Okay, I can pelt you with this piece of wet lemon from my drink, if you insist."

"Tell me the best thing about it."

"You didn't make me cut any ceremonial ribbons or open those little curtains they put in front of commemorative plaques. Those things are so fiddly! They get stuck!"

"There's a bottle of champagne in the fridge at home. You can smash it against my truck and launch it into the creek for its maiden voyage, if you ever feel the need."

"You're too good to me!"

"I'm just a beautiful person, Mish, what can I say?"

They smiled at each other and it lasted a few seconds too long. Got sort of tangly and warm, and Misha's breathing caught in her chest. She didn't know what to do next, and hoped that Brant would do it for her, without giving her another second to think. Something unexpected and dramatic and sexy and—

He was the first one to break their eye contact. Misha almost heard the snap. He looked down with a frown, dragged his keys out of his pocket and muttered something about getting back before dark.

"You must be tired." He stood without waiting for her answer, and maybe he was right about the tired thing, because her energy level suddenly went dead flat.

On the long, winding drive back to Inverlochie, she dozed off in the passenger seat and stayed asleep until Brant stopped to open the farm gate. Even then, she kept her eyes shut for some seconds longer. It was just too hard to rouse herself, but she knew that soon she'd have to. It was the passenger's job to open the gate, and Brant was waiting for her.

"Sorry," she mumbled to him. "I'm going to get out and do it, I really am. Just let me wake up a bit, first."

"It's okay. I'll do it." His voice sounded gravelly and reluctant.

"No."

Silence. Except for the engine ticking.

After an interval she opened her eyes and found him leaning his head and arms on the wheel, making no move to get out of the truck. "Are you asleep, too?"

He twisted his head and looked at her, his eyes their usual smoky hue. "No." She looked back at him, and neither of them moved. "I'm awake." He sighed between his teeth. "I'm just not in any hurry to open the gate."

They kept sitting. The shadows had grown long by this time, and the light had done the gorgeous green-and-gold thing that it did most evenings. Any minute, the sun would dip behind a tree or a hill in the west and the shadows would pool together and grow blue and cold.

"Why, Brant?"

"Don't want to be a sheep farmer today," he said.

"No?"

"Nope, I'd rather be royal. Or maybe just a duke. Something easy, with no pressure."

"You wouldn't. And I'm not even going to get into the issue of pressure. But why?"

He sighed again, and started to get out of the car. She leaned across and put a hand on his shoulder, flattened her mouth stubbornly and frowned at him, demanding an answer. "Why?"

He sat slowly back, leaving one leg on the ground and the truck door half open. A puff of breeze tossed the top branches of the big eucalyptus tree that overhung the gate, and a flock of sulphur-crested cockatoos squabbled in another tree near the creek. A car went past with its headlights on against the fading light, and in the truck's side mirror Mish saw the driver lift his hand in one of those Australian country greetings that people gave whether they knew each other or not. Instinctively, she gave him a royal wave in reply.

Silence.

"I think my new ewes have got foot rot," Brant said.

Foot rot.

New to her personal universe.

"Haven't they been wearing their pool shoes in the hot tub change room?" she teased him gently. "I'm sorry, Brant, I don't know what foot rot means."

She took her hand away, but her body stayed where it was, a little closer to him than it had been before.

"It's caused by a kind of bacteria."

He pulled his leg back into the vehicle, let the door swing shut and twisted to face her. The truck cab felt as if it had shrunk to half the size. Because the sun had gone, now, and the light was fading?

"It spreads really easily in warm, damp soil," he went on, "and we've had such a warm autumn and such good rain. It ruins their feet and makes them lame. It can get really serious, and there are strict regulations about reporting it. When I bought them, they came certified against disease."

"So shouldn't they—?"

"But I see some of them limping. I've checked a few feet and they don't look right. Reddened and inflamed, with the horn separating from the hoof. Which can be foot rot, or it can be a couple of other things. And the new ones have crossed tracks with the ones I'm selling, which means those could be infected, too. I had someone in from the Pastures Protection Board to take a sample last week, and thought I'd hear the verdict today. Thought I'd know one way or the other if I'm going to be slashing six figures off my cash flow this year, because if the stock are infected I can't follow through on the contracted sale. Phoned the P.P.B. first thing this morning, as soon as their office opened. But they've lost the sample and they have to take another one, which means another week of doubt. And waiting. And if it is foot rot, then the effort and expense of getting rid of it is massive. And today I'm sick of it, Misha. Just sick of it. On top of the wool prices, and the drought we had. I had to get out of the house. We had a great day. But now we're back. I'm back to this. And I'm sick of it."

He sounded that way—heartsick and tired to the bone. Misha was amazed at how well he'd managed to keep it to himself, amazed at all the times he'd still managed to be funny with her, or patient when she did something wrong with the sheep, or generous in entertaining her.

"Nu hasn't said anything," she blurted out, wanting to say all sorts of other stuff as well. That he mustn't worry. That she'd help.

Which was naive and idiotic, because she'd flown in as a brief visitor, and she would fly out again soon, back to her own life, immune to his problems.

They both knew it.

Knew it despite this strange, shrinking truck cab that kept pushing them closer together.

"I haven't told her," Brant said. "She'll think it's her problem, and it's not. I'm buying out her share in the farm—hoping to—if I can afford it—after the wedding. Chris has a big bank loan. There's a chunk of his land, beautiful pasture, that he'll have to sell off if he can't pay the loan down. If I can give Nu her capital share from Inverlochie by the end of September, they'll be well set up, but if this foot-rot thing is confirmed…"

"Is it fatal? Isn't there a cure?"

"There is, but it's a heck of a lot of work, and it's expensive. You can't spray sheep like fruit trees. Every animal will need individual treatment, every hoof will need to be cleaned out. Footbaths, hoof-paring, culling of the ones that are slow to respond to treatment. I'll probably end up selling hundreds of otherwise fine animals straight to slaughter at rock-bottom price." He shifted suddenly. "This isn't your business. Let me open that gate."

He leaned on the door, but again she held him back. This time, her hand hit the bare flesh on his forearm, instead of the shirt wrapping his shoulder. She left it there a little too long, and he had time to look down at the now-ragged manicure on her fingers before she snatched them away.

"You've been carrying this on your own for how long?" she asked.

"Since the day you got here."

"Ah. I guess that explains a couple of things from that afternoon."

"Yes. Sorry. I was a bit of a yob."

"That's boy spelled backwards, have you noticed?"

"Is it? Should probably be something else spelled backwards. D-a-e-h-k-c-i—" He stopped. "I'm going to open the gate. We can't sit here forever just because I don't want to get home and start thinking about my limping sheep."

"What can I do, Brant?" She slid her hand up his arm, feeling the chemistry and knowing that he did, too.

"Well, you could open the gate…"

"All right. Okay. You're right. It's not my problem. But I wish you'd at least talk to Nu."

"No. Don't tell her, okay? And don't *hint*." He mimicked her accent and raised the pitch of his voice. "Nuala, I don't want to betray your brother's confidence but I should tell you there's something you really need to talk to him about, relating to sheep feet."

"Is that what you think I'd do?"

"You might."

"When you've asked me straight out to say nothing? Of course I'll respect that, Brant!"

He whooshed out a breath, then took another one. "I know you will. I'm sorry."

"It hurts me when you think badly of me. It hurts me quite a lot." Somehow, her hand had landed on his knee, now.

When had she put it there? And the truck cab had gotten so small she was amazed that either of them could still breathe.

"Does it?"

"Yes."

"Open the gate." He closed his eyes. His hand came down on top of hers. It felt so warm. "Please?"

"Open your eyes."

He did, and they looked at each other. She turned her palm up and curled her fingers, and their grips locked together. His eyes fell to her mouth, and she could feel his gaze like the touch of warm fingers.

"I don't know how it feels to have lame sheep, Brant, but I know how it feels when you can't talk about what's going on inside you or about what you're afraid of. I know how it feels when you have to hide it and lie about it and pretend everything's fine."

He answered harshly, "It would be more useful if you knew how it felt to have lame sheep."

"Oh, shoot! No, it wouldn't!" She blinked back sudden tears. "It wouldn't, Brant! You've told me all this, and it's important. Now don't push me away, just because I haven't been studying the sheep-disease manual since I was six. Just don't push me away!"

He heaved out a huge sigh. "Yeah? What am I supposed to do, then?"

They both knew. Misha was the one to say it. .

"Pull me closer," she whispered.

Silence

"Open the gate," he told her.

"You don't want me to."

"No, but what I want doesn't count. How can it?" Except that he'd already settled her shoulder into the crook of his arm and reached to touch her. His whole body eased against hers in all the places where they could touch, and it felt magic and right and so important. "How can it?" he repeated.

"It counts for me," Misha said.

"For now, it does."

"Yes, for now." She cupped his jaw, her nose only an inch or two from his. His mouth was like a magnet. "I thought the whole point of this, of us sitting here, was that you didn't want to think beyond now."

He groaned and began to kiss her.

No games. Just the hunger.

For a moment, she simply accepted his mouth over hers, cajoling and imperious and single-minded. She gave in to its demands and let her lips fall apart, let his tongue find hers. She felt paralyzed by the strength of her body's reaction.

When she responded, it was like a leaf getting swept away in a current of water. No choice, no other way. She tasted him, letting her tongue sweep the inside of his mouth in an almost desperate level of intimacy, letting her body press hard against his, as if no kiss could ever go deep enough to satisfy her need for him, or his for her.

Time stopped, and the rest of the world went away. This was so unspeakably precious. Worth everything. Worth more than anything she'd ever had or known or felt in her life. It had to be a kind of magic. Nothing else explained how she could have gotten this far in her charmed existence and never felt so right in a man's arms before.

Gian-Marco hovered at the edge of her mind, as insubstantial and unreal as a shadow. She'd never felt this way when he had kissed her. There was no logic to a feeling like this. The feeling just *was*. This kiss felt like nothing else in her life. She would cross oceans for this. She would fight battles. The earth's magnetic field might shift for the sake of this kiss.

It went on forever, until they were breathless, until Misha couldn't tell where her body ended and his began.

She wrapped her arms around his neck and whispered, "Do you have any idea what this is doing to me?"

"Some. To me, too." He kissed her neck, his face warm and slightly rough against her skin. "Misha…"

"I'm only talking because…because otherwise we might sit here all night."

"Would that be bad? I don't care."

"There are better places."

He drew back a little and looked at her, and she realized just how long they must have been here locked together because she could barely see his face, it was so dark outside. "Is that what you want?"

"Yes."

He looked at her some more, and she wasn't quite sure what he could see in her face, or what he wanted. Finally he said, "Open the gate." It sounded more like a prayer than a request.

She climbed out of the car, her whole body throbbing and shaky and dizzy and dazed, her legs moving like rubber. She unhooked the tarnished metal chain and swung the gate open, then stood leaning on it as Brant drove through. He lifted his hand from the wheel and waved and smiled at her, and the smile almost melted her into the ground. She swung the gate back, hooked the chain, climbed in the cab, and Brant said, "I don't think I can drive."

"No?"

He stopped the engine, put on the brake, leaned against her once more, not even kissing her, just holding her with his face pressed into her neck again and his arms almost trembling. "Can you feel my heart?" he said. He took her hand and laid it against his chest. "You must be able to feel it."

"I can only feel mine."

"The same? Just pounding?"

"Yes. Who knew? We both need a coronary care unit."

"We need a bed," he said bluntly.

"That brings us back to the driving problem."

"I'd better try harder this time."

Misha helped, by resting the whole of one forearm along his thigh, and her head on his shoulder. It seemed to work. He got the car going, remembered to turn on the headlights this time, stalled the engine going up the hill after they'd crossed the creek, swore beneath his breath.

"We could walk," she suggested.

"No…"

When they came around the bend and first glimpsed the house through the trees, it looked dark. "Nu must still be at Chris's," Misha said.

"I forgot about Nu. Yeah, she's not here, is she?" He screeched to a halt beside the house and couldn't find the light switch inside the mudroom door. Misha had to grab on to the waistband of his jeans while she waited, because she couldn't bear to lose the contact and he forgot about the light and kissed her again.

For a long time.

Finally, they made it as far as the kitchen and found a note on the bench. They read it together, with their bodies pressed against each other like two trees growing in the same place.

Gone to Sydney with Chris. Back Monday. He has Tom Andrews checking the place so no need to go over. Have fun. Love, Nu.

"Shall we have fun?" Brant asked.

"No, let's be miserable." Misha pillowed her head on his shoulder, within kissing distance of his jaw. "So much more unusual and interesting."

"Okay, but miserable together."

"Definitely together."

"Are you hungry?" He rested his chin on her hair, and it felt like a kind of shelter, the place where she belonged, the place that would keep her safe.

"No," she told him.

"Good." He didn't move, and at first that was okay.

She stayed, feeling the safety and the bliss. But then she realized that he was struggling. His body had stiffened and he wasn't giving as much.

"Are you going to carry me to your bed?" she prompted him, pressing her hips against him.

"Where's Gian-Marco in this, Mish?" he said abruptly.

She sighed. "He's in Europe."

"That's not an answer."

"Yes, it is," she insisted, fierce about it. "He's in Europe and I'm on the other side of the world. I don't know what he's doing, but no doubt it's something involving a woman. He doesn't know what I'm doing, but he probably thinks I'm doing something, too, involving a man. So I will. And then we're even."

"Is that what this is about?"

"No. Of course it isn't."

"So what's it really about?"

"Boy, you want me to have all the answers tonight!"

"Yeah, because I sure as hell don't have any."

Silence.

Time for her to say to Brant, actually, we're not engaged anymore. Nuala's minding the ring for me. I haven't told Gian-Marco yet, and it can't be publicly announced until I get the go-ahead from the palace. But I can tell you, because I know you won't say a word.

There would be a kind of protection in staying silent, though, wouldn't there? She could fly out of here in another week or two and Brant wouldn't need to know how big a piece of her heart she was leaving behind. Which might be handy if she didn't know that, either.

Protection versus honesty.

Safety versus risk.

She thought about it, listening to Brant's strong, thudding heartbeat against her ear. He didn't move. Finally, she heard herself say in a thin voice, "Brant, if you're thinking this is the same as what happened ten days ago, after we looked at those photos—"

He cut her off. "I don't care if it is, or it isn't." She felt his arms tighten until the breath squeezed out of her lungs. "Don't tell me, okay, because I just don't care. If you want to do this, if you're still engaged to him but you want to do this anyway, then it's your business. I don't care." His teeth gritted over the words. "This is here and now. I'll take whatever you're offering."

"Bed. Take me to bed."

He lifted her up without a word and carried her toward his room, pressing hot, hard kisses against her hair and temple and cheek with every step.

Chapter Eleven

He shouldn't be shaking this hard, Brant knew.

What would Misha think? She'd feel it, because he had her whole body pressed against his chest as he carried her to his room, not even feeling her weight.

And what would she think tomorrow, when she was rational again, about his admission that he didn't care about Gian-Marco, that all his scruples had flown to the four winds in the face of his need, and he'd take anything he could get?

Brant thought of himself as a strong man. He knew he was strong. Physically. Emotionally. All the ways a man could be strong. He worked hard. He honored the people he cared about, looked after his stock and his land. He did the right thing, and he usually knew pretty fast what the right thing was. He was generous when people needed him, and tough if anyone tried to run him around.

He had choked on tears last week when he'd thought he might lose his beloved dog, but he would have put a gun to

Sox's head and shot her to relieve her suffering if he'd thought she had taken a lethal, irreversible dose of that bait. He knew he wouldn't have flinched. He'd had to shoot animals before.

This meant strength, in his world—knowing when to be tender, knowing when to be tough.

None of this fitted with what he was feeling now, and with what he had just said to Misha about her relationship with Gian-Marco Ponti. He was the kind of man who took everything on his own terms, not someone else's. He'd never needed to beg in his life.

"Put me down, Brant," Misha whispered when they reached the doorway to his bedroom.

There. She'd come to her senses.

Or she was pushing him to come to his.

He still didn't care. He wanted this too much.

"No. I won't put you down." He bundled her tighter, feeling the curve of her rear end against his arm, and the squash of her breast against his body.

"But I can't kiss you properly like this." She leaned her head against his shoulder, and he felt the caress of her breath against his neck as she whispered to him, "I can't…take off my clothes. Or feel enough of you against me."

Oh, geez.

She meant *that?*

This was still *yes?*

He put her down in a half a second and they folded against each other, breathing hard. He stroked the silk of her hair and buried his face in it, inhaling her soft scents. She splayed her hands against his backside and pulled him close, showing how much she wanted him. He had to fight not to crush her with the strength of his arms, because it felt as if he could only get enough of her if he wrapped her tighter and tighter. He was still shaking.

He'd never wanted a woman like this, or felt so out of his

depth. He'd never made love to someone with such a total bedrock of awareness that it couldn't last, that it was only a fling. He just wasn't that type. He didn't look for endings until they happened. He only slept with a woman if he cared enough about her to think that there might be more.

Liking and desire went together in his heart, but in this case they also went nowhere.

She lived in Europe.

She was—probably—engaged to another man.

She was a bloody princess.

He should have way more pride.

And he didn't care. What he felt about her was so powerful that it overrode everything else.

He kissed her the way he'd kissed her in the car by the gate, engulfing her mouth with his, drinking the taste of her yet still hungry for more. She made some sounds in her throat, little protests that seemed to say this was too much, but that she wanted more of it anyway.

Oh, she wanted more? So did he! He wanted her sweet, swollen heat against him, wanted to push into her, hear the sounds she made, claim her with the invasive intimacy of everything he did to her body.

Misha wanted it, too.

She told him so in the way she moved, snaking against him, letting him feel her body, and told him so again in her shallow, unsteady breathing. She crossed her arms and lifted her blue top over her head, making her breasts pull upward in her cream lace bra. They looked so beautiful, high and neat and round. He cupped her, feeling the peaked nipples and aching to kiss them, stroking them with his thumb, outlining the swelling curves with feverish fingers.

She smiled at him, unsnapped the bra, dropped it from her shoulders in a single cat-like whip of movement that made her bounce. Then she tossed the bra aside, showing off the essence of her female shape with a mixture of sauciness and delicacy that made him laugh even as he bent and touched his lips to the tender, darkened skin. "Misha, you're so beautiful," he whispered.

"So are you. I want to see you." She let her eyes travel from his mouth and down to his neck and chest. "And I want to touch. Everything."

He heard his T-shirt rip as he pulled it over his head, then she stepped toward him and helped him with his jeans, freeing him to the teasing, silken caress of her fingers. He didn't think this whole thing was going to last for very long. He doubted he'd be able to summon the patience or the restraint.

"Your jeans now," he said.

"Just the jeans?"

"And what's underneath." He could hardly get out the words.

And she could hardly breathe. He watched her shimmy her jeans down over her hips, leaving a semitransparent piece of net and lace that matched the forgotten bra. It outlined the shape of her—that peachy rear end and the swollen triangle between her thighs.

Outlined it so beautifully that he added quickly, "No, leave those on," and stepped close to her again and touched her through the lace and felt her quiver.

He was right to guess that it wouldn't last long.

Neither of them could wait.

They fell onto the bed, panting out their impatience like animals with four pairs of hands each. He touched her everywhere, used his mouth on her, tasting heat and musky sweetness. She would have marks on her neck in the morning, but neither of them cared. He found a contraceptive in the drawer beside the bed and stumbled over an apology for his slowness in getting the packet open.

"Don't apologize," she said. She rolled toward him. Her hair tumbled over her eyes and she brushed it back, watching his face. "You're taking responsibility. That's enough."

When he was ready, she reached for him and lifted her

hips toward him and still he didn't tell her to get rid of the lace, he just moved it aside and pushed into her, powerful and slow. He heard her gasp out his name, but he couldn't say a word, and for a timeless interval of heat and pulsing and darkness and climbing, climbing urgency, they both had everything they wanted in the whole world.

"Now I'm hungry," Misha said, because she could think of a few other things to say that seemed too scary, and that she might regret.

"Thank you," Brant drawled. "The earth moved for me, too."

Misha slid up, propped herself on her elbow and ran a finger down his nose. "Hey, are you saying my bedroom manners need work?" She kissed him, and rested her hand on his chest. "Weren't the non-verbal signals extravagant enough? This mattress will never be the same again. The earth did move. It shook."

"Good." It came out like a growl.

"Are we spoiling it now?"

"No." He pulled her head down to his chest and wrapped his arm around her. He whispered, "But don't get hungry yet. Please? Let's just stay here awhile."

This felt so different.

She had an uncomfortable, unhappy flashback to Gian-Marco. Some men rolled over and fell asleep after they'd made love, she knew. Others jumped up and charged into the shower, as if the deed was something you needed to wash off before contamination set in. Gian-Marco fell into the second group.

Brant was in a group of his own. He stayed. He held her. Pulled the quilt around her shoulders to keep them both warm. Squeezed her a little bit. Kissed the first place his lips found. Cupped a hand gently against her breast. Traced the outline of her mouth with the tip of his finger. Told her a story about Sox getting so excited one day when he called her to the truck that she misjudged her enormous flying leap into the back of it and landed on the ground on the far side. "If you ever want to see a visibly embarrassed dog, that'll do it."

"This is what you're thinking about? Flying dogs?" she teased him lazily. "I'm scared about your subtext. What can possibly be the association here?"

"Well, I think that's what would probably happen to me if I tried to jump into the back of a truck right now. I'd overshoot."

"This is a way of saying…?"

"It feels very good, that's all."

"It does," she agreed. "Okay, I promise not to be hungry for another half hour."

"Make it an hour, and…you know…there might be time for something else."

"Ooh."

An hour and a quarter, actually.

Or an hour and a half, if you counted the shower they eventually…and very lazily…shared.

"Now I'm hungry," Brant said, so they had a silly, giggly time in the kitchen scrounging emergency rations that Misha had never tasted before, like instant cups of soup and freezer sausage rolls and packet macaroni and cheese. Postbed junk food had a lot going for it, she discovered.

Later, she slept in his bed.

Because he asked.

She loved that.

He captured her outside the bathroom just as she was about to go to her room, wrapped his arms around her and nuzzled her ear. "Will you stay with me all night? Is that… against the rules, or anything?"

"There are no rules," she whispered back, loving the clean smell of him and the reined-in strength as he held her, as if he was afraid she might break if he squeezed her too tight…or as if he was afraid she might say no. "I'd love to stay with you."

* * *

On Monday, just before dark, Nuala came back from Sydney and Brant's perfect interlude in a fool's paradise came to an end.

Chris dropped his fiancée at the house but didn't come in for more than a quick greeting to Brant and Misha because he wanted to get home and check his animals. Nu was so tired he refused to let her go with him. "I know what you're going to be like tonight."

Nu was indignant. "Not that bad!" But she never slept well in the city, because of the traffic noise, and, of course, her mind had been buzzing as usual with the details of the wedding. Chris no doubt had the right idea.

"Come over tomorrow, first thing," he told her. "You know I'll be up."

They kissed quickly, and he climbed back in the car. Visible through the kitchen window, Nu stood watching him until the vehicle disappeared into the trees. You'd never guess that they'd known each other most of their lives.

"It was so good that we went," she told Brant and Misha a few minutes later.

The two of them were making a real dinner together tonight, because somehow over the past five days they'd been too busy to cook and had eaten all the emergency rations. They'd been riding again. They'd hired a canoe and gone paddling on the Murray River, getting very wet and slightly sunburned, and bringing spicy Thai food home to eat as night fell.

They'd done the essential work around the property, but very little more than that. To be honest, Brant had neglected a few things, and he still didn't care. The Pastures Protection Board guy had come back to take a second sample from a ewe's foot, blaming the lost sample on someone else. He was blunt about what he saw. "There's definitely some infection in this one."

"But it's not spreading as fast as I would expect if it was foot rot."

"Yeah, well, it would be if this was November or February. You're bloody lucky the weather's much cooler."

Brant had felt stressed and sick to his stomach for the next hour, and then Misha had brought an afternoon picnic up to the mustering yard on the back of the four-wheeler and they'd zoomed up to the top of the hill together. She'd spread a blanket on the ground in the sunny lee of the round granite boulders and they'd peeled off each other's clothes right there in the open air and climbed halfway to heaven.

He'd tried to get a few things done. A couple of repair projects had fizzled out because Misha apparently found Brant particularly appealing in an old flannel shirt with a hammer hooked into the back pocket of his jeans. This, he didn't get. "I do actually own a suit, Mish," he'd said to her. "I'm not a total Neanderthal, and I really feel I should prove it to you sometime."

"One suit?"

"Well…yeah. I only need it a couple of times a year."

"And it's personally tailored by Giorgio Armani?"

"Mish—"

"Don't answer! I'm teasing! I like you in the shirts and jeans, Brant. They're…real."

Real.

He, too, valued things that were real. And everything about the past five days had felt real to him. Real kisses, real laughter, real conversations, real heat…

But now Nuala was back and he remembered that reality could show more than one face.

"He understands now," she was saying, still talking about Chris and the wedding. "And he likes everything I decided on. He still thinks it's going to cost too much, but he knows how much Mum and Frank want to, and that Frank can afford it, so he's letting it go."

She yawned and covered her mouth. Her skin looked

slightly papery with fatigue. Apparently they'd only stopped for petrol on the drive home, and she hadn't succeeded in dozing off when Chris was driving.

"And have you calmed down yet?" Brant couldn't help asking.

"I'm slightly less crazy about the whole thing. And we've settled on a florist and on the design and wording of the invitations, which were the last two really important things that had to be done at this point—"

"So for the invitations did you go with sage?" Misha cut in. Either she cared, or she was a good actress.

A good actress, Brant decided half a second later when she put her hand softly on his backside behind the open refrigerator door where Nuala couldn't see. She kept the hand there until the last possible moment, then closed the fridge door and shot him a sly, smiling glance.

"Sage and gold on cream," Nuala said, scrabbling in her bag for some lip cream. "I love it. I mean you'd have to see the shade of sage to picture how it's going to work."

"You are joking!" Brant had to say. "There are *shades* of sage?" Misha brushed past him on her way to the sink and he felt the nudge of her breast and the tickle of her fingers at his waist.

As always, he wanted more of her than this.

Now.

He wished there were a hundred shades of sage, and that Nu and Chris had had to ponder each and every one. They should have stayed in Sydney another week.

"No, no, it's really called something else." Nu waved her hand impatiently, then put the lip cream away. "But as far as I'm concerned, it's a shade of sage. I'm not obsessing about this, you know, the way some brides do! Gosh, but my lips had better not be this dry in September!"

"No," Brant said with heavy irony. "You're not obsessing at all. Heaven forbid anyone should think that."

His sister stuck out her tongue, and he hoped she hadn't seen the moment just before that where he'd returned Misha's earlier gesture from behind the fridge door, with embellishment and with no camouflaging white goods in the way. He really wished Nu had gone to Chris's tonight.

He wished it more thoroughly when the three of them sat down to eat and he kept wanting to look at Misha or touch her under the table but couldn't because he knew Nuala would see. He didn't want any of this to be a secret, but somehow, without even asking, he knew that it was. He knew this was what Misha herself would want.

Lifelong love a princess publicized.

Brief illicit flings she kept to herself.

If Brant had consulted only his own feelings, he would have shouted this whole thing from the rooftops.

And, yeah, did he know how much trouble he was in?

Down to the very last drop.

"So what have you two been up to while I've been away?" Nu asked brightly. "Brant, I hope you've kept her entertained and haven't just made her work!"

"He's kept me thoroughly entertained, don't worry," Misha said, and Brant could hear the mischief in her voice—nothing too obvious, just meant for him.

Oh, hell, he wanted to look at her! It was as if a puppeteer had a string attached to his head and was pulling it sideways. He looked. He just couldn't stop himself, and found Misha looking at him, her lips softly parted, her blue eyes shining and her fingers brushing her neck just the way he wanted to do. They smiled and looked quickly away.

Nuala frowned.

"We went riding and canoeing, and we climbed the big Polish mountain," Misha said quickly, as if she thought there could have been something significant in Nuala's frown. "The one we can't spell. He was awful, Nu, he wouldn't tell me beforehand how you get to the top and I had this mental picture of ice picks and harnesses and the works, and when he found out that's what I was picturing, he tried to tell me, no, they have kangaroo pouches to rent."

"That's my brother," Nuala said lightly. "Awful." An odd expression screwed up her face, then her look grew more guarded. "You must have been dreading the kangaroo pouches, Mish," she teased, with a slight edge. "You obviously believe every word he says, which you absolutely shouldn't. Seriously. I'm warning you."

"Dreading them," Misha agreed. "And thanks for the warning. But we had a great day. Didn't we, Brant?"

"Just about perfect."

"I'll wash up," Nuala announced at the end of the meal. "Brant, could you dry? Then I'm going straight to bed!"

"I think I will, too," said Misha, and her tone was so innocent that Brant had no idea if it was a secret invitation or not.

She disappeared, which gave Nuala just the opportunity she turned out to have been angling for.

"What is going on around here, Brant?" she hissed, as she jetted hot water into the sink, wetting the front of her shirt. She made a sound of irritation at the mess, then squirted in an overdose of lime-flavored detergent that smelled artificial and unpleasant. "What happened while Chris and I were gone? What the hell do you think you're doing?"

A week ago, Brant would have thought she'd somehow guessed about the problem with the sheep. Tonight he knew better, but hedged anyway.

"Well, I'm thinking of putting in a second bathroom," he said. "And getting a dishwasher."

"Oh, stop! Do you think I didn't notice? Over dinner? The way you and Misha looked at each other? From the moment I got back, I could tell there was some kind of atmosphere, but I didn't put it all together until that look. Which was unmistakable."

Brant could find no words.

Which was fine, because Nu was still in full spate.

"If you hurt her, I'm warning you, I will *not* forgive you for it! I cannot believe it! She is so vulnerable at the moment, because of Gian-Marco's infidelity, and you must know that. If she's somehow trying to pay him back by getting involved with you, then it's going to backfire on her big-time, because she's just not the kind of person who can do that."

"No?" he croaked out.

"She'd be a mess. She was already a mess when she got here. If you make everything worse…! If you take advantage of her doubts…! You had all those opportunities with the women who wrote to the magazine, and you couldn't be bothered, could you? It wasn't enough of a challenge, or something. But Misha, who deserves way better—and who is, let me tell you, Brant, *so* far out of your league it's almost a joke—Misha, of all people, is the one you pick."

Brant picked up a clean wet glass to dry, his whole body operating on automatic. He couldn't even feel it move. "Why…" He stopped and cleared his throat. "Why do you assume I'm only in it for the challenge? Or that I'm taking an unfair advantage?"

"Well, aren't you? Come on, get out a clean tea towel, that one's already half-wet. You've had your chances with women, Brant. You're thirty-four and you're not married and Mum and I—"

"Oh, hell, you and Mum have been talking?"

"She asked me a couple of weeks ago why I thought you still weren't married."

"And what did you say?"

"That I assumed you didn't want to be. Because you easily could, if you did. Gaby Fry, Alison Carter, Mary-Theresa Gordon." She ticked off a couple more names of local girls he'd been out with over the years—girls he'd liked but had still somehow known weren't right for him as a long-term thing. "You have a lot to offer, you're stable and you are a good-looking man, Brant."

"Oh, shoot, this again? Magazine-cover material. I know. You don't think I like it, do you? And if you really think I'd play it up and use it with someone like Misha, even if I had the power…" He shook his head, his stomach knotted and sour.

She ignored him. "You're funny, you work hard and you know how to play, too. And right now, yes, you're playing. That's all I can conclude. You know she's only here for a few weeks. You're taking advantage of her when she's vulnerable and I'm not going to let you do it."

"Why do you assume I'd hurt her? Why do you think that's the way it would work?"

"I said. Because she's vulnerable. Just because she's a princess… She still has a heart."

"Yes, she does." He didn't really know what was going on in that heart regarding Gian-Marco, but he knew the heart was there. He'd felt it, beating hard and warm and true against his own skin. "But you're right about one thing. She's out of my league. And don't worry. I know it."

"The only thing in your favor."

"You are being incredibly unfair." The words strained in his throat. He'd been unprepared for this attack, and his defenses were all over the place. "Can you stop? Please? Now? I am not in the mood."

Nuala turned off the water too suddenly and the pipes thumped. She pivoted and stared at him, her mouth dropped open. "How am I being unfair? What are you saying?"

Her eyes glittered with suspicion and fatigue. Her cheeks were too pink.

"Nothing. I'd just prefer to talk about something else, that's all."

"No, you have to tell me what you mean." She stamped her foot like a spoiled five-year-old.

"Why? So you can ride roughshod over that, too?" He threw the wet dishtowel down. "Leave the washing-up till the morning and go to bed. Chris was right to avoid you tonight. You get very, very ratty when you're tired, Nuala. Let's both hope we've forgotten all of this in the morning."

But he saw how wide her eyes were, and he knew she'd guessed how deep his feelings ran. Let her stew on it. Let her feel guilty or horrified or sorry for him or whatever she wanted to feel. He wasn't going to talk about it. Couldn't stand the idea of admitting to any of it in words. He was going to bed.

Chapter Twelve

Misha must have heard him coming along the corridor past her room, after the blowup with Nuala.

His bedroom door opened quietly as he stood there in the old black martial arts pants he wore as pajamas, and he heard the whisper of bare feet on the wooden floor. He'd stripped off his undershirt and was on the point of climbing into bed, his gut sour after Nuala's illogical attack. Turning to the door, he froze at the sight of Misha, the shirt still balled in his hands.

"Hi," she said. "Is this okay?"

She had on a drifty, ankle-length white nightgown that he hadn't seen before. It was made of some fine fabric that was almost transparent apart from panels of almost equally transparent lacy stuff in various places. Across her breasts, for example.

He nodded in answer to her question, but couldn't speak.

"I mean, Nu looked so tired she'll be out cold in three minutes." She hesitated and almost stammered. "B-but if it's not okay, just say."

"Of course it's okay," he said softly. He dropped the shirt on the floor. "If it's okay for you. You're the one who—" He stopped.

"Finish," she commanded, her slight smile totally assured and her voice taking on a cooing note. She did that, sometimes—spoke as if she was so used to being obeyed that she didn't even think about another possibility and could word her orders with perfect sweetness.

He finished, as ordered, gritting his teeth. "The one who has the most to lose."

She frowned. "I guess. I'm not thinking that way right now."

He could have done without those last two words.

Right now.

All of this was only about right now for her. A royal holiday romance that would come to an end the day she left here, if not before. She probably didn't have a clue that he'd begun to envisage more than that.

She closed the door silently behind her, then wrapped her arms across her body. The nightgown floated around her legs in the brief draft made by the door, and settled again. Its sleeves came down to her wrists and the neck was high. If it hadn't been for the open working of the lace and the semi-transparency of the fabric it would have been a very chaste garment indeed.

She came toward him.

"I hadn't picked you for a Victorian maiden in your night wear," he said, to keep her back until he decided if he could really do this tonight.

Or ever again.

She dismissed the maiden idea. "It was a gift from the Langemark Lacemakers Guild on my twenty-first birthday. I love how floaty and soft it is." She gave her sexiest smile. "But sometimes I wear gold silk with tiny little straps and a hemline that barely gets to my thighs."

"Do you?"

Okay. He could do this tonight.

And as many times again as she wanted.

He'd face the future when it happened.

She came closer and he reached out for her, discovering fabric so thin it was like soft tissue paper. He brushed it lightly against her skin as he ran his hands down her back, stopping at the creases of her thighs. He was already aroused, and she would feel it.

"Mmm…" She sighed against him and he could hardly breathe.

He brushed his mouth against her neck and felt her shiver with expectation and need. After only five days of this, he knew so much about her body and her responses, the way they matched his own and the way they surprised him. She loved it when he kissed her neck. And when he touched her breasts so softly. She loved it when he breathed heat against her swollen nipple through the delicate holes in the lace. And when he whispered his intentions in her ear.

"Now?" she whispered back.

"You can strip first, if you want."

"That's good, too." The nightgown disappeared in a saucy flash.

Her body whipped as she removed it, her breasts jiggled and he groaned. They fell on the bed. He lay on top of her and she began to touch him lazily, as if they had all night. He could handle all night. Mmm, and he could handle her fingers running down his back, and her thighs parting to accommodate his burgeoning size.

"What was Nuala talking to you about in the kitchen?" she asked lazily.

"She was a real pain. Grumpy as a bear with a sore head." He rolled to the side as he spoke. He couldn't touch her properly like this, squashing her into the mattress.

"And?"

"Nothing. I'll be glad when she's bloody married."

"You think that's what's going on with her? The wedding?"

"I think it had better be, or the marriage isn't going to last. I didn't have her down as the type who'd think she had the answer to everyone's major life questions purely by virtue of the ring on her finger, but there it is."

Misha didn't press him for more detail, which was good because he would have said too much. And all of it wrong and impossible. "We can forget Nu," she whispered.

"Who?"

She laughed. "Exactly!" He felt a ridiculous spurt of pleasure at having entertained her, even in such a minor way. "You…" She ran her finger down his nose. And down. And down. "Oh, you."

"Me, what?"

"Just you. You make me feel happy."

As if this was all that mattered.

Brant decided to pretend it was, just for tonight.

Again.

His sixth night in a row of "just tonight." He wondered how long he'd be able to maintain that delusion, how many more nights of this they would have, and then she reached up and held his face between her hands and kissed him, and for the thousandth time he didn't care, just gave himself to her sweetness, her eagerness and her heat.

"Are you asleep, Brant?"

Misha knew he wasn't. She could feel it in his body, hear it in his breathing. The clock beside the bed said it was four in the morning, and both of them were lying awake in the dark. She couldn't see his eyes, but somehow knew that he'd been staring blindly at the ceiling for a while.

"Sorry," he said.

"No, it's okay, you didn't wake me." She eased against his

body. "Well… Maybe you did. But in a good way." He felt resistant to her slyly sensual movement. She wondered what Nuala had really said to him last night in the kitchen. Nu could be overprotective sometimes.

And sometimes she was right.

Had she guessed just how much had happened while she was in Sydney?

Would Misha tell her?

Telling her felt too hard. The instinct to put the right spin on it ran deep. A princess wasn't supposed to make mistakes in love, and she already had a huge one of those, zooming his way around the Formula One circuit in Europe at this very moment, with blondes and brunettes dangling from his arm like charms on a bracelet. How much of what she was doing with Brant was simply running away from all of that?

Oh, but running away felt good!

His body had softened into her curves, now. She slid her thigh over his and stroked his chest. It felt familiar and good. If the communication between their bodies was all that counted, then she might just keep running in this direction and never go back.

"Come here, woman," he growled at her and she moved on top of him, letting her nipples brush his chest and running her fingers into his hair.

"Yeah?" she whispered. "What do you want from me?"

"Show me what's on offer."

And she did.

Misha fell into a doze again afterward, and didn't waken until she heard Brant moving around the still-darkened room and felt the cold space in the bed beside her. The clock read five-thirty.

"What's up?" she asked him creakily.

"I am. Couldn't sleep any more. It's almost morning."

"Spoken like a farmer."

"That's what I am." There was an odd note in his voice, and she immediately thought about his stock, and the concerns he'd shared with her last week.

"Are you going out on the four-wheeler to do a check?"

"No. Thought I'd head to the track and watch the horses being worked. There's a race meeting next Saturday, and Trans Pacific and Santari are both running. I want to know what Rae thinks about their form."

Misha scrambled quickly to her feet. "I'll come with you."

For a moment, she almost thought he was going to tell her no, but then he nodded. "Eat breakfast when we get back?" he suggested.

"My stomach won't wake up until nine."

He nodded again, and she knew something wasn't right. What was he thinking about? His sheep?

Out at the track, he relaxed, which meant that Misha could, too. Her moods had become so attuned to his now that she knew more than Nuala did about what was on his mind. She leaned on the white-painted wooden rail beside him and watched as a thoroughbred and rider galloped toward them. Once again she was astonished as she had been so often over the past couple of weeks at finding herself here, now, in a moment like this.

The rail was slick with dew, and the wet grass at her feet had already soaked the toes of her running shoes. The morning sun had only just floated above the horizon, and the air was cold enough to make the sweat rise as steam from each horse's back, but there was something exhilarating about being here, something about the sheer beauty of such highly trained yet spirited beasts perfecting what they were born and bred to do.

It was like being on a film set or behind the stage of a theater. This was a part of horse racing that only a few people got to see. She could watch it over and over again and never lose interest, she thought.

At a full gallop, the horse came past. The jockey stood high in the short stirrups and leaned close over Santari's neck, his knees knocked together. He slowed and dropped into the saddle, then wheeled around and came back at a trot toward where Rae stood watching.

"There," she said, turning to Brant. "Nice?"

"Beautiful," Brant agreed.

The jockey called out something to Rae about the horse's run, and she nodded. "Give him a good cooldown, Joe, before you bring him in."

"You think he can keep it up over the full sixteen hundred?" Brant asked.

"I'm sure he can. But we'll see on Saturday. I've got him in the Class Four."

"Stacking it against him, there."

"He has the potential, Brant, and word is getting out. He's going to be running as the favorite. We should race him a couple more times this prep, then spell him so he's ready to be back in full work by spring, and then we should enter him in some bigger races. Why hold him back?"

"What do you think, Mish?" Brant asked her.

She spread her hands and laughed. "I think this is the best fun. But if you're asking whether Santari's a good racehorse, you have a trainer for questions like that. Or else you could find a pair of dice. They'd be bound to give you a more accurate forecast than I could. I thought he looked beautiful, that's all."

They followed Rae into the stables and her apprentice jockey led the next horse out for its morning trackwork, while Misha walked up and down the stalls looking at the others. They were such fabulous animals. Trans Pacific had just been taken for a swim in the round and luridly green concrete equine swimming pool, and Rae's stablehand dried him down with the efficient pull of a long, bendy metal sweat scraper. Its serrated edge groomed away old hair and left the horse as sleek as polished mahogany.

"Why are racehorses always groomed so perfectly?" Misha asked.

"Because a lot of people bet on the prettiest." Rae grinned. She now stood in a horse stall that passed as an office-cum-coatroom, making handwritten notes about feeds on a computer printout. "And don't you perform better when your body feels good? Brushing them is like a massage."

"Do they know they've done something good when they win?"

"Some of 'em do." She gestured at a big bay in the opposite stall. "This lovely boy over here does. The day after a win, he holds his head up, he's so proud of himself. When he loses, he's hanging his neck down to his knees, doesn't want to look at anyone. Some of 'em you don't know what's going on in their heads, what they think about it all."

"Who else have you got running next Saturday?" Brant asked.

"Just my Extra Fresh in the thousand-meter Class Two. He practically rolls over and cries for his mother if he's tried over sixteen hundred, but on a sprint he's going to be hard to beat at the weekend, and he doesn't mind a slow track if we get more rain."

"And how many people know that?"

Rae looked at him and paused, the pen still in her hand. "Not that many, now that you ask."

"Yeah?"

"He looked like such a stayer when I first put him in work last year, and he won a couple of times at the longer distances—small fields, nothing too impressive—but I've never raced him at this distance. He got an injury and he's had a big holiday and this will be his first run since we've brought him back up, but every day in trackwork he's been telling us, 'I'm a sprinter!' so this time I'm going to listen to him and let him prove himself. But I don't think the bookies or the punters have caught on to his potential, yet."

"Any idea what odds he'll get?"

"He's up against a couple of promising Canberra horses, as well as one of Len Radic's mares who rocketed home at Albury at this distance a couple of weeks ago. I'll be surprised if he's shorter than ten to one. Looking for a home for your five dollars?"

"Might be. At that kind of a return." Brant added slyly, "As long as he's a sure bet."

Rae laughed. "If you believe any horse is ever a sure bet, I've got a nice little opera house up in Sydney I could sell you at rock-bottom price. Great location, right on the Harbour. The roof looks like white sails, you might have seen pictures."

Brant laughed, too. "See you on the weekend, Rae."

On the drive back to Inverlochie, Misha asked him, "What was all that about Extra Fresh? You're going to put your five dollars on him, not on your own horses?"

"They're running in different races. I can put money on all three."

"Five dollars at ten to one, I like the profit margin."

"It does have a certain appeal," Brant agreed.

He reached a straight piece of road and floored the pedal, bringing the four-wheel drive up to over a hundred kilometers per hour. There was a bend coming up and he knew he'd have to slow, maybe even brake, but right now he wanted the speed.

This morning, watching the apprentice taking Santari through his paces, he'd felt envious of the man. He needed something like that—a thundering gallop around a wide, deserted loop of lush grass, blowing the cobwebs out of his brain, along with the stress over his stock, the annoyance at Nu, and his gut knowledge that she was one hundred percent right, in the important half of what she'd said.

The princess was out of his league.

He shouldn't have let Misha into his bed last night. He should have remembered his pride. He'd awoken with this knowledge at four, and she'd still been lying beside him, her body soft and deliciously warm. That was when he should have fled the room and drowned this frustration in some early-morning work. He shouldn't have made love to her again. He shouldn't have let her come with him to the track.

And the visit to the horses and their trainer hadn't helped, anyway. He felt even more restless, brooding and stubborn, and craved something that would burn up some adrenaline, some extravagant, risky action on his part that would make a difference *now,* to his future prospects and his current mood.

Waiting for bad news always tortured him.

Waiting for rain. Waiting for the market to improve. Waiting for the verdict on the hoof infection. Waiting for Misha to leave. Too much waiting. Too little he could do about it, except blow out his frustration in some pointless extravagance of speed.

"Woo-hoo, Brant, did you want to jump up on Santari the way I did?" Misha teased him. "I've never seen you go this fast."

"Yeah, I could see you on a racehorse," he teased back. "And you're about the right size. Ever consider a career as a jockey?"

She laughed. "I almost asked Rae this morning if I could give Santari a try, but she looked like a woman who knows how to say no."

"She's pretty protective when it comes to her horses."

He approached the bend and slowed as required, accepting his responsibility to play things safe when it came to the crunch. Beside him, Misha sighed and settled back into her seat, and they didn't talk for the rest of the journey home.

Chapter Thirteen

"Sorry I was so ratty last night," Nuala said to Brant.

She had waited until Misha was settled with coffee and a newspaper, following their dawn visit to the track, and had dragged Brant into her bedroom and closed the door.

"That's fine," he told her quickly, because he didn't want to talk about it. He reached for the door, but with one small sidestep Nu got there first and blocked it off.

She fixed him with an earnest gaze. "I stand by what I said, but my delivery could have been better."

"Apology accepted. Now can I have the door?"

She still didn't move. "I mean it, Brant. Either you're going to hurt her because this is just a fling for you, or even worse…what you sort of didn't say last night…"

"What I *didn't* say?"

"What was written all over your face."

"Can we leave my face out of it?"

"She *is* out of your league. That was the wrong way to put

it. Too harsh. But it's realistic. My friendship with her…it's like a vacation for both of us. We get a taste of each other's worlds. But I can't see how those worlds could ever connect permanently. I mean, wouldn't it turn Inverlochie into a hobby farm? You're so proud of this place." She shook her head, then added on a desperate rush, as if she knew how much he would hate hearing the words, "I really, really don't want you to get hurt, either."

"You're too good to me," he drawled.

"Don't take it the wrong way."

"Do I have to pick you up and lift you sideways, Nu? I've got things to do this morning."

"Just…be careful."

"I promise not to drop you, is that good enough?"

"You really don't want to have this conversation, do you?"

"You are so perceptive."

Nuala sighed and opened the door with exaggerated courtesy. "Okay, big brother." She looked at him with a less exhausted version of that wide-eyed, searching expression she'd given him last night and he felt like a complete fool, and a naked one at that.

He escaped out of her room and into the fresh air, breathing it like a prisoner released after a twenty-year sentence. He spent the whole morning cleaning and paring sheep feet, and with the help of Sox and Mon separating any animals with suspect hooves so that he could muster them down to the shearing shed and give them a night on the dry wooden floor.

If this wasn't foot rot, then a spell of relief from his wet, green paddocks might help. He should probably have tried it days ago, and he should definitely have worked harder at cleaning out their hooves, particularly after the latest bout of rain and unseasonable warmth.

He'd been…yeah…distracted.

There were at least sixty ewes and their lambs milling

around the big wooden shed by the time he'd finished, and there were two more big paddocks of sheep he hadn't had time for, yet.

The really stupid, incomprehensible problem about the entire morning was that the foot-rot scare had begun to seem like the least of his troubles.

"Honey?" said Queen Rose over the phone on Friday morning. On the far side of the world, she sounded as if she were in the next room.

"Mom?"

"Can you talk? Are there people around?"

"No, I'm all by myself."

Misha took the cordless phone and walked to the window. The four-wheel drive was absent from its usual crooked parking spot, and she couldn't see the other farm vehicles from here. She knew she was alone in the house, however.

Nuala was over at Chris's, as usual—she'd stayed the night there—and Brant was already out with his sheep. Since Nuala and Chris's return from Sydney on Monday, Brant had told Misha in no uncertain terms, "You're not here to work yourself into the ground, but this is my livelihood and I need to get a few things done. Don't sit around bored. Take that rental car of yours and go into town for coffee, or down to Albury to shop."

Today, she planned to do just that, but it was still only seven in the morning. Thinking about the time difference between here and Langemark, she realized out loud, "Mom, you must be up late over there."

"We've just had the summer closing of parliament." Which always entailed a huge formal banquet, Misha knew. It could run well past midnight.

Her heart jumped as she understood what this meant. "So the new divorce laws had their vote?"

"They only just squeaked into the schedule. It was the

final item before the formal closing, and the debate went on a lot longer than expected. Another half hour and I don't know what they would have done. Held it over until fall, or convened an extra session after the formal closing."

"And did the new laws pass?"

"Yes, but it was close. It could easily have gone the wrong way. And tonight at the banquet Christian and Graziella announced her pregnancy. She's not quite at the three-month mark yet, but she had an ultrasound and she says the baby's turning somersaults in there. Her doctor thinks she's doing great."

"In other words…"

Her mother took a deep breath. "Yes. Honey, if you've made a decision and you want the palace to issue a statement, it can go ahead."

Misha's stomach dropped to her knees. She hadn't expected this to be such a big moment, but suddenly it was. Her hand shook slightly as she slid open the French door that led to the veranda, and stepped out into the fresh morning air. The sun still hung in the trees to the east, and it was chilly. She shivered and began to pace as she and her mother talked.

On the grass, a pair of crimson rosella parrots searched for seeds. Nuala had told her a few days ago that crimson rosellas mated for life, and since then she'd realized how often she saw the pretty birds in pairs, feeding or flying together. It seemed like an omen somehow.

"Artemisia Helena? Are you there? Are you all right, sweetheart?" her mother said, her voice sharpened by a concern which was also reflected in her use of Misha's full name. "Have you decided yet what you're going to do?"

She struggled to speak. "I need to talk to Gian-Marco face-to-face. I can't do it by phone."

"But you do want to call it off?"

She reached the end of the veranda and turned, took a deep breath. "Mom, has Dad ever cheated on you?"

"Oh, honey, that's not a question I ever wanted you to need to ask!"

"I'm not suggesting—"

"I know you're not. You're asking me if all men are like Gian-Marco and I hate that you'd even think that. Your father and I have been each other's one and only since the day we met—and I think the fact that he'd played the field a little before that day only helped him to realize how special we were together, so I've never held it against him or asked for details! You're worth more than this, Misha, you deserve better than a man you can't trust."

"This is what you've thought all along, isn't it?"

"I've thought you could do better. I know you can. But I understood the attraction, and I wasn't going to stand in your way if it was what you really wanted. Sweetheart, I think you're always going to need a little speed and action in your life, a little excitement, and that's not wrong, but you have to be so careful about where you go looking for it. You have to see below the surface."

"This has been such a mess. I need to fly back now, don't I? It can't go dragging on. There's too much riding on it. I need to talk to Gian-Marco, then to people like Mette Janssen and the bishop at St. Margrethe's."

"The palace can take care of all that."

"No," she told her mother firmly. "Not all of it. Some people deserve to hear from me directly. Don't say anything to anyone until I get back, will you? Except Dad, of course."

"Not even to Christian and Graziella?"

"Not yet. I'd rather tell them myself. I'll book my ticket this afternoon, for the first flight I can get."

"Tomorrow," her mother assumed.

"You're cute, Mrs. Queen. I'm on my unescorted Michelle Smith passport, remember? You've forgotten all about that lowly level of existence. Doors don't just fall open, nor do seats on international flights instantly free up."

Mrs. Queen ignored her teasing and urged seriously, "Soon, though."

"Soon," Misha agreed.

She added a visit to a travel agent to her list of things to do in Albury, and then thought about Brant and everything she'd be losing and letting go of when she told him goodbye. They'd known each other for just over three weeks.

None of it seemed real, and she wanted her mother's arms.

"As soon as I can," she said, her voice fogging up, and she paced up and down the veranda for a long time after she'd pressed the End Call button on the phone.

"Sunday," the travel agent in Albury told her later that morning. "Unless you want the stop over in Tokyo, or the flight changes in Singapore and Athens, in which case Saturday. No? You'd rather the direct Melbourne-Bahrain-Langemark, on Langemark Air? It's a small carrier, but they have a great reputation, don't they? Much better food!"

"Their mushroom risotto is pretty good," Misha agreed, not really thinking about it.

The travel agent confirmed the reservation and Misha paid with her unlimited funds credit card. Then she went and bought Snowy Mountains souvenir T-shirts for her little nephews, bottles of local award-winning wine for her father and brother, a range of Australian-grown teas and coffees for Graziella, and a silver souvenir teaspoon for Mom.

Mom had begun collecting spoons as a child, and still did. Forty years ago, the spoons had rattled around in an old cookie tin in Mom's Colorado bedroom. Now they had their own display room at the palace, lined with gleaming chrome and glass cases featuring interior track lighting and midnight-blue velvet shelves. Recent acquisitions tended to have been bestowed by visiting heads of state and were made of solid gold.

And yet, Misha realized, Mom's pleasure in her collection hadn't changed. There was some essence to the experience that had stayed exactly the same. Fingering the little silver spoon in its flimsy box, Misha somehow felt there was a message for her in Her Majesty's Spoon Collection, but she wasn't quite sure what it was.

She ate lunch at a café—pumpkin soup, a bread roll, hot tea and a piece of chocolate-caramel slice—with her head buried in a crime novel she'd just purchased at the nearby bookstore. Driving back to Inverlochie, she thought about telling Brant that she was leaving in less than two days and almost had to stop the car because her legs suddenly didn't work right.

"This is crazy!" she said aloud to the car and the road, and managed to keep going safely.

Brant wasn't at the house. Hardly a surprise, since it was midafternoon. The dogs weren't around, either, which meant the three of them were probably out in a paddock somewhere, so she hitched her floaty skirt up to her knees by tucking in handfuls of fabric at her waist, took the little two-wheeler motorcycle that he often rode himself and went looking for him.

The weather was exactly as it had been the day she'd first arrived here twenty-three days ago. Sun shone in a blue sky. A breeze teased at her clothing, sometimes dying back, sometimes rising in innocuous gusts. Huge fluffy white clouds surfed the heavens. As she roared up the track, one of them crossed the sun, darkening the grass and chilling the air, but it was soon gone. You never would have known that this was early June, and officially winter now.

Misha bounced over the grass on the noisy machine and got some exhilarating air as she went over a stock grid too fast and momentarily took off. Whee-ee! She didn't see Brant or the dogs in the mustering yard, but finally found him in the shearing shed, down beside the creek where the original farmhouse had once stood, along with an abandoned cottage now almost covered by renegade roses. She left the motorcycle parked beside the four-wheeler, with the helmet dangling on the handlebars.

This was the first time she'd been inside the shearing shed. It was a funny old building, classic in its design, due for renovation. She'd passed several of them on other properties in the area and appreciated their odd charm, now. Climbing the rough concrete ramp on the outside, she heard the clatter of hooves on the slatted wooden floor and then Brant's impatient voice cursing the animals.

"You bloody stubborn moron!" Somehow, he still managed to sound kind of *fond* of his sheep as he said it. It was very cute.

Inside, he didn't see her immediately and she took advantage of the fact to pause and watch him. Light spilled into the musty interior through various holes and openings, making the space look like a theater, atmospherically lit. There was a strong smell of damp wool and lanolin that Misha had gotten used to now, and actually liked.

Brant wore an old, collarless blue cotton business shirt with the sleeves taken off at the shoulder seams and the top two buttons missing, and he'd been working hard enough to oil his skin in a sheen of sweat which glistened in the dusty shafts of light, etching the clean lines of his muscles.

He saw her and pushed a ewe quickly down the ramp that led to the ground-level yard. They waved to each other without a word. He picked up a water bottle and tipped his head back to pour a long stream of cold liquid down his throat. He let it splash over his shirt-clad chest and shoulders, then grabbed a towel from a table and buried his face in the thick fabric. He moved it roughly over his bare arms to buff away the smears of sweat and water-dampened dirt.

Misha couldn't drag her gaze away. He emerged from the towel with the ends of his hair curling still slightly damp against his neck, threw the rectangle of fabric aside, crossed the lanolin-stained floor and came up to her.

"Hi," she said at last.

"Hi." He looked at her outfit of peasant skirt and blouse in various ocean colors, accessorized with beaded peacock-blue slides and a little turquoise jewelry. The whole thing pretty much said exactly what it was—incognito princess dresses down for a day out in a country town. "So you went to Albury?"

She nodded. "I got—" She stopped.

Some souvenirs for my family.

She couldn't say it, because she knew where it would lead—to the fact that she'd booked her flight home for Sunday, and she couldn't…didn't feel ready to…just *couldn't*… tell him this yet.

"—a few things," she finished. "A crime novel. But it's too gory and dark. I should have paid more attention to the blood dripping down the cover. How are things here?"

"I'm looking at a few hooves, cleaning them out and paring them back, trying to work out if keeping the lame ones in here on the dry floor overnight is doing any good."

"But you thought you'd get a result from the P.P.B. on their test today, and know for sure."

"I phoned them first thing this morning. Monday, they're saying now."

Monday.

"So you have to wait the whole weekend?"

And I'll be gone before you have an answer.

"It isn't foot rot," he said. "I really don't think it is. And I don't think it's O.I.D."

"Tell me what that stands for," she commanded.

"Ovine interdigital dermatitis. Forget it right now. You're never going to need to say it."

"Ovine interdigital dermatitis," she repeated at him, and stuck out her tongue.

"I think it's shelly hoof. See? If you'd waited you could have said that one, instead. Much easier."

She laughed. "I like that disease best, so far. You're right. It has the prettiest name. The sheep grow cute little seashells on their feet. Let's definitely go for that one."

"Okay, agreed. We'll tell the P.P.B. guys to forget the sample, we've made our own decision. Hey, or we could invent a completely new disease."

"Inverlochie limp."

"Rain-dance fever."

"I think we have a great future as official disease namers, and we're really onto something with this."

The word *future* echoed in Misha's head after she'd said it, spoiling the light moment. It carried too much weight. It acted like an invisible force field, keeping her out of Brant's body space so that there was no danger they'd kiss. He seemed to sense the force field, also. He rocked back on his heels a little, and leaned a hand on one of the wooden columns that supported the roof.

They looked at each other.

"So…I'm about done here. Is there anything you—" he cleared his throat "—want to do?" A chorus of sound came from the sheep and he turned to look at them, frowning and glaze-eyed.

"I booked my flight home," she blurted out. "For the day after tomorrow."

The beat of silence that followed her words stretched out for too long. They both understood the importance of her announcement, and there didn't seem to be any easy words to say. She'd intended to skirt around the subject for a little longer, and then to bring it up more carefully, with some prefacing remarks about how much she appreciated and valued—

Oh, forget it, it was done now.

And prefacing remarks would not have made it any easier.

"Let's go outside," Brant said finally.

Misha followed him, noting the deep thrust of his hands into his pockets, and the tight lift of his shoulders. He headed for the creek, which looped lazy and slow toward its confluence with the Murray River some miles downstream.

There was a fallen eucalyptus tree lying at an angle to the

creek bank, its leaves and lesser branches long gone and only its trunk remaining, now polished by the weather to a smooth, hard silver-gray. The trunk had the girth of a race-horse and the same quality of silkiness and sheen. They both hauled themselves up on it and sat side by side.

Misha kicked off her shoes and let them fall onto the narrow band of grass between the log and the water. She felt fluttery and churned up in her stomach, scared of what they might say to each other. And what they might hold back.

"So that's good news," Brant guessed at last.

"Yes."

He was right.

Of course he was.

Of course it had to count as good news.

"But you'll have to tell me why." His voice held a rusty note. His usual directness had gone. "I know it was complicated. You haven't told me—"

"I'm not going to marry Gian-Marco. I should be telling him that before I tell you, but... It still is complicated. He hasn't called. Neither have I. I—I don't even know where he is. I'm going home to Langemark, then I'll take it from there."

"You can't announce it yet, right? Or the palace can't? You told me all this, but I haven't—I've tried not—Well, I just haven't thought about it."

Misha knew why. They'd both put considerable energy into pretending that Gian-Marco Ponti, and in fact her whole life in Europe, just didn't exist, and that only Inverlochie was real...which hadn't been that hard, because Inverlochie felt like the realest place she'd ever been.

"Parliament voted on the new laws last night and they passed," she told Brant. "Christian and Graziella announced her pregnancy. I'll talk to Gian-Marco and find out if he has a preference for how the broken engagement is handled publicly. I probably shouldn't have hidden out here for so long."

"So long? Three weeks?"

"I needed it."

"Three weeks isn't long."

"No. But sometimes it doesn't take a long time to make this kind of journey. If that makes sense."

"The journey toward knowing what you have to do."

"That's right."

It took longer to separate all the tangled strands of feeling, however. Misha knew she would only begin to do that once she returned home. And even then she knew that Inverlochie was a place she never wanted her heart to lose for as long as she lived.

And she wouldn't lose it, she remembered. Nuala was still her best friend, and Nu planned to spend her life on Chris's farm just a few miles away.

She imagined herself visiting occasionally, down the years. Seeing Nu's kids. "Gosh, you've grown!" Briefly shaking off the suffocating formality of her public life in Europe and snatching some precious private days. Nu and Chris would organize a barbecue and Brant would come over. "Misha, this is my wife. Fifibelle, my sweetheart, let me introduce you to Princess Artemisia and her husband Count Ladislaw of Stetzenberg."

Or something.

Her imagination really didn't stretch as far as naming or picturing a future wife of Brant's or a future husband of her own.

It didn't even stretch as far as returning her rental car on Sunday and taking the first flight from Albury to Melbourne.

"But is it okay if I still come to the races with you tomorrow?" she asked Brant, as if he'd banned her from all his activities now that she was about to leave.

"Sheesh, of course it is, Mish! Why wouldn't it be?"

Ah. Why?

Because she suddenly understood what she'd really been asking.

Is it okay if I still kiss you?

Was it okay?

It had to be.

She let her body ease toward his just a little. Not enough to touch. Possibly not even enough for him to notice. Then she froze, her shoulders hunched and her fingers resting on their tips on the gray eucalyptus trunk.

Maybe it *wasn't* okay for her to still kiss him.

It was crazy for her to still want to, she realized, now that real life was timetabled to start again at exactly nine-fifteen on Sunday morning, which was when she'd have to steer her little red rental car around the puddles on the track to Inverlochie's gate for the last time.

Change the subject, Mish, and change it fast.

She opened her mouth and took a breath, ready to launch into some inane question about what they should do for dinner, the two of them, because Nu had already said she and Chris were going out. Before she could frame the first word, Brant twisted around and pulled her into his arms.

Why am I doing this?

Brant knew it was crazy and self-destructive. But then a proud and stressed-out sheep farmer getting involved with a European princess had been both of those things from the very beginning and the knowledge hadn't stopped him.

He had this bizarre, wrongheaded sensation that, yes, he was working against the clock but that, like a horse coming from behind in a big race with several hundred meters to run, this was still somehow *winnable*—that if he kissed Misha just right, made love to her just right, said and did all the right things between now and Sunday morning, then she'd stay and everything would fall into place.

Logic told him it wouldn't happen, but he refused to listen and kissed her harder, deeper, sweeter, with his heart totally on the line.

How much did she know about how he felt?

Her lips had parted with the first touch of his mouth and she'd sighed against him as if she'd been waiting for him to take the lead. She touched his neck, her fingers delicate and soft, not teasing but exploring. He leaned his cheek against her hand and kept kissing her, letting her hair brush his face, wondering if that dousing of ice-cold drinking water back in the shed had done enough to freshen him.

It hadn't.

"Mmm," she said, pulling away. "I'm kissing a sheep."

He heard the laugh in her voice.

Oh, *hell!*

Seconds later, she'd tipped them both off the log, down the short grassy slope of the bank and into the cold, clear water. They both gasped and he let out a yell as they came to rest half-sitting and half-lying on the coarsely sanded bed. It was shallow, up to Misha's breasts in her sitting position.

"I shouldn't have done that!" She took in a gasping, laughing breath and fell back to soak herself up to the neck, then came forward on all fours to push Brant farther under.

The water wasn't really that cold—nowhere near enough to make him forget what he wanted. He'd already grown used to it and it felt great to wash off the rest of the grime from the shearing shed. He dunked his head and let the water comb through his hair, then sat up, scrubbed his hands with the rough sand, rinsed them off and used them to clean his face.

"Fresh as a daisy," Misha said.

"So I can kiss you again now?"

"Please kiss me," she said softly. "I might die if you don't."

They almost crawled toward each other, pushing against the smooth braiding of the current. Misha's gypsyish clothing was plastered against her body, and her hair streamed with water.

She was still laughing and it made her clumsy. Gracefully

clumsy, if that was possible. Her backside swung, taut and neat beneath the sodden skirt, as she pushed against the water. One hand gave way beneath her for a moment in a patch of soft sand, and she had hair dripping in her eyes. None of it seemed to trouble her one bit. She had the spirit of someone with ancestors as gutsy and determined as Brant's own.

Maybe he *could* still win this, he thought hazily, watching her teasing mouth.

Maybe he really could. As long as this kiss was perfect.

She twisted to kneel in the current and he eased her onto his angled thighs, holding her close. His lips met hers, cool and wet, and she tasted of creek water, earthy and clean at the same time. He pushed the wet hair back from her forehead then closed his hand over her breast. It was taut from the cold water, and the soaking fabric of her top and bra clung like a second skin.

He barely even felt the water, was only aware of it because of the way it changed her body. She felt like pure marble, like a mermaid, as supple as the current itself. He touched her everywhere he could reach and his tongue swam in her mouth. Minutes passed, and he lost all sense of time. He felt her pull him to his feet, and on the way up he wrapped his arms close around her hips and kissed her through her wet clothes from her lower belly to her throat before reaching her mouth once more.

She was shaking. So was he, probably, although he couldn't feel it. He had wild thoughts about taking her right here. Pushing her skirt out of the way and just taking her. On the fallen eucalyptus trunk. In the water itself. In that patch of mud on the bank. Could he? Would that make this kiss into the perfect thing he wanted?

She pressed harder against him and he tightened his own arms, deepening the hungry exploration of his mouth, sliding his thigh between her legs. She pulled back from the kiss, holding his face between her hands and showering more kisses—short, feverish ones—on his jaw and temples and nose.

"B-Brant," she said, "I'm s-sorry but I'm s-so cold. I d-don't think I can do this."

Oh, hell.

"Cold?" he echoed stupidly, then stepped back and looked at her.

This was why her body trembled. Despite the warmth of his mouth, her lips were blue, and goose bumps stuck out all over her skin. When he took his arms away, she immediately wrapped her own around her, but it didn't help. She looked stiff and miserably uncomfortable.

"Let me get you out of here," he mumbled. "I'm so sorry!" He began to help her toward the bank.

"It was my f-fault. I p-pulled us off the log. Was okay at f-first, but not now." She could hardly get the words out, her mouth was so numb.

The sun had gone behind a cloud. There was a bank of them building in the west, which would probably mean more rain overnight. What time was it? After four? And it was June. It would be dark in just over an hour. He felt the chill now himself. The breeze freshened and she couldn't control her shaking.

On the dry ground, they both felt colder. The wind was sharper up here, beyond the shelter of the creek's banks, and it cut through their wet clothing, ripping their body warmth from their skin and blowing it away. His brain felt as numb as his fingers, and it took him too long to realize that the only sensible thing to do was to go directly back to the house. There was nothing here to warm them, and no way to get dry.

"We'll take the four-wheeler," he said. "Never mind about the other bike. It can stay here. You ride behind me and that way at least you won't get the headwind as we ride."

"I'll be f-fine once we're back at the house."

They huddled together and ran shivering to the four-wheeler, which he had trouble starting because his fingers had stiffened so much. Why hadn't he felt the cold before?

Easy—because he'd been too busy delivering the perfect kiss.

Ironic.

Sad.

It was probably the worst kiss of her life.

On the rough journey back to the house, he saw that the bank of clouds had already built thicker in the west. The sun had well and truly disappeared behind them, gone for the day. The wind cut through his wet shirt like a knife, and he doubted that his body would give Misha much shelter.

She'd had to drag her wet, clinging skirt up to her thighs in order to straddle the bike, which meant that her legs were bare, and they'd put her shoes in the storage hatch at the back because she couldn't grip them with her numb hands or slide them onto her soaking feet.

He had to help her off the wide seat when they reached the house.

"I'm s-sorry, my legs are so stiff. They just won't move. This was my fault, B-Brant."

"No," he told her tersely as he lifted her to the ground. "It was mine."

Nuala agreed with him. He saw Chris's car parked out front, and found the two of them in the house, having coffee and talking about seeing a movie tonight. Nu took one look at Misha's purple, shivering body and said, "Brant? What have you done to her now? Has she been helping again? Mish, you mustn't. *What* can have made you this wet?"

Brant held back the information that he was as wet and cold as she was. "We fell in the creek."

"Fell?"

"It was my f-fault," Misha said again. "I pushed him."

He started toward his bedroom, knowing he couldn't afford to get sick. He needed to get warm as much as Misha did. "Run her a bath, Nu, can you? Fill it. Hot. And make her some tea."

"Yes, your lordship, and what are you going to do?"

"Get into some dry clothes." He squeezed the hem of his shirt and water dripped onto the floor. "See this? It's not sweat."

Nuala looked at them both as if she were a harried mother, dealing with a pair of very naughty children.

Chapter Fourteen

It rained heavily overnight.

The track was graded Heavy for this afternoon's race meeting, and by the look of the sky it could get worse as the day progressed. There were patches of blue, but the clouds were low and the wind was cold. Winter had arrived with a vengeance, several days after its official start date.

The gray, unpredictable weather suited Brant's mood down to the ground. It had taken him two hours to really warm up last night. He'd been stubborn about it. Nuala had lit the fire, but he made Misha sit close to it, and since he didn't trust himself to sit close to *her*, this meant he had to retreat beyond the reach of its radiance.

"Make yourself some packet soup," Nuala had suggested. "Or let me do it."

She'd relented in her intial assumption that Misha's frigid state was his fault, but her offer of soup came to nothing because Brant and Misha had eaten all the packet soups last week, and hadn't yet bought more.

Chris had identified the best movie option, and he and Nuala announced their intention to go into Albury early and eat Chinese beforehand. "Who's coming with us?" Nu had asked. "Misha?" Pause. "Brant?"

"I won't," he'd said quickly, so that if Misha wanted to go but *didn't* want to spend time with a country-bred man whom she might never see again after Sunday and who had effectively attempted to, let's face it, *kiss her to death* that afternoon, she was free to do so. "But Misha…?"

"Yes, Mish, please come," Nu had said.

And Misha had gone.

Brant had spent a wakeful night assuming she wouldn't come to the race meeting and telling himself this was a good thing, but when their paths crossed over lunch, she asked him, "So when's the first race? What time do we have to leave?" and, so help him, he just didn't have it in him to turn her off.

They arrived at the track at one.

Misha wrapped her dusty pink Mette Janssen coat more closely around her and jammed her matching Arne Norte velour hat lower over her ears, being careful not to pull on the suede rosebuds and assorted bits of trim. She'd dressed up a little today, not to conform to high fashion or her royal role, but because the coat and hat were the warmest garments she'd brought with her and she'd had her quota of almost freezing to death for this month, thanks.

Brant's immediate interpretation of her action with the coat and hat was to tell her, "You shouldn't have come."

"It's going to be fun," she answered firmly, but inside she wasn't so sure.

Yesterday's life-threatening kiss in the creek still hung between them like an icy mist. Brant had been distant and different ever since. At first she'd thought it was simply the bone-chilling cold. He'd insisted on her taking that bath, and

Nu had filled it so enthusiastically that by the time she was done there was no hot water left.

Brant had kept saying that he was fine. He'd put on dry clothes and was standing by the fire when she emerged from the bathroom, but then he'd made way for her so she could have the heat, and…oh…just hadn't been in the mood to talk, or something. He'd sat as far from her as he could.

He'd still been moving his hands stiffly, at that point. She knew he must have almost frozen on the four-wheeler, coming back to the house. He'd been up early that morning, as usual. He was probably just tired and needed some time to himself.

So she'd said yes to Nuala's suggestion of Chinese food and the movie, hadn't gone to Brant's room last night when she returned home, and planned for today to count as a fresh start.

A final fresh start, since she was leaving tomorrow. She'd spent most of the morning packing.

But a fresh start required a shared commitment to the issue, and Brant wasn't playing ball. Something was seriously wrong.

"Made a decision on our five dollars for the first race?" she asked him. They were running out of time. The horses were already parading beside their strappers in the mounting yard.

"I'm not betting," Brant said. "Not on this one."

Misha stayed upbeat. "Well, I am. And I'm going to be a total girl and go for the prettiest horse, which is number five. American Prairie. Look at her, she's a supermodel, with that dark mane and sassy gait."

American Prairie romped home, and Misha was wealthier by fifteen Australian dollars. She was as happy about it as if it had been a thousand times that much. Santari ran in the second race, and Brant didn't place a bet on him, either. Misha put on another five dollars, and he won easily by about eight lengths, but he'd been the clear favorite so she only pocketed a gain of three dollars. Once again, she was thrilled.

"What was that horse Rae was telling you about the other day?" she prompted Brant, still foolishly looking for a way to lift his mood and bridge the distance.

Being brutally honest with herself, she wanted to spend tonight in his bed. It felt so wrong that they'd barely touched each other today. She wanted the bittersweet delight of a final night together, and knew that a part of her seriously hoped tomorrow might never come.

"Extra Fresh?" she went on. "Oh, I see he's in Race Three, coming up. Aha, I've guessed your strategy now. You're saving all your five-dollar bills for today and sinking them on him." She tried a grin and waited for his reaction.

"I'm thinking of backing him for eighty thousand," Brant said.

"What?" She felt a sudden chill. "I heard that wrong."

"You didn't," he said casually. "He's at ten to one for the win, and Rae seemed pretty confident about him."

"She offered to sell you the Sydney Opera House at the same time, remember?"

"I could make a tax-free profit of $720,000 in one afternoon, and stop worrying about the farm. I wouldn't owe anyone a cent. I'd be my own man."

"You could lose. You would be very *likely* to lose. Brant, you don't make bets like that."

She'd met people who did—oil and technology billionaires who sank a million on a single race and shrugged when they lost, and decaying European aristocrats with a serious gambling problem who traded on their family name and made doomed, desperate attempts to restore their fortunes with flashes of mystical intuition.

But Brant was different.

She felt cold.

He must not do this.

She couldn't understand why he'd even consider it. She knew there was an element of the risk taker in him. It was something they shared. But the risks they both loved weren't of this type.

She looked up at him, feeling every inch of the distance between them, trying to work out what was going on. He stared out at the track, where the horses from the second race were still cantering back toward the stands after their run. There was a grim calm to his expression, and she felt as welcome beside him as a buzzing fly.

"Brant?" she said. "Don't."

"Why not? Because I might lose? That's a bit pathetic, isn't it?"

"Because you know as well as I do that it's not a courageous act. Some people think it is, but it isn't. It's deluded and desperate and not right. Five dollars…pocket change… a reason to cheer for a pretty horse, yes, but—"

"Stop, can you? It's not a decision that needs your involvement." He looked at her—glared at her, really—and she wanted to cry the way she would have cried if he'd slapped her in the face.

She felt as if he had slapped her.

No. As if he'd closed the door on her when she was begging for him to let her inside.

"I *want* to be involved!" she insisted. "You brought me here for a fun afternoon."

"I've tried to provide a fair bit of entertainment for you over the past three weeks, Misha, but you're leaving tomorrow and this is my life, not yours."

"Are you doing this…because I'm leaving?" she dared to guess, and immediately felt like a foolish, pampered princess who thought the whole world revolved around her, because he just laughed.

"It could have a little more to do with bank loans and diseased sheep, don't you think? You talk about desperation.

Well, I am desperate. I don't want to borrow money from my stepfather or from anyone else—"

Me, she realized bleakly.

"—and Rae is confident that Extra Fresh can win."

She should let it go, at this point. A part of her—the princess part—was convinced that she should. The princess should smile politely at Brant the way she'd smiled at oil billionaires at Ascot in the past and say, "Good luck, then. If you win, will there be champagne?"

Uninvolved.

No reason to care.

But the woman who existed totally without reference to the princess part of her just couldn't do it.

"But you think it's shelly hoof!" she said instead. "And you'll know for sure on Monday. Why pick now to act like some Regency rake in a historical novel?" She took a shaky breath. "Why are you so *angry* with me?"

"I'm not," he said sharply. "I'm angry with myself."

"Why?"

"Because of yesterday."

"Because we got wet and cold, kissing in the creek like a pair of teenagers? That's something to laugh about."

"Because—" He stopped, shook his head and turned away, and she thought she heard him mutter the word *perfect* under his breath.

Perfect afternoon.

Perfect emotional mess.

"I'm not letting this go!" she told him.

"Do you have a choice? I'll say it again. This is not your decision. It is not even your business. If I want to place the bet, then I will."

"Well, I don't have to stay and watch you do it!"

"You have my permission to leave, Misha."

"I don't need your permission. And I am."

She turned on her heel and pushed through a group of

people heading toward the mounting yard before he could see that she was about to cry. She knew he wouldn't follow her. That was the whole point. His bet wasn't her business, Inverlochie and his entire life weren't her business, and her emotional response wasn't his.

She was leaving tomorrow, she'd never belonged here, and he'd decided to cut short the whole messy, awkward process of saying, "Thank-you and good-bye" by disengaging half a day ahead of time. She'd be sleeping in her own bed tonight.

Circling through the pavilion, she found the side exit and pushed through the open gate, then realized she'd have to call a taxi if she wanted to get back to Inverlochie. She found a helpful race club official who gallantly did it for her, then stood in the cold wind waiting for it to arrive. It took a long time, and she heard the voice of the race caller announcing that the last horse had gone into the gate for Race Three just as the driver pulled up beside her and enquired, "Smith?"

"That's me."

As the taxi drove away, she couldn't help craning to try and watch the race. The horses had come into the turn, but she didn't have a clear view. Trees and a shed got in the way. What colors was Extra Fresh wearing? Was he leading the field?

It was no good. The taxi turned a corner and she couldn't see.

"You're a long way out of town," the driver told her when they reached the road that led to Inverlochie.

"Yes, another ten kilometers, roughly, and another kilometer of track to the house. But I'll just get you to drop me off at the gate."

"Save a couple of dollars?"

"That's right." She thought the driver would probably take one look at the mud on the track after last night's rain and refuse to go farther, anyhow.

She ruined her shoes and blistered her feet walking it.

The house was empty. It was just after three o'clock. She went to Brant's computer and tried checking the results of the race on the Internet but they weren't yet posted on the website she found, not even the ones for the first race. Maybe nothing would appear until the whole meeting was over.

The wait seemed unbearable. She'd always hated waiting. If there was going to be bad news, just let it happen, please, so she could take whatever action she could to deal with it and then get on with her life.

Had Brant placed the bet?

Had Extra Fresh won?

She couldn't stand the uncertainty, and, princess-like, identified the service she needed and went directly to it—she called the local branch of the national betting agency and got an answer to one of her questions.

Extra Fresh had run second.

She felt ill, wanted to draw down eighty thousand Australian dollars from her unlimited credit account to give to Brant today, but she knew this would be the worst thing in the world she could possibly do, for him or for herself.

Instead, she changed into farm clothes—mostly Nuala's—unchained Sox and took her for a fast, bumpy, aimless ride on the four-wheeler, across the muddy paddocks. Nuala must have taken Mon over to Chris's because she wasn't in her kennel.

"Why is he doing this, Soxie?" she asked the dog, as Sox stood sentinel behind her on the seat of the bike. "It's to push me away, isn't it? It's his way of telling me, just in case I was in any doubt, that I'm not a part of his life, and he can stuff it up any damn way he wants to, no matter how much I might want to help. Well, great. Okay. Message received."

Message *not* received.

She zipped into a paddock she hadn't been in before, at the far reach of Inverlochie's acreage, and saw some sheep trying to get to a mud-verged, brimming pond for a drink.

They were Brant's valuable rams. She recognized the fact even at a distance because of their curling horns.

One of them was in trouble. The others had found the tiny stream which fed the pond and were drinking from that, but this independent fellow had tried to go across the mud and he was stuck on a steep, sticky, eroded section that led down to the water. Coming closer, she saw that one whole side of his woolly body was slicked with mud and he was lying sideways, bawling his frustration as he repeatedly tried and failed to haul himself to his feet.

"This is not my business, Sox," Misha told the dog.

Sox had a different opinion. She jumped down from the four-wheeler and said with every movement of her athletic kelpie's body, "Tell me what we're doing to rescue the ram, Captain Princess."

"We're going back to the house. You're getting chained up, I'm leaving a note for Brant about the ram, because it's his problem, then I'm going to Chris's to see Nu and we're having a girls' night. I don't care where. The local male strip club, maybe. A biker bar in Melbourne. It's only, what, three or four hours' drive? Maybe we can get tattooed."

"Nope," Sox said. "Not going back to the house."

"Yeah, I'm just making that up," Misha agreed. "You can read my mind. But I've never hauled a ram out of mud before. Any ideas?"

Sox panted.

"Panting is limited as a mode of communication, do you realize?" She switched off the four-wheeler's engine and climbed off it.

The other rams barged away at her approach, and the stuck one tried to do the same, then sank back into his sticky prison. He was getting tired. How long had he been here? She knew that Brant usually checked all his paddocks every morning, but the animal could have got stuck since. How long could a sheep survive in this position?

She went closer, and this time the ram stayed quiet, too exhausted to struggle. Assessing his position, she doubted she could pull him free just using her own strength, even if Sox somehow understood how to help her. But if she used the four-wheeler?

She checked the rear hatch and found rope. Tie it to the ram's front feet, maybe—the ones he again tried to haul himself onto, while his back legs were thoroughly stuck. But would that damage his quite slender legs?

"Am I insane, Soxie?"

Sox panted her total approval of Misha's existence, which suddenly made her want to cry. "You have no idea I'm leaving, do you? No idea how much I totally and utterly do not belong here."

She was going to free the ram. She felt as stubborn about it as Brant had been this afternoon at the track. She was going to prove to him that she could belong here if she wanted to, that she understood Inverlochie's place in his life and would never want to change that. And she wasn't going to do it in some stupid, ineffectual, ill-thought way, either. She was going to think it through and get it right.

Nu's jacket.

She pulled it off, assessing its potential as a sling, and decided, yes, if she could get it around the ram's back and armpits—leg pits?—she could attach the sleeves to the rope and…

Then what?

The four-wheeler. Attach the rope to that, and if she could position the four-wheeler in the right spot, she'd have enough traction, Sox could bark up a storm at the ram and then the silly thing would do some of the work himself. She actually thought that between the three of them, they could do this.

And it seemed important. Eighty thousand dollars' worth of proof that when she and Brant said goodbye to each other tomorrow morning, it shouldn't be said with bitterness and failure but with care.

She cared about this place.

She cared about his life.

She cared about *him!*

She looked at the terrain, the four-wheeler and the ram's position, and then moved the vehicle. It was a little hairy, getting it into the right spot on such steep, slippery ground. Getting Nuala's jacket around the ram was a struggle, too, and she hoped it would hold. She knotted the sleeves to the rope and the rope to the four-wheeler, and this was easier, even if the knots themselves would have earned her a failing grade on a camp-craft test.

"Okay, now, Soxie, do you know what we're doing? What's all that stuff Brant says to you? Wa-ay back, back around. All that sheepdog stuff. Do you know what I'm talking about? Could you just stand there behind him and bark so he gets the idea?"

She straddled the four-wheeler and started the engine, then took a deep breath. "Here goes, guys."

It worked. At first.

Sox barked, the ram bawled and began to slither, the four-wheeler moved slowly forward, skidding in the mud. And then it tipped and fell. The engine stalled on the way down. Misha landed in the mud, her torso on the downward side of the slope and her leg pinned beneath the four-wheeler.

Behind her, the ram bawled and struggled, tangled itself briefly in Nuala's jacket and then the jacket slipped over his back and he lolloped away, indignant and skittish and heavy with mud but free.

"We did it, Soxie!" Misha said. "Uh, not sure if I can get the bike standing up again, though."

She couldn't even get herself standing up. It was just ridiculous, she thought at first. Silly. All she had to do, surely, was slide her leg out, or maybe dig it down into the mud a bit deeper and then slide it out.

She looked at her mud-smeared, diamond-encrusted

watch, and it read three forty-five. Later than she would have thought. She must have spent a good twenty minutes working over the ram already.

Sox barked at her. "It's not as easy as it looks, girl," she told the dog.

She pulled, and something hurt. She pulled harder and it hurt more, so she stopped. She tried the digging-down idea, but the rest of her body had no traction in the mud, especially tilted downhill as it was, and after a further fifteen minutes of theorizing and struggling and swearing and catching her breath, she had to accept what had happened.

"Sox, I'm trapped. Can you go get help?"

Chapter Fifteen

When Brant got home from the track at four-fifteen, a taxi had pulled up at Inverlochie's gate, and a man stood beside it, along with a small wheeled suitcase. He was arguing with the driver in fluent but exotically accented English.

"How am I supposed to get to the house?" he yelled. "I can't even see it. And it is about to rain." He saw Brant pull over beside the taxi in his four-wheel drive. "Is it you who lives here?" he demanded.

At this point, Brant recognized him. "Yes, this is my place," he said.

"So he's your problem now, mate?" the driver asked tersely.

"Yep. No worries." He turned to the newcomer. "Gian-Marco, isn't it?"

The man nodded, his dark eyes flashing and his lips pouted like a child's. He looked like a Formula One version of the young Elvis. "If I had known it was this difficult to get around in outback Australia, I would have hired one of those battery-operated toy cars they offered me at the car rental."

"This isn't the outback, mate," the taxi driver drawled, saving Brant the trouble.

"I'll put your luggage in the back," he said to the racing driver. "Mind opening the gate?"

"Sure." Gian-Marco walked toward it, and the taxi drove off.

Brant loaded the suitcase and went through the opened gate. Gian-Marco shut it behind him and climbed into the front. "Let's just confirm. Am I in the right place?"

"If you're looking for Misha, yes."

"This is the house of her friend Nu."

"That's right. I'm her brother. Nu's brother," he added stupidly, as if Gian-Marco might otherwise have thought he was Prince Christian of Langemark. "I'm Brant."

"And where is Misha?"

"Did you tell her you were coming? Did she call you?"

"No. I wanted to surprise her. To be honest, I felt a little threatened by some…" He stopped, took out a folded piece of paper from his jacket pocket and thrust it into Brant's field of vision as he drove. "Is this you?"

Brant glanced at the piece of paper, then batted it away. "Wait till we get to the house. I can't look at it now. Is what me?"

"Hot new Aussie man."

This wasn't making any sense.

Well, nothing much would make sense to him at the moment, Brant recognized, after the horrible afternoon at the track—his stubbornness, his need to stir up a fight and prove to Misha that she didn't belong. His heartbeat quickened. They would reach the house in another two minutes and he'd have to face her.

With Gian-Marco Ponti in tow.

"Hot new Aussie man?" he echoed blankly.

"Only one magazine picked up the story, because, really, you can't know it's her, the picture is so blurred. It could be anyone. But the magazine says it is Misha. Princess Incognito Heals Her Broken Heart Down Under With Hot New Aussie Man," he quoted on a drawl. "Even if it's true, it's still trash, as always. But I thought it was time she and I ended the hostility, since we are getting married in three and a half months and most of the population of Langemark is involved in organizing the wedding."

Brant stopped the car, five hundred meters from the house. "Show me that."

He snatched it from Gian-Marco's obliging hand, his whole gut in a tangle of painful knots. The picture was less blurred to his eye than the racing driver had suggested. He knew at once when it must have been taken, and from where.

It showed himself and Misha standing in the front yard here at Inverlochie. Her blond hair was tossed loosely around her shoulders and they were grinning at each other. She had something in her hand that was hard to identify, unless you already knew what it was.

Brant did.

It was her brown curly wig.

The photo had been taken from almost exactly this spot, from the passenger-side window of a car travelling in the opposite direction, the day Shay and the photographer had done the story on him for *Today's Woman* magazine.

"Why are you here?" he asked Gian-Marco.

He shrugged. "To see if it's true. To tell her I've finished with Ariane. To get her back."

She doesn't want you back.

"So you do know that you've lost her, then?" he asked.

Gian-Marco laughed. "There's a very short distance, my friend, between losing a woman and having her crawling on the floor with her arms wrapped around your knees begging that you'll take her back."

"Is there? I wouldn't know. I don't treat women like that."

"Maybe you should," Gian-Marco said.

They didn't like each other.

Surprise, surprise.

Brant wrenched the four-wheel drive back into gear and gunned the remaining distance to the house.

"Where is Misha?" the racing driver asked again, the moment Brant had switched off the engine.

"I don't know," he answered, through gritted teeth.

It was the truth. He had no idea if she'd come directly home after their argument at the track. She might be halfway to Melbourne by now. The thought gave him a bitter, self-destructive kind of satisfaction. They both knew she had to leave. It might be easiest if she'd already gone, without a messy goodbye.

"She must be here!" Gian-Marco said.

"Oh, because you've shown up wanting her?"

"No, because the taxi driver said this was the second trip he'd made to this place this afternoon, and his first passenger, a very attractive blonde, had been happy to walk from the gate."

That sounded like Misha.

"Right," Brant agreed. "Then I guess she's here."

Except that she wasn't. Her rental car was parked out front, but the house was empty and silent, and when he called out, there was no reply. He abandoned Gian-Marco and checked the dogs, but their kennels were empty, too.

Drops of rain began to fall. He took his phone out of his pocket and called Nuala to find out if she'd taken the dogs, but she must have gone out in a paddock with Chris, because her phone was out of range and Chris's landline didn't pick up, either. Walking around to the carport at the side of the house, he discovered that the four-wheeler was gone.

"Is there a chance of coffee?" Gian-Marco asked, back inside. He seemed impatient and dissatisfied, but not the least bit concerned at Misha's absence.

Brant made the coffee quickly, because around here you acted hospitably toward guests, even ones that you didn't want. He poured a mug for himself, but after one sip he couldn't drink it.

"Misha must have gone for a run on the four-wheeler," he told his visitor. "Because it should be in the carport, and it isn't. Why the hell didn't you tell her you were coming? At least call from Melbourne, or something."

"I like the element of surprise. Take my advice, if you're ever in a situation like this. When you surprise a woman, you learn how she really feels. Besides, I wasn't sure when I'd fit the trip into my schedule."

"Well, she's leaving tomorrow. If you'd left it another couple of days your two planes would have passed each other in flight."

"She's leaving? What has she said?" He looked more alert and tense, suddenly. "She's gotten over her stupid attitude to the attention I get from other women, then? And the business of Ariane? It meant something for a while, yes, but it's over, now. A man is entitled to one last piece of freedom before he marries a princess, I think!"

"Look, this is between the two of you. I'm not going to get involved."

He *wasn't* involved. He'd signalled the fact pretty strongly to Misha herself, this afternoon, and he didn't regret it. Felt icy cold when he thought back on it, but didn't regret it, all the same.

Outside, he saw the rain coming down more heavily, and listened for the sound of the four-wheeler coming back. It was after four-thirty now, and the light had begun to go.

"Where is she?" Gian-Marco asked, showing his first sign of concern.

"I'm beginning to wonder the same thing." Brant frowned and looked out the window, then found himself saying, "She wasn't in a great mood when I last saw her," which earned him a sharp look from the Formula One driver.

"So she's punishing you? Giving you a scare? Just what she did to me by flying out here in the first place!"

"It's not." Brant knew Misha's reasons for coming here, and he trusted them.

"Listen, I don't care what's been going on with the two of you," Gian-Marco said, "if this is her attempt to pay me back for Ariane, if there is any truth to the story in the magazine. I want her back, but I'm not going to stand here waiting for her. I have a reservation at a motel." He checked a printed travel itinerary and read out the name of the place, pronouncing it uncertainly. "Could you run me there?"

With pleasure.

It was located in Holbrook. Not far.

But then Brant thought about Misha, the missing four-wheeler and the fact that she still wasn't back, and felt his spine begin to crawl. "Just let me make a couple of phone calls, first."

He tried Chris's house, and this time Nuala picked up. "I took Mon, but I didn't take Sox," she said, in answer to his question. "What do you mean Misha isn't back?"

He explained, avoiding any detail concerning their argument over that massive, crazy, self-punishing bet. "And Gian-Marco's here," he added.

"*What?* Listen, I'm leaving here right now and coming home. If you go looking for her, leave me a note saying which paddocks you're checking first, and I'll check the rest."

Brant put down the phone and Gian-Marco picked up his suitcase. "So? You know the name of the motel to tell Misha, when she deigns to return?"

"I'm going out to look for her." He felt his anger rising, along with his alarm. "Don't you want to help? Or at least wait to see if she's all right?"

Gian-Marco made an impatient sound. "Of course she's all right! She's like a little cat, that one. Nine lives." He grinned suddenly, his olive-skinned face lighting up with wicked appreciation. "And she tries to live all of them at once."

It was the first thing he'd said about Misha that Brant actually agreed with, and the first moment he'd been able to understand a part of why she might have once fallen for this man.

"She does a pretty good job of it, too," he said to Gian-Marco. "But if she's a cat… Cats don't like the rain."

It had grown even heavier, like a silver-gray curtain where it overflowed the gutters on the roof of the house and poured down to the ground. He remembered how quickly she'd started to shiver yesterday in the creek. Why would she stay out in this? Not to punish him. Gian-Marco was wrong. She never behaved that way.

His pulses quickened and an urgent energy flooded him. "I'm going to look for her. Something might have happened. You can wait here, or come with me."

Gian-Marco unleashed a rapid flood of Italian, half under his breath, and began an impatient pacing through the room, drawing in long mouthfuls of coffee at frequent intervals. "I'll wait," he said. "What use would I be?"

"There's more coffee in the plunger," Brant told him, then grabbed a rain jacket and a helmet from the mudroom and left the house.

The two-wheeler motorcycle was still down at the shearing shed, he remembered. Jumping into the four-wheel drive, he drove down there, his wheels slithering in the mud as he took the bends too fast and tried to scan the paddocks as he went. At the shearing shed, the iffy starter motor on the bike gave him its usual trouble and he cursed it until it finally started.

It was a difficult little machine to ride in these conditions, but it offered the best way of reaching the rougher parts of the farm. He stuck to the grass whenever he could, circling through this lowest paddock first and sending up jets of water when he wheeled through the sheets of rainwater spreading wider on the ground. No sign of Misha, the four-wheeler or Sox.

Now that he was right out in the weather, his sense of urgency soared and his stomach began to jump. Gian-Marco was an egocentric idiot to put this down to female gamesplaying. Something must have happened to her.

Something *had* happened to her.

He knew it deep in his gut, suddenly, and the knowledge went beyond his awareness of the accident rate of four-wheelers on farms and the increased danger in these conditions. He knew with every cell in his body that something was wrong, and could almost feel her need for him. She was out here somewhere, waiting for him to come, and he had to find her.

Oh, dear God!

He gunned the motorbike faster, until his own safety was in question, and had to fight to slow himself down, act rationally, think about where he should look and how the sight of her and the four-wheeler might be distorted by the fading light and thickening rain. He combed the creek paddock, the hill paddock, the front paddock, and then he went around the hill, over two more grids and across toward his far boundary fence. That was when he saw Sox come charging toward him.

"Oh, hell, where is she, Soxie? Have you been with her? Show me, girl, come on!" He felt newly energized by finding the dog, but ill at the fact that Sox was alone.

She wagged her tail and jumped up on the back of the bike. Feeling the continued thumping of her tail, he knew he must be heading in the right direction, and rode farther into the paddock until he saw Misha and the four-wheeler at last— both on their sides, sodden wet and muddy, on the steep slope of bare earth leading down to the dam he'd had bulldozed last spring.

Was she moving?

Was she conscious?

Was she…don't even think about it…alive?

"Misha!" he called out to her through a bone-dry mouth.

He couldn't hear a reply over the sound of the bike's raucous engine, and his level of fear climbed still higher.

Oh, dear God, if I lose her…I can't lose her…I might only see her a handful of times in my life after tomorrow, but as long as she's all right… That's all that matters. She just has to be somewhere in the world, *safe*, for the rest of my life.

He skidded to a halt on the grass and almost lost control of the machine. It fell over, and he didn't care. He ripped off the helmet and dropped it on the ground, struggled to say her name, and at last, just as the sound left his mouth, he saw her move.

"Mish! Oh, hell, Misha!"

"Tell me the truth, Brant," she called weakly. "Your dog has never seen any old episodes of *Lassie* on cable TV, has she?"

"*What?*" He lunged clumsily toward her, slipping again on the grass.

"She stayed right by me." Sox rushed up to her again, panting, and she patted the dog in a series of weak, shaky caresses. "She was a sweetheart. She kept me company. I think she would have stayed with me all night. But I wanted her to go and find you…like Lassie always did…and she wouldn't…and I started thinking…that you'd never come."

She was crying now, gasping, jerky sobs that shook her shoulders and stopped her from breathing. He gathered her into his arms, his heart light with relief and his head dizzy, and began to kiss her wet, muddy, ice-cold face, but then she hissed and told him, "Don't. It hurts if you pull on me. That's why I couldn't get free. As soon as I try to pull on my leg, it just hurts worse and worse." Her voice cracked again on the last word.

"Oh, lord, I have to get this thing off you!" He knew it

would be too heavy for him to lift on his own, especially in these conditions and especially in the controlled way that would make sure he didn't hurt her any further. He cursed himself for not insisting that Gian-Marco come with him, and knew he'd only avoided pushing the issue out of his own distaste for the other man's company.

Having done some first aid, he also knew that if her leg was seriously crushed, then it could be dangerous to remove the weight without medical help, but for the life of him he couldn't remember the detail on that. How long would it take to get an ambulance out here, anyway? What was the safest thing?

His relief, a minute ago, had been premature.

"Can you move your toes?" he asked. "Do you have feeling down there?"

"Feeling? My whole leg is half-frozen! I might never get the nerve endings back the way they were."

"But you can feel sensations? Cold? Mud? Pain? Move your toes for me, Mish."

She understood the implication behind the questions and nodded slowly. Seconds later she announced, "I can move it fine. I can feel mud oozing on it, and it only hurts when I try to pull it. I—I really don't think it's crushed. Just… pinned."

He reached down and squeezed her hand, but couldn't speak.

Searching the darkening landscape through the rain, willing himself to stay calm and rational, he found a thick, iron-hard eucalyptus branch torn from a big tree in some long-gone storm and now lying on the ground. He rolled a football-sized, lichen-covered granite rock down the slope and positioned it on the mud, then balanced the branch on top of it and slid the end of the branch under the side of the four-wheeler.

Would it hold? Would the mud be too soft? What if he had to leave her on her own again and go back to the house?

"I'm going to lever it up," he told Misha, hiding his doubts. "But I won't be able to move it completely. When the pressure's gone, slide out."

Fast, he wanted to add, but didn't.

If the branch gave way, or his own strength did…

He couldn't think about it.

With branch, rock and Misha in the right positions and ready, he pushed and the four-wheeler moved. She clenched her teeth and let out a high-pitched groan of intense effort as she dragged her body down the slope.

"Free?" he grunted. His whole body was shaking with the strain. He heard a crack as the branch began to break.

"Yes! Free!"

"Keep going!"

She rolled through the mud just as the wood cracked and splintered, dropping the four-wheeler back onto the ground. They were both shaking, while Sox ran anxiously back and forth between them.

"Can you stand? Oh, hell, Misha!"

"I'm okay. I'm okay," she sobbed. "Oh, thank God you came! Thank God you could get it off!" She stood awkwardly, the half-numb leg unable to bear her weight as yet. He checked it for bleeding, saw the hard dent in her flesh where the four-wheeler had pinned her, but the skin wasn't broken and neither was the bone. "Don't let me go…"

"As if I would." He held her hard, supporting her and making a vain attempt to warm her with the press of his body. "Why were you under that four-wheeler?"

"There was a ram stuck."

"Where?"

"There in the mud. You can see the marks where he was struggling. I got him out. I rigged up a sling with Nu's jacket, and moved him enough so he could free himself, but the slope was too steep and the four-wheeler tipped. I think the ram's okay. He went off with the others. I don't know where they are, now." Her knees began to buckle as she tried to survey the darkening slopes in search of him.

The rain poured down on them both, and he could feel how cold she was, and how precarious on her feet. It was almost dark. "Shh," he soothed her. "Forget about the ram. If he went off with the others, he must be in pretty good shape. I'll check them in the morning. Let's get back to the house."

Where Gian-Marco was waiting.

He didn't know how to tell her.

"First, Brant…"

"Yes?"

"Did you place that bet?" She stroked his face and looked at him, her eyes narrowed.

He didn't want to talk about it now. "Extra Fresh ran second."

"I know. I checked with the betting agency. Did you place the bet?"

"It's not—" he began.

"Don't *tell* me it's not my business!" She fought her way out of his arms and staggered two lopsided paces, rubbing at her leg. She gave a sob, part anger, part frustration, part pain.

He grabbed her back again and pulled her close. "Misha… You can't walk properly yet. Don't let's—"

"I've just spent an hour and a half stuck in the freezing mud proving that your life *is* my business," she yelled, gripping his arms and shaking him. "So damn well *tell* me if you placed a bet that would have left you eighty thousand dollars in the hole!"

He sighed. "No. I didn't. Okay? Happy?"

He felt the relief flood through her body as he held her, and knew he couldn't hold back the news about Gian-Marco any longer.

"I put a hundred dollars, win or place, on another one of Rae's horses in the next race," he said. "It's the biggest punt

I've ever made in my life and it didn't made a dent in how I felt, didn't help at all, but she came in third, so I made a profit of twenty-five dollars. Which is…so irrelevant I can't believe I'm wasting the words." He took a breath. "Then I got home, Mish, and there was a taxi standing at the front gate…"

"Madre del dio! Look at you!"

"If you'll excuse me, Gian-Marco, I'll just freshen up a little before we talk."

He burst out laughing at this, cutting right through Misha's attempt to erect a force field of royal manners. "Can I tell you that you still look beautiful?"

"Be my guest."

She walked steadily to the bathroom, concealing her utter lack of preparation for any of this. Brant hadn't placed that huge, horrible bet at the track, which counted as one check in the plus column, but he'd said nothing in response to what she'd told him about rescuing the ram—about proving to him that this place was her business. She'd given away so much, and he'd stubbornly and deliberately ignored it all.

And now Gian-Marco was here in Brant's living room, with a newly arrived Nuala keeping a suspicious watch over him and ready to say something one hundred percent supportive but massively tactless at the first opportunity.

My worlds have collided, and one of them is going to get destroyed….

The shower helped a tiny bit. She actually warmed up faster than she had done yesterday, because at least she'd been dressed appropriately in the first place this time, and even without Nu's jacket, the wool sweater she had on beneath it had helped her retain body warmth.

Wool was like that, she'd learned since coming here. It was one of the few fibers that remained an effective form of insulation when wet.

Under the streaming hot water, she laughed at herself.

Feeling proud and possessive about the favorable properties of wool fiber?

Oh, shoot, she was in deep here!

Nuala brought her the clothes she'd asked for and she dressed in the bathroom. A princess didn't dart along the corridor to her bedroom wrapped in a towel when she had the male representatives of the two radically conflicting halves of her life waiting for her in an adjacent room.

"Are you okay?" Nu asked, through three inches of open bathroom door.

"I'm fine, thanks."

"I'm not asking Princess Artemisia Helena of Langemark, I'm asking Mish."

"In that case, no, I'm a total mess. But at least my leg's stopped tingling. I think it's going to have a pretty big bruise."

There was a beat of silence. "If you need to stay at Chris's tonight…"

"I—I have no idea, Nu."

"You wanted your ring?"

"Yes. To give back to him."

Nuala handed it through the steamy opening in the doorway. "I'll let you get dressed."

When Misha emerged ten minutes later, she saw only Gian-Marco. "Where are Brant and Nuala?"

He shrugged. "She has driven him in some vehicle to pick up some other vehicle from beside some kind of shed. Being tactful."

"Nu is rarely tactful. That's why I like her. I get tired of tact. So we'll just cut to the heart of this, shall we?"

Gian-Marco laughed and came toward her, his hand ready to caress her face. He had a good line in caresses—little strokings on the inside of a woman's wrist, gentle pinches of a cheek or chin, the ball of a thumb run along a lower lip. They'd always worked, somehow, even when Misha had known from the beginning how well practiced and frequently repeated they were.

She'd appreciated his expertise.

She liked people who were good at what they did.

Today, she cut him off, circling her own fingers around his wrist and then taking his hand. "I'm breaking off the engagement."

"Ba-by, don't get hysterical…"

She smiled. "Don't try that stuff, okay? It's stopped working. I'm not building up to a fight or a scene, here. I'm not playing games. I'm just giving you back your ring." She took it out of her pocket and gave it to him, depositing it in the palm of his hand and curling his fingers over it with a kindly pat.

I'm immune, she thought. I'm free of him. His charisma and selfishness and glamor, and all those little moments when he makes an effort and creates a connection, makes a woman feel as if she's the only one in the world. It's all gone. Coming here was the right thing, no matter what happens next.

Because she never would have had the freedom and space to make this emotional journey under the public eye at home.

His eyes glinted and challenged her, as he spread his hands. "Misha-a-a, no…"

"It's not a game."

"No?"

"I know you love to think it is." She looked into his face for signs of hurt or panic, but couldn't find any, confirming her instinct that this was more about ego for him. "I know you want me to appreciate that you've flown all this way out here to…whatever. Sweep me off my feet. But the engagement's off. I'm flying home tomorrow. I'll arrange everything with the palace. If you want to make a statement of your own, can you run it by the press office first?"

He got angry. "This is stupid, Misha! It has gone on long

enough, hasn't it?" He wrapped an arm around her waist and pulled her hard against his groin, letting his eyes sweep down her body so that she could see the thick curve of his black lashes. "You and I, we understand each other. You like a bit of excitement as much as I do. Are you really going to tell me that a few stupid photos in the press—which you've been a victim of yourself, now, you saw the cutting I brought—is going to ruin what we have? We're getting married in September and I can't wait. Don't you remember how I proposed to you? Don't you remember how good it was? We can live our whole lives like that."

He gave her his gorgeous, heart-stopping grin.

She pulled away. "Brant said you needed someone to run you to your motel in town. I'll get my keys."

"I won't stay there. There's no point now I've seen you. Drive me back to Melbourne, and we can have a luxurious night in the best hotel. We can go to dinner, drink champagne, go clubbing and fly out together tomorrow. Which airline are you on?"

"No, Gian-Marco."

"Okay, okay, the motel, then, since you are being stubborn tonight." He'd backed down so quickly that she knew he planned to seduce her into a different arrangement once they were alone in the car.

She gritted her teeth. "I'll get my keys."

Nuala dropped Brant at the four-wheel drive parked beside the shearing shed and wheeled around at once to head back to the house. "I don't trust that man alone with her," she explained, yelling the words through the driver's-side window of her own vehicle.

"But you trust Misha, don't you?" Brant said. "Leave them on their own a little longer to work it out, Nu."

She hadn't heard.

He followed her along the muddy track, holding back his

speed. Nu could play the fifth wheel if she wanted, but he was staying out of the way. It was a contradictory decision. Every cell in his body wanted to charge in there like a wounded bull, boot the Formula One driver out of his house, take Misha in his arms and tell her, "Stay. Don't go tomorrow. Don't go, *ever*. Just stay."

But he wasn't going to do it.

No matter what happened with Gian-Marco, Misha needed to go home to Langemark and he needed to prove to himself that Inverlochie was still a profitable concern without taking help from anyone else.

Back at the house, the rain had temporarily stopped, although the trees still dripped in the darkness. Must be time to eat, but no one had even thought about it. He climbed out of the vehicle and met Misha coming out of the house.

"I'm driving Gian-Marco to his motel," she announced in a brittle voice that was far too bright and upbeat. "Want me to pick up pizza on the way back?"

"Misha, you have to go with him," Brant heard himself say.

In the light spilling from the house, her eyes widened. "*Go* with him? You…you want me to? You can't!"

"You have more to talk about, don't you? You have to work out a press statement for the palace. You're supposed to be getting married in three and a half months. There must be…protocol. Don't turn it into a mess by not communicating with him properly, because you know it'll all go public."

"Brant—"

"You'll regret it. Do this right. You're leaving tomorrow anyway, first thing in the morning. You're packed. What's the sense in staying any longer?"

Misha heard Brant's relentless logic in disbelief. Nuala had come into the house a few minutes ago with the air of a suspicious dog face-to-face with the mailman. Now she was standing guard while Gian-Marco went to the bathroom.

He'd be out any minute. Misha intended to deliver him to his motel, pick up pizza—she really wanted pizza—then come right back here and…

"A whole night's not worth anything to you, Brant?" she whispered. "Our last night?"

"I think you should leave," he repeated. "I think it would be easiest…for both of us…if you leave tonight."

His stubbornness goaded her, and stripped everything down to its starkest level of truth.

"I don't want to leave at all," she blurted out. "I want to stay."

"No." His jaw looked as if it had turned to stone. "That's only postponing the inevitable. And you're braver than that, Mish."

"Am I?"

"Yes. You have to go. You have to talk to Gian-Marco to-night and fly back to Langemark tomorrow. That's your life. You have to live it, work it out."

"I'll talk to Gian-Marco, then I'll come back here. With pizza."

"You have to leave, and start living your life. You're already packed. So go with Gian-Marco now. Forget the damn pizza."

He meant it.

She could see it in the way he held his body, the way he didn't look at her, and she could hear it in the way he kept repeating the same thing over and over. He'd made up his mind. He was ending it right now, and the last night she'd wanted so badly because…because even another hour with him would be precious and worthwhile…it would never happen.

She heard Gian-Marco behind her. "Ready?"

"Gian-Marco—"

"I am dead on my feet. We'll talk in the car."

"I'll get your bags," Brant said.

"There are still things I haven't packed. Last-minute things."

"Pack them. We'll wait." He said *we* as if he was some kind of prison overseer, standing by to make sure that the execution went ahead. "Do you need Nuala to help?"

"No, it's just a few things to go in my carry-on bag." She couldn't even think, and knew she was bound to leave something behind.

Her hairbrush in front of the mirror.

A discarded sweater on the arm of a chair.

Her heart, bleeding.

"Put your suitcases out in the corridor and I'll load them in," Brant said steadily. "Go, because it's already getting late."

She couldn't speak, just nodded and fled on shaky legs toward the house.

Chapter Sixteen

"Oh, sweetheart, it's so wonderful to see you!"

"You, too, Mom. It's—it's such a long flight!"

Queen Rose enfolded Misha in a mother's warm, familiar hug, in the morning room at Rostvald Castle, traditionally the summer residence of the Marinceski-Sauverin family for over three hundred years. The aroma of rich coffee filled the air, and two members of the royal staff waited for the resumption of their planning meeting with the queen, who was dressed impeccably as usual, in a cream angora cardigan and pearls over a silk blouse and linen skirt. Outside, the early-summer sunshine shone brightly on the gravel walks and beds of formal flowers, and the air felt steamy and mild.

"I'm sorry I didn't come to the airport," Queen Rose said. "But you know how it is."

Misha knew how it was. If ever the king and queen met a flight at Rendhagen's international airport, the runway was closed to all traffic for at least an hour, and every incoming or outgoing passenger experienced major disruption and delays.

"You've put on some weight, I think," her mother said.

"I've been eating well and working hard."

"Working?"

"Around the farm."

"Nuala expected that from you?"

"No, of course she didn't expect it, but you know me. I get bored. It was different. Great, actually."

"But you're on edge. You're tired…" She looked at Misha, then turned to her staff. "We'll pick up after lunch, I think," she said. "I'd like some time with the princess."

The two women nodded and told Misha cordially that they were happy that her break had been a success, then left the room.

"Gian-Marco showed up," Misha said as soon as the heavy gold-and-cream-painted door had closed behind them. "The day before I left. He'd seen an article in the press."

"Oh, I know the one. Only one magazine picked up the story, thank goodness. The others must have thought the picture of you was too blurred, which it was. The palace issued a statement saying there was no truth to the report. It really could have been anyone."

"You didn't tell me about seeing it."

"I didn't see the point."

"So you didn't believe it either."

"Hot New Aussie Man?" Mom quirked her mouth. "Should I have?"

"It was, um, Nu's brother. That's all." Misha managed to make her voice sound casual, even though she couldn't say Brant's name.

Her mother accepted the statement. "You were telling me about Gian-Marco," she said.

"I told him the engagement's off. He had…uh…a little

trouble coming to grips with the idea, but he's got a handle on it now."

She knew her mother would recognize a certain amount of understatement.

And she hated to think back on her drive into Holbrook that rainy, horrible night. Just two nights ago, she registered in disbelief. Here in Langemark, it was still only Monday morning. Gian-Marco had laughed at her as they drove. He'd ridiculed her, tried to seduce her, made promises to her, sworn that once they were married he would be utterly faithful, insisted that if she went through with cancelling their wedding she would break his heart.

She'd stayed firm.

He'd moved on to insulting her—*frigid, naive*, and *neurotic* were the words she remembered—and had slammed the car door when they reached the motel. Gritting her teeth, she'd stayed long enough to make sure he was successfully checked in, and then she'd left. She hadn't told him where she was going.

Melbourne.

Three and a half hours through the increasing rain, farther from Inverlochie…and Nu's brother…with every swish of the windscreen wipers.

She'd checked into an airport hotel, thankful that she'd learned from Gian-Marco that he would be flying on a different airline when he went back, with London his final destination in readiness for the British Grand Prix. Right now, she didn't know where he was. Midair, possibly.

"Can we draft a formal announcement right now, Mom?" she said quickly. "While it's being vetted, I'll call Mette Janssen and the bishop at St. Margrethe's." She thought of a few more people who deserved to hear the news personally. The director of the Langemark National Orchestra. Some of the younger and livelier members of Europe's various royal families, with whom she was friendly. "I want to get it public and over with as quickly as possible, and when the dust has settled I want to—"

She stopped. She had no idea what she was going to do next. Ahead of her, the summer dragged. Her schedule had been filled with planning meetings about the wedding—all of Nuala's concerns about menu and decor and guest list, magnified tenfold in the case of a princess.

Those cancelled meetings would leave a gap, as would her scheduled trips to the US in July and Hungary in August to watch Gian-Marco race, also to be cancelled now. She had her charity work, various public appearances, the usual wardrobe and scheduling meetings, twice-weekly riding sessions.

All of it seemed pointless.

The only thing that held any appeal was the time she always spent with Christian and Graziella's two boys in summer. Graziella was a slightly overprotective parent, and Misha liked to tease her sister-in-law a little, just occasionally, by getting the boys wet and muddy in Rostvald Lake, or hyping them up with chasing games right before bedtime.

"Graziella's still feeling pretty queasy," her mother said, as if she'd read Misha's mind. "Maybe we could have the boys here for an extra couple of weeks and leave her in Rendhagen to rest."

For a moment her spirits lifted. "That would be great!" But then she frowned. "And after that, Mom, I have to find something real to do, something that has a direction and a goal. I can't live my life like this, or I'm eventually going to meet someone else like Gian-Marco who's wrong for me, and repeat the pattern all over again. I—I couldn't bear that. I don't want to."

She couldn't picture such a man right now. She could only see Brant, who felt so right—him and his world—but who'd sent her away without even a final night together. He'd shaken her hand before she climbed into her rental car on Saturday night, in the same distant, smoldering way he'd shaken it the afternoon they'd first met.

"You're flying back to Australia at the end of August for Nuala's wedding…" Mom said.

Misha was all too aware of this. She said with desperation creeping into her voice, "By then, I have to know what I'm doing next."

For the first time, she began to have the tiniest inkling that Brant might have done the right thing in sending her away.

Brant gave himself three weeks and three days—the amount of time that Misha had spent at Inverlochie. He hadn't heard from her, and hadn't expected to.

He knew that Nuala had had an e-mail, though, because on Tuesday morning she confronted him at breakfast, flourishing a sheet of paper printed out from the computer, demanding to know, "What the heck is Misha asking me about, here? Do I know if you've had a result on the test sample from the P.P.B.? What test sample from the P.P.B., Brant? What does she mean?"

"I had them come out and test the new ewes for foot rot."

"*What?* We have infected sheep? And you didn't tell me?"

"We don't have infected sheep. It's shelly hoof. I got the result yesterday. It has delayed the contracted sale on the other ewes, but their feet are still in good condition so it hasn't affected the price. They'll be going this week. The new ones will need a bit more work. I was getting pretty sure it was shelly hoof even before the P.P.B. got back to me, so I've been doing some cleaning and paring, but there's more still to do. Time lost, but not money, apart from a couple of days' worth of contract labor."

"And you didn't tell me?"

"You can help with the hooves if you want."

"You didn't *tell* me!"

"Boy, I will be so glad when this wedding is done with!"

"This has nothing to do with the wedding, Brant."

"But it has to do with your future, and Chris's. What would you have done if it had been foot rot?"

"Told you that you couldn't buy out my share of Inverlochie at the price we agreed."

"Exactly."

"You're horrible!"

"Because I want to safeguard your future with Chris?"

"Because you keep me so totally out of the loop!"

"Yes, because when I tell you things, you start yelling."

"What else aren't you telling me?" Nuala demanded. "Misha sounds a bit strange in her e-mail. What did you two talk about on Saturday night, while I was babysitting Gian-Marco? What is going on?"

It was a long three weeks and three days.

At the end of it, Brant bought a plane ticket to Europe, and this time, since Nuala didn't want to be kept out of the loop, he told her what he was doing.

Her reaction was terrifying—she barely said a word.

Delivering him to the airport in Albury, having promised that Sox, Mon, the chickens and several thousand sheep would be fine under her care in his absence, she gave him a huge hug. "You're a good person, Brant."

"Not horrible, after all?"

She hissed in a breath through her teeth. "I just hope you have a chance at what you want, that's all."

"You don't think I have the ghost of a one, do you?"

Nuala pressed her lips together and shrugged. He fought her pessimism in his heart halfway around the world.

Two little boys needed a garden hose jetted over them before they even went onto the pristine sandstone-paved castle terrace, let alone inside. Misha took them around through the castle's kitchen garden, where tender green lettuces and spinach plants sat in military rows almost ready for picking, and the frond-like leaves of carrots grew taller every day.

The royal trio startled the head gardener. This was his domain, not theirs. He hurried toward them, frantically wiping his dirt-stained hands on the back of his pants. "Your Highness…"

"We got a bit wet," Misha announced. "We need a hose."

"A hose?"

"To wash off."

"The water is cold."

"So was the water in the lake. We'll live."

"Your Highness…" He picked up the length of green plastic, but couldn't bring himself to hose down a toddler prince, a princess and the four-year-old who was second in line to the Langemarkian throne.

Sensing his scruples, Misha kindly took it from him and squirted her nephews, raising a series of happy, hysterical shrieks and ending up half-drenched herself as they splashed her.

"Your Highness…" the head gardener said for the third time.

She turned. "Seriously, we're fine, we're—" She stopped.

"Hello, Misha."

Brant.

Not possible. Simply not possible. She'd had three e-mails from Nuala since she'd left. Nu had said nothing about this! Nu would have warned her. Someone on the castle staff would have warned her. All of Nuala's family and contact details were on file for security so it was no surprise that Brant had been allowed in, but… how could he be here?

Then she saw Mom's principal private secretary rounding a turreted corner of the castle, wringing her hands nervously, and realized that this was the warning. Miss Heiningen had been looking for her, but it was Brant who had immediately known to follow the sound of the shrieks.

"Um, we're a little wet," she told him.

"I know," he said. "I've seen you this way before."

He was grinning.

And at the same time frowning.

Misha wasn't thrilled with the frown.

"Take…" she said to Miss Heiningen. "Take…"

Oh, shoot, she'd started shaking. He'd come. He'd just shown up. And she was thrilled and scared and all over the place.

"You want me to take the boys." Miss Heiningen looked slightly appalled at the request, because they still weren't very clean. Her training gained the upper hand, however. "Come along, darlings," she said to them, polite and bright. "A little more under the hose and then we can go inside via the—the—"

"Scullery," Misha suggested. The stone-floored space offered further washing possibilities, and was her own favorite entrance to Rostvald Castle. She suspected that Miss Heiningen may never have used it.

When the secretary and the two sodden princes disappeared in that direction, and the head gardener took himself discreetly to a distant toolshed, she discovered how hard her heart was beating, and that she hadn't taken a decent breath in quite a while. Her denim shorts had patches of moisture all across the front, and so did her pale pink T-shirt.

She looked down.

Yep. Semitransparent in several places.

But Brant had seen her looking worse.

"You didn't tell me you were coming. I didn't…miss a message, or—I—I know I didn't."

"Somebody told me recently that surprising a woman can sometimes be a good idea, when you want to find out how she really feels."

"How she feels?" Misha echoed shakily. "Oh, lord, can't you tell? I can't believe it." She pressed damp hands to her burning cheeks, and then a fist to her beating heart.

"Wh-what are you doing here?" she asked him, still aware of the frown on his face.

"Feeling slightly encouraged by the fact that you still get messy even when you're living in a castle." He came closer.

"That is not an answer."

"Make this easier for me, Mish, please?" he muttered, taking her hands. She stepped back about two inches and shook her head, panicking totally. "I've come all this way. I left you alone for nearly four weeks, but now I need to know. What were they for you, those nights we spent together? And the days? A holiday fling? Or something real? You have to tell me if I have this all wrong."

"You were the one who sent me away," she whispered back. She gripped his hands harder, and his familiar warmth and scent surrounded her. "I said I didn't want to leave, that I wanted to stay, and you refused to listen. I so much wanted one last precious night together, and you said no. You kept telling me over and over, you have to go, you have to go. As if you didn't want me at all."

"No, sweetheart…"

"I drove all the way to Melbourne that night, wondering how it had happened, how I could have made it different. Miserable about it. And still worrying about those damn sheep!" She gave a shaky laugh.

"How could I let you stay, when you'd only come to Inverlochie because of another man, and because you needed the space? Your real life is here, and my real life is on the farm. You had to come back…"

It sounded too much like another rejection, and yet he'd flown halfway round the world to deliver it. Had she gotten it wrong again?

"…even if only to sort out your future so you could leave again," he finished.

"Leave again?"

"Yes." He dropped his voice so she could barely hear. They

were still gripping each other's hands, their arms twisted together and their thighs touching. "To be with me. To live in my world."

"You want me with you?"

He swore under his breath. "Misha, I've wanted you since about the second day after we met, but I know it's crazy. It's impossible. You know how I live. I'm not rich or powerful or famous. Nu said something… she said that even if something could happen between us, it would turn Inverlochie into a hobby farm and I don't want that. I'm successful in my own terms, but not in the eyes of the world."

"You're successful in mine."

"Yes? I'm just a farmer with land and family and animals and friends that I care about."

"You think that's not the best kind of success? It's where my own mother came from."

"I hoped…I didn't know. But I had to give it a chance. If there was a hope in hell that you felt the same, that my priorities were important to you, that my life…my way of life…meant something to you, I had to give it the best shot I possibly could. But I had to give you a chance to say no, too, to get your feet back on the ground."

"And that meant sending me away…" She'd begun to understand this herself—that she had more to prove to both of them than rescuing one ram in a muddy paddock could achieve. She'd done so much difficult thinking since she'd been back in Langemark.

"Yes, and then coming after you." He parted his lips and brushed them across hers. Her whole body began to tingle, and to remember. "To see if three weeks could count for something, to see if they were still important, and if you wanted to try to make this work."

"I do." Because she knew now that it was real. "Oh, Brant, I do!"

They held each other. With the beautiful castle rising behind Misha, and the lake sparkling through the trees, Brant's arms were what felt like home—her place of safety, her place of belonging, her future. He kissed her more deeply, his mouth so perfect and right in the way it moved on hers, but their kiss was only the beginning. After a moment he pulled away and looked into her eyes.

"Don't promise too much yet. We have a lot to work out. I'm not going to let you rush it, or rush it myself. We can't mess this up."

"We're not going to mess it up." She touched his face, tracing the lines of his lips, cupping his jaw. "Oh, Brant, I will do anything not to mess this up!"

"Me, too," he muttered, his mouth warm against her hair. "Whatever it takes. With my whole heart, and every breath in my body."

And she knew he meant every word.

The bride looked so beautiful. She swept onto the dance floor with her new husband, calm and confident and smiling. They squeezed each other's hands in a gesture of commitment and reassurance which said more than words, and then they began their first dance as man and wife.

At the bridal table beside Brant, Misha's vision grew blurred.

Nuala had almost gotten through her wedding day at last. It had gone without a hitch, every bit of it beautiful, and incredibly the universe had not come tumbling down around her.

"Our turn," Brant whispered to Misha as she watched Nuala's gorgeous silk dress floating and swirling through the room.

He pulled her lightly to her feet and they joined Nu and Chris, Frank and Helen McLaren, and Chris's parents on the dance floor. "Do you think there's a chance Nu will get back to normal after tonight?" he whispered to her.

"Do you want her to?" she whispered back.

He looked at her in astonishment for a moment, because indeed Nuala had been pretty emotional—translation, unbearable—over the past few months, but after some thought, he said slowly, "You know what, I guess in a way I don't. When she isn't hysterical over the wedding, she looks pretty happy."

"She does," Misha agreed. She whispered a kiss against his jaw and added, "But not as happy as me."

"No? Got some more detail on that statement for me?"

But she only smiled at him.

He knew how happy she was. And he knew why.

He'd stayed at Rostvald Castle for six weeks over the summer—six weeks of sun and sailing on the lake, hiking and horseback riding in the woods, picnic meals and formal functions, playing with the little princes and taking anonymous minibreaks in picturesque little hotels dotted around Langemark, or in nearby Denmark and Sweden.

Eventually, of course, he'd had to fly home, but this time they had both known that their separation was only a temporary thing. Misha had her ticket to fly out for Nuala's wedding, and when she had shown up at Inverlochie this week as planned, several days ahead of time, Brant had seen the mountain of luggage she'd brought with her and his eyes had lit up.

"Planning a long stay?" he'd drawled.

"I've cleared my calendar until November. I hear there's some shearing to do."

Nuala and Chris would be flying to an island in the Pacific tomorrow morning for a two-week stay, but Misha felt as if she and Brant were already on their honeymoon. Only one thing remained to complete her certainty about the future— the fateful words from Brant himself.

She knew him pretty well by this time, and when he bent his head even closer toward her as they danced, she knew what he was going to say. Other people had joined in the bridal couple's first dance, now. Chris's two sisters and their husbands, relatives and friends all circled on the floor.

Misha's heart felt as light as Nu's swirling dress, and she didn't need hot-air balloons, champagne and a huge diamond ring this time around. She needed exactly what she had—people she cared about nearby, and a private moment in the middle of a crowd, with the man she loved.

"Is it our turn, Misha?" he whispered, just as he had before they started to dance. "Our turn for this next? You know how much I want it. Will you marry me?"

"Yes, oh, yes!" she said, and they danced until they were laughing and dizzy.

Later, when Nuala threw her bouquet, Misha leaped into the air like a basketball player and caught it in one hand.

Epilogue

They were married the following June.

The sun shone that afternoon, making the king's hair gleam with distinguished shadings of silver beside Misha in the royal horse-drawn coach on the way to St. Margrethe's Cathedral. "So, sweetheart?" he said gently, the rhythmic clip-clop of hooves forming a backdrop of sound that kept his words private despite the two footmen and the coach driver, for her ears alone.

"So, I'll be glad when it's over," she answered.

"But it's what the people wanted. We had to do it this way, so the whole country could celebrate."

Thousands of people lined the streets, waving the flags of Langemark and Australia, cheering and calling out their good wishes. Misha knew that Brant would be able to hear them from where he waited in the cathedral, and she felt a flutter of nerves, knowing how much it had cost him to put himself through all of this—the preparations, the protocol, the publicity, the television cameras in the cathedral and the foreign dignitaries at the bridal banquet.

"And it's your farewell," her father added quietly.

Because she and Brant were not returning to Langemark after their honeymoon in Hawaii. It had been announced to the people of Langemark that Princess Misha would be making her home in Australia and giving up her public duties. She and her husband would visit, of course, but her role as a princess would be very much a part-time one now.

"Is that really okay, Papa?" she asked, with a sudden pang. "I know you and Mom love him, but would you have preferred to find a role for him here?"

The king was silent for a moment, then he began slowly, "When your mother married me, she married a kingdom as much as a man. When she and I talked about you and Brant, we realized that you were doing the same. The challenge will be just as great as the one your mother faced, and the rewards will be just as rich. We had no doubt, when we thought about it, that you would rise to such a challenge, and that it was the right thing." He squeezed her silk-clad shoulders. "But we will miss you so much."

He pressed his lips together and couldn't speak. Waving an absent hand at the cheering crowd, he took a moment to gather himself and finally put on a smile. "This reminds me... I commissioned your groom to buy a gift, and I wanted to give it to you before we reached the cathedral, so we are running out of time."

They had rounded a corner and there was St. Margrethe's, the guard of honor, the crimson carpet and the coach containing Misha's attendants just pulling up in front.

"A gift...now?" Misha said.

"This may be the only time in the whole day when you and I are alone." At a moment like this, the well-wishing crowds didn't count. "You are wearing the St. Sebastian diamond tiara for your wedding, but when you take it off, you'll need to replace it with something very different. Think of me when you wear it, sweetheart, and think of your mother, and know how much we love you and wish you well."

He placed the gift in her lap. It was light, a round box wrapped in white and gold paper. She pulled the end of the ornate bow and slipped her freshly manicured nails beneath the seam in the paper, reached for the box lid, lifted it aside... then laughed.

Her father the king had commissioned her groom the sheep farmer to buy her a brand-new Australian sheep farmer's broad-brimmed felt hat. She lifted it up and the crowd saw it and cheered. "What do you think?" she asked the king. "This? Or the tiara?"

"They both suit you admirably, my dear," her father said.

Then the royal coach pulled up beside the sweep of pristine carpet and Misha alighted and went to meet Brant, to pledge her life and her heart to him. He was waiting for her, with a smile on his face and a light in his eyes that she vowed would keep burning forever.

* * * * *

Page-turning drama…

Exotic, glamorous locations…

Intense emotion and passionate seduction…

Sheikhs, princes and billionaire tycoons…

This summer, may we suggest:

THE SHEIKH'S DISOBEDIENT BRIDE
by Jane Porter

On sale June.

AT THE GREEK TYCOON'S BIDDING
by Cathy Williams

On sale July.

THE ITALIAN MILLIONAIRE'S VIRGIN WIFE

On sale August.

With new titles to choose from every month,
discover a world of romance in our books written
by internationally bestselling authors.

It's the ultimate in quality romance!

Available wherever Harlequin books are sold.

www.eHarlequin.com

HPGEN06

**Hidden in the secrets of antiquity,
lies the unimagined truth...**

Introducing

a brand-new line filled with mystery
and suspense, action and adventure,
and a fascinating look into history.

And it all begins with DESTINY.

In a sealed crypt in
France, where the
terrifying legend of
the beast of Gevaudan
begins to unravel,
Annja Creed discovers
a stunning artifact
that will seal her destiny.

*Available every other
month starting
July 2006, wherever
you buy books.*

GRA1

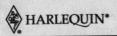

HARLEQUIN®

American ROMANCE®

IS PROUD TO PRESENT A
GUEST APPEARANCE BY

QUILL
BOOK
AWARD
WINNING
AUTHOR

NEW YORK TIMES bestselling author

DEBBIE MACOMBER

The Wyoming Kid

The story of an ex–rodeo cowboy,
a schoolteacher and their journey to the altar.

"Best-selling Macomber, with more than
100 romances and women's fiction titles
to her credit, sure has a way of pleasing readers."
—*Booklist* on *Between Friends*

**The Wyoming Kid is available from
Harlequin American Romance in July 2006.**

www.eHarlequin.com   HARDMJUL

If you enjoyed what you just read,
then we've got an offer you can't resist!

Take 2 bestselling
love stories FREE!

Plus get a FREE surprise gift!

Clip this page and mail it to Silhouette Reader Service™

IN U.S.A.	IN CANADA
3010 Walden Ave.	P.O. Box 609
P.O. Box 1867	Fort Erie, Ontario
Buffalo, N.Y. 14240-1867	L2A 5X3

YES! Please send me 2 free Silhouette Special Edition® novels and my free surprise gift. After receiving them, if I don't wish to receive anymore, I can return the shipping statement marked cancel. If I don't cancel, I will receive 6 brand-new novels every month, before they're available in stores! In the U.S.A., bill me at the bargain price of $4.24 plus 25¢ shipping and handling per book and applicable sales tax, if any*. In Canada, bill me at the bargain price of $4.99 plus 25¢ shipping and handling per book and applicable taxes**. That's the complete price and a savings of at least 10% off the cover prices—what a great deal! I understand that accepting the 2 free books and gift places me under no obligation ever to buy any books. I can always return a shipment and cancel at any time. Even if I never buy another book from Silhouette, the 2 free books and gift are mine to keep forever.

235 SDN DZ9D
335 SDN DZ9E

Name	(PLEASE PRINT)	
Address	Apt.#	
City	State/Prov.	Zip/Postal Code

Not valid to current Silhouette Special Edition® subscribers.

Want to try two free books from another series?
Call 1-800-873-8635 or visit www.morefreebooks.com.

* Terms and prices subject to change without notice. Sales tax applicable in N.Y.
** Canadian residents will be charged applicable provincial taxes and GST.
  All orders subject to approval. Offer limited to one per household.
  ® are registered trademarks owned and used by the trademark owner and or its licensee.

SPED04R   ©2004 Harlequin Enterprises Limited

Stability is highly overrated....

Dana Logan's world had always revolved around her children. Now they're all grown up and don't seem to need anything she's able to give them. Struggling to find her new identity, Dana realizes that it's about time for her to get "off her rocker" and begin a new life!

Off Her Rocker

by Jennifer Archer

Available August 2006
TheNextNovel.com

HN53

HARLEQUIN®
Next™

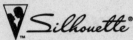

COMING NEXT MONTH